RINGS OF HONOR

RINGS OF HONOR

ANTONIO FRANCESCA

Rings of Honor

Copyright © 2022 by Antonio Francesca. All rights reserved.

No part of this publication may be reproduced, stored in a retrieval system or transmitted in any way by any means, electronic, mechanical, photocopy, recording or otherwise without the prior permission of the author except as provided by USA copyright law.

The opinions expressed by the author are not necessarily those of URLink Print and Media.

1603 Capitol Ave., Suite 310 Cheyenne, Wyoming USA 82001
1-888-980-6523 | admin@urlinkpublishing.com

URLink Print and Media is committed to excellence in the publishing industry.

Book design copyright © 2022 by URLink Print and Media. All rights reserved.

Published in the United States of America

Library of Congress Control Number: 2022905906
ISBN 978-1-68486-151-4 (Paperback)
ISBN 978-1-68486-152-1 (Hardback)
ISBN 978-1-68486-153-8 (Digital)

15.04.22

CHAPTER ONE
November 1934

A line snaked around the icy corner of Walnut and Mulberry Street in the iron bound neighborhood of Newark, New Jersey. People huddled into their large overcoats, breath swirling in front of their faces, both avoiding the record cold wins and the glances of people passing by. No one was proud to be standing on a soup line, waiting hours for a bowl of warm tomato soup.

Donato Petrucelli waited with his family. Gone was the vibrant middle-aged man with a perennial twinkle in his eye. The last couple years had beaten him down, causing him to enter his not so golden years prematurely. Glaring at the front of the line, he wondered how much longer he would have to endure this humiliation. Tugging his brown woolen cap over his ears, he hoped for warmth.

His wife, Teresa, gently touched his arm with her threadbare glove, but he continued to stare straight ahead. Her expression was gentle, and her eyes still held the promise of hope, even after all the hardship her family had endured.

"At least Danny's working," she whispered. "We can be thankful our eldest found a job."

"Yes," Donato said, matching her quiet tone. "I am."

"You'll get your job back."

"I know."

"And Tony'll get work too."

Donato glanced behind him, smiling wanly at his youngest son. "From your mouth to God's ear."

Tony Petrucelli had turned twenty last week. He was a clean cut handsome boy with unruly shaggy black hair. He didn't return the smile. "Pop, can I go?" he grated. Out of respect for his father, he attempted to hide his revulsion at his surroundings.

"What?" his father hissed. "No. You will stay here."

"But…" Tony's voice caught in his throat.

Donato glared at his youngest and turned back to face the brown coat two feet ahead of him. No more words were needed from the Petrucelli patriarch.

Tony stared down at his feet. The agonizing, slow paced shuffling of the entire line made him want to bolt with every fiber of his being, but the gnawing hunger in his stomach, along with his father's order, checked that urge. Just barely.

His sister, Maria Petrucelli playfully ruffled his hair. At twenty-one she was an incredible beauty. Her delicate features were that of a model, even if she was far too thin. She tossed her long, wavy tresses over her shoulder and leaned in close. "Just think of the warm soup, Tony. We'll get there soon." Her dark eyes sparkled with optimism.

Tony shot her a grateful look. No matter the circumstances, she always seemed to find the silver lining. Even standing on this degrading line on this dreary street, he felt much better standing next to her. His urge to bolt diminished, and his shoulders relaxed.

Maria grinned as she helped ease her brother's tension.. Rubbing her hands together, she whispered, "I heard Danny did well last night."

"Yeah," Tony exclaimed loudly, forgetting where he was for a moment. Blushing, he realized his tone was inappropriate and lowered his voice. "Yeah, he did good."

"Boxing's fine, but it don't pay like real work," Donato grumbled, not bothering to turn around. "He should focus on his job."

Tony groaned and rolled his eyes. "Pop, Danny works plenty! Plus, he'll get paid extra when he boxes a real match."

"So, what was last night then?"

"Practice."

Donato let out a grunt. "Waste of time."

"Nate 'Lights Out' Rubin's has managed to make a living," Tony said stubbornly. "He's fighting regular and feeding his family."

Donato spat on the ground. He turned around to face his son; his features showing his obvious disgust. "Don't talk to me about that mocky kike," he gritted out.

"If that Jew boy can do it, certainly Danny has a shot," Tony answered rebelliously. "Rubin's a thug."

Maria politely turned her head away from their conversation. As she glanced through the sea of faces behind her, their hopeless looks made her shudder. A few of the men returned her innocent gaze with lascivious smirks. Fear crept into her features, and she blushed profusely. Turning too suddenly, she stumbled over her feet as the line moved forward.

Tony caught her by the elbow, helping her to regain her balance. He looked into her eyes, puzzled by the fright he saw there. "You're trembling. What happened?"

"Nothing," Maria replied quickly. She gave him a quick smile, in an attempt to remove his concern.

Tony wasn't fooled. He looked around and spotted one of the culprits. The man hadn't been able to wipe the lewd look from his face in time and realized his error too late. Tony glowered menacingly and walked over to him. Growling low, he said, " I'll knock your teeth out if you don't take your eyes off my sister."

The man paled at the threat and stammered out an apology before jamming his hands in his pockets, limiting his gaze to his shoelaces.

Satisfied, Tony rejoined his family. Maria leaned against her brother gratefully. They shuffled forward a few more steps before stopping again.

"Tony, I'll get you work soon," Donato promised quietly. "Old man Larson'll find a way to hire me back. When he does, I'll bring you in with me."

" Sure, Pop," Tony said, trying not to sound too bored at the prospect. "But I'm thinkin' I can be Danny's manager."

"Focus on getting real work, son," Donato replied dismissively.

Seeing that Tony wasn't about to let the subject go, Maria asked, "What about me, Father? I can work, too."

"I'm sure we can find work for you, my daughter," Donato replied fondly. "It's good you want to help."

Teresa shook her head. "You'd do better looking for a good man to marry. Pretty girls don't ever need to work."

" Oh mamma," Maria sighed in frustration.

Teresa raised a silent eyebrow at her daughter.

They continued their forward shuffle in silence until they reached the front of the line. Mob boss Philip Cantalupo's men were doling out tomato soup and crackers. They were under strict orders to take care of the Italians in the neighborhood. Of course, it was just a fraction of the money Cantalupo raked in each week, but the charity was needed and was gratefully received.

Tony wrinkled his nose at the bowl, but mumbled a respectful thank you to the portly man serving up the soup before ambling down the street. Looking at the men behind the table, he knew they were well taken care of. Any member of the Cantalupo family had money no matter what the economic climate. He dreamed of being invited to join that life but had no connections to make that possible. That day will come…one day.

He stopped a few paces away from the table and closed his eyes. He could almost smell his mother's chicken parmesan.

As if reading his mind, Donato whispered into his ear, "I miss your mother's cooking too. I swear to you, I'll get my job back. Larson's a good man. He'll come through for me."

Tony nodded bleakly. "You're great baker, Pop. I miss those days."

Teresa patted her son's arm. "This is only temporary. Things will get better."

"You're mother's right." Donato nodded and took a sip of the watery soup. Grimacing he continued to walk down the street with his family. "We could go home to the old country," he said quietly.

" Father, please," Maria implored. She couldn't stand the thought of her family going back to Italy and living under Mussolini's fascist ideology.

" Why not? Mussolini takes care of his people," Donato said stiffly. "Not like FDR."

Teresa guided her husband forward, and the two children fell behind. "Don't worry, Maria," Tony whispered when he was well outside his father's earshot. "We're not going anywhere. Pop just talks. You know that."

Maria sighed. "I know. I just…"

"I know," Tony said. He shot her grin and continued, "Danny was pretty amazing last night. I think he's ready."

Maria's eyes glanced forward to be sure her parents were still ten paces in front of them. "Ready for?"

Tony nodded. "A real fight."

"He told me he needs another six months."

"No way."

"Don't rush him. He's methodical. You know Danny."

"Yeah, I know Danny. He sometimes needs a swift kick in the- "

"Tony!" Maria exclaimed, causing her parents to turn around. She blushed and waved to them, mouthing, "Sorry." She shot her brother a scathing look, blaming him for her embarrassment.

"Well, he does," he said with a grin, ruffling her hair playfully.

Just like the Cantalupo Family provided soup for the Italian neighborhood, the Temple Beth Shalom provided for its parishioners almost every day. Nate Rubin, struggled not to hang his head in shame as he stood in line with his father, Jules. His Mediterranean good looks were not marred by his hunger; he still maintained his washboard stomach. His brown eyes mirrored his frustration in not keeping his father off the soup lines.

Although his bouts earned him some money, his recovery time was too long to make the pay regular. He had just spent the rest of the last purse on the electricity bill yesterday.

"When's your next fight?" Jules asked him. He didn't quite look his son in the eye but focused on his cheek instead. He tried to make his voice sound casual, not wanting to put too much pressure on his son.

Nate studied his father. In better times, Jules was a meek man but now that he had lost another ten pounds, it was as if he was disappearing from view. He forced himself to smile at his old man. "Next week."

Jules nodded vigorously, attempting to hide his relief. "Good, good."

They shuffled forward and stopped. Nate hated waiting on this line and felt a tremendous shame that he couldn't support his father. If he didn't need every ounce of strength he could muster for his fights, he'd skip the soup for himself. But in those smoky backrooms, it was every man for himself. He couldn't afford to lose a pound.

His last fight only lasted twenty minutes. Nate slammed his opponent with a right cross, knocking him out cold. Despite the match being so short, Nate still got some nasty bruises on his ribs. He wished he didn't have to wait so many weeks between fights.

The fights brought in about $250. Half went to his manager, who took care of all the expenses. Too many expenses. If Nate didn't know Manny was on the up and up, he'd deliver a few uppercuts to him, but Manny was as good as they came. The last decent manager in town.

The men around Nate gave him plenty of space. No one would look him directly in the eye. Not that he cared much, but it was clear they didn't exactly approve of his profession. Good Jewish boys didn't box. It was too uncivilized, too provincial.

Nate grunted and moved forward a half a pace with the line. "You visit the dock again this morning?"

"Yeah," Jules said. "Not hiring today."

Nate nodded. "Good that you're trying and not giving up." He patted his father on the back affectionately. "In the meantime, I'll just have to get more fights."

Jules looked up at him, his expression filled with worry. "I don't like those smokers you fight in."

Nate barked a laugh, causing the men around him to press back further away from him. Glowering at them, he shook his head.

"What part don't you like? The fact you can't see nothing on account of the cigar smoke or is it the gambling you object to?"

Jules shrugged and shook his head. "It's okay, I'm not complaining. You bring home money. I just worry about you getting hurt. That's all."

Nate sighed and berated himself for speaking harshly at the already deflated man. His father couldn't take much anger. He counted to five and forced his voice to calm down. "I'll be fine, Pop. It's my opponents you should worry about."

Jules laughed uncomfortably. "Word on the street is you're good."

"You could always come and see for yourself," Nate suggested.

Jules shook his head. "Too violent."

"That's okay, Pop. You don't have to come. Maybe someday."

"Yeah, maybe someday."

"In the meantime, we need to get you a job."

"It's all I really want. That and your health."

CHAPTER TWO
March 1933

Teresa Petrucelli carried a large steaming plate to her dining table with pride. Now that they had money coming into the household again, she could feed them all. There were usually at least three pots going at one time; the Petrucelli house always smelled of good Italian cooking. Teresa got down on her knees daily to give thanks for their good fortune. Hopefully, the soup lines were a thing of the past.

As she approached the long table, her family looked up to her with a silent reverence, savoring the sweet smell of her famous lasagna. She looked around at her family and sighed with pleasure. They were beginning to gain weight, losing the gaunt look of starvation.

"Ah, *amore,* that smells wonderful," Donato breathed.

"I can't tell you how much I missed your meals," Tony said, his stomach echoing his sentiment

"You only mention it every time she cooks," Maria said teasingly.

"I'll never take it for granted again," Tony vowed.

"We have a lot to be grateful for. Now that my men are working, we can eat properly again," Teresa said, her eyes misting. She turned back to the kitchen to retrieve the salad, dabbing her eyes with her sleeve. When she came out again, carrying the large plate of antipasto, she made sure her eyes were free of tears.

"We're lucky we can all work together as a family," Danny Petrucelli commented. He smiled warmly at his father, returned the sentiment with a nod.

Danny Petrucelli, at first glance, looked different from his younger brother. His face didn't have the olive tone that Tony had, and he stood a half a foot taller at almost six-foot. His dirty blond hair was cut short and had blue eyes that made him look more Irish than Italian. In fact, his birth name was Donato Jr., but with the strong American flavor epitomized in the large Italian section of Newark called the Ironbound, European birth names changed quickly, not to mention the popularity of the song "Danny Boy", Donato Jr. quickly became Danny.

"Old man Larson really came through," Donato agreed. "I knew he would. And of course, you too, Danny."

Danny shrugged sheepishly. "I just kept talking to Mr. Demaio and he finally found you a spot. And Tony's in part time now. I'm sorry I couldn't get your old job back. I mean loading trucks all day is exhausting and I know its boring."

"Of course, I'd rather be in the kitchen," Donato said. "But I'm very happy to be earning again to complain. My back hurts now and then, but I just ignore it."

"Do you think they might find something for me?" Maria asked. "Maybe something clerical?"

"I'll keep asking," Danny replied.

Donato looked at her with a smile. "We're doing well now. You don't have to work. You're help to your mother. That's enough."

"But I love working. Not that I don't love helping Mamma," Maria added quickly. "Besides if I'm home all day I'll never find a nice man." She tossed a hopeful glance to her mother to see if she would support her desire to work with that reasoning.

Teresa laughed, seeing through her daughter's ploy. "Maria, if you really want to work, you may. I just don't want you to lose sight of the important things in life. Would you deny me the chance to plan my only daughter's wedding? Or, be there at the birth of her first son?"

Maria let out an embarrassed laugh. "Mamma, you're getting a little ahead of me, don't you think?"

Teresa grinned. "Someone has to set goals!"

"Yes, Mamma," she replied quietly.

Danny leaned in and whispered loudly in his sister's ear, "Good answer." The rest of the table laughed.

"How's the training going?" Donato asked Danny.

"Great!" Tony cried out enthusiastically. Danny'll be ready by June."

With an exaggerated look of surprise, Donato said to Tony, "My, Danny, how your voice has changed."

Everyone laughed at his quip, and Tony blushed. "I'm his manager," he stammered defensively.

"Oh really?" Maria teased. "I wonder what Willie would say about that."

"Willie Greene's his *trainer*. I'm his *manager*," Tony said.

Danny remained quiet and studiously avoided his brother's gaze. Instead, he focused on his father. "Training's good. There's this guy they're looking to put me up against. Thomas Gardner."

"Isn't he tutsune? A Darkie?" Donato asked disgustedly.

"Yeah, Pop, he's black. So?" Danny sighed in irritation. "It's a boxing match."

"They shouldn't let *them* fight," Donato said scowling.

"The fight's going to be in mid-June," Danny said quietly. "Might not be him anyway."

"At least he's not fighting a kike, Pop," Tony chimed in.

"Thank God for small mercies," Donato muttered.

"Maybe I'm just grateful to be fighting at all," Danny said under his breath.

The family fell silent for a few uncomfortable moments as their patriarch fumed. Tony looked from his brother to his father and wanted to put peace back into the family. "Hey, Pop, I read that the Yankees have a kid out in San Francisco; they say could come here and start this year. And guess what? He's Italian! What do you think about that?"

Even the comment about the up and coming great Italian baseball player Joe DiMaggio couldn't deter Donato once he got off on his favorite subject. "The Yankees are owned by Jews," he muttered, his eyes glinting with anger. "If they get an Italian, it's only for show. Believe me if he's good, I mean real good, they will never give him a chance. And even if they ever gave him a chance, they wouldn't pay him what he's worth."

Tony nodded. "Yeah, they'd rip him off."

"Pop, when did you come to America again?" Danny full well knew the answer but was eager to get him away from the unpleasant discussion.

Donato's eyes were boiling over with impassioned rage. He took a while to hear Danny's words but when he met his son's interested gaze, his heartbeat calmed down and his features softened. "Now there's a story." A soft smile touched his lips.

"Tell me, Pop," Danny said, relieved to see his father's anger dissipate. He returned Donato's smile. "I love to hear it. How did you learn English?"

"Back when I was in Italy, it was hard. There were no chances for any of us. I had a neighbor, Valentino Ruggerio. He was a seaman and used to come home and tell us all about his travels. He taught me English.

"I came to America about twenty- five years ago. I met your mother just after I arrived. It was a good omen. We married quickly, and Danny you were born two years later," Donato said with a grin.

"How'd you meet Mamma?" Maria asked, casting a conspiratorial smile at Danny. She was happy to hear her father speak of pleasant things.

"At church, of course," Teresa said proudly. "Like any good girl does."

"Your parents were happy to have me as part of your family," Donato said straightening his shoulders. "I was a good catch."

"Yes, and you still are," Teresa said. She looked at her husband with the same rush of love she had felt as a teenager back in that church, peeking out from behind her fan in the pew. She remembered how handsome he looked, how confident he was and how he had made her blush when he looked deep into her eyes with passion. She couldn't help the warm sensation that overtook her and blushed anew.

CHAPTER THREE

Danny ran through the streets of Newark; his mind filled with images of what his first fight would be like. He knew Thomas Gardner by reputation only and found his adrenaline rushing every time he thought of the upcoming bout. The man was known for his knockout punches.

He trained daily after work and running was part of that routine. Traversing the Italian end of town, Danny passed scores of neighborhoods like his own, filled with two-story wood frame houses that in many cases nearly touched one another. This gave way gradually to tenement buildings and then business and warehouses. Many minutes had passed just as Danny reached a Jewish neighborhood, the red sun ducked behind the hills to the West.

He came up on a soup line outside a Temple and slowed down. No one waiting looked him in the eye. They seemed to focus on the pavement for the most part. He stopped short when he saw the stocky Nate Rubin. Staring in disbelief, Nate cast a glance his way. Blushing, Danny stammered a greeting.

Nate tipped his hat cordially and said, "Hello."

"Saw you at the fight last week," Danny said. "That's one powerful uppercut you got."

Nate allowed a smile. "Thanks. You fight?"

Danny nodded. "I'm up against Gardner in three months,"

"He's okay. You run every day?"

"Of course."

"Haven't seen you before."

"I usually stick to my neighborhood," Danny said.

"Make sense. What's your name?"

"Danny. Danny Petrucelli."

"Good to meet you, Danny," Nate said shaking his hand.

The two fell silent. Danny felt a bit silly standing there next to the line, but he didn't want to leave. Nate Rubin was one of the best fighters in Newark. His style was like Gardner's; they were brawlers. Nate relied on his tremendous power to knock his opponents out quickly. His matches tended to end abruptly, sometimes as early as the first round.

Although Danny didn't frequent smokers, he did see him beat Rusty Lane three months ago. Rusty was fun to watch because he was a swarmer, pummeling his opponent with a barrage of jabs. His relentless attacks could overwhelm his opponents very quickly. Nate simply took the beating and when Rusty was out of steam, he delivered a crushing uppercut, knocking Rusty out before he hit the mat. It was the most exciting fight Danny had ever seen.

"Where's the fight? Maybe I'll swing by," Nate said with a shrug.

"East Ward Boxing Club."

"You know Willie Greene?"

"Yeah, he's my trainer."

Nate nodded, contemplating Danny with a new look of respect, "You could do worse."

Danny wrinkled his brow, taking offense to Nate's choice of words. He was about to open his mouth to tell Nate just how amazing trainer Willie was when a black Packard slowed down next to the line, causing him to lose his train of thought.

The car was shiny and new, not a speck of dirt on it. Everyone on the line stared at the car as if looking at a mirage in the middle of a desert. The market value of that car could feed all their families for the rest of the year. It was hard not to feel jealous.

The window rolled down, and Danny could see an olive-skinned man in the driver's seat. He looked to be in his late twenties. Danny felt the hairs on the back of his neck stand up. Although the driver's face was in the shadows, he knew instinctively the man was up to no good. Danny shot a nervous glance over to Nate, who was glaring at the car.

"You know this guy?" Danny whispered.

Nate nodded slowly not taking his eyes off the Packard for a moment. "He's come around before."

Suddenly something flew out of the window and splattered onto the sidewalk between two men. Danny's jaw dropped open as he realized it was a rotten tomato. Two more followed, hitting a man in a tattered brown coat. The man didn't say anything but removed a handkerchief and cleaned himself off and passively continued to shuffle towards the eventual soup table.

Laughter erupted from the car as it squealed away from the curb.

Danny stared after it. "I can't believe that. Who is that jerk?"

Nate's eyes were locked on the Packard as it continued down the street. "Nick Martens. He's some big shot soccer player from Argentina."

"Why would he do that?"

Nate turned to look at Danny, contempt filled his voice. "He runs the walnut Street Athletic Club."

Confused, Danny asked, "What does that have to do with anything?"

Nate stared at Danny for a moment before he snarled, "Scram, will you? Go back to running in your neighborhood. You don't belong here."

Danny's mouth opened to say something, but he closed it when he saw the dangerous glint in Nate's eye. He took a step back, turned around, and jogged home.

"Pass that olive bread," Tony said with a mouth full of spaghetti.

Teresa gladly handed over the sliced bread still warm from oven. Olive bread was her signature item. Whenever her neighbors or friends threw a party, they hinted that Teresa might bake her bread for them. Teresa would always blush modestly and assure them she would bake a few extra loaves for the occasion.

"Someday, we'll go back to the old country," Donato said. The dreamy quality of his voice might have been influenced by the half a bottle of Chianti he had polished off himself. "You can cook, *mi amore*. And my sons can farm the land like my parents once did. We would be free under Mussolini- free to live the good life and have it all."

The family was silent, each focused on the meal in front of them. Donato's was the only one with an empty plate. Growing up in a large family and being the youngest of five children, he was accustomed to eating the remains of a meal. Eating slowly was a luxury one couldn't afford, it meant you went hungry. Inhaling his food was a difficult habit for him to break.

"Why did you leave, Pop?" Danny asked mildly.

"Huh?" Donato asked. "What do you mean why did I leave? Leave where?"

"Why did you leave Italy and come to America?"

Donato scowled at his eldest son. "Why do you think? There was no chance for a real life back then. No chance to live the life I deserved to live, to have the life that I wanted to make for me and my family. You think I could have married your mother? No way! Her parents would have laughed at me."

"Okay, Pop," Tony said gently. "You've done what you set out to do. No need to leave, right?"

Donato scoffed. He drained the rest of the wine from his glass and reached for the bottle. "We can do better now. Italy's different with Mussolini at the helm. He's changed things all around, made it possible for us all to prosper there. We don't have to worry about the kikes taking over like we do here."

"Yeah, those filthy kikes piss me off," Tony said.

"That's enough," Danny said, his voice low.

Tony looked at his brother in disbelief. "What did you say?"

Danny gritted his teeth and glared at Tony. "I just can't listen to this anymore."

Tony snarled back, "You're not turning into a kike lover are you?"

"What the hell's that supposed to mean?" Danny asked, his face mottled with red splotches. "You can't be that ignorant."

"Who you calling ignorant?" Tony shouted.

Danny studied Tony grimly for a moment before he stood up. Shaking his head, he said quietly, "Today when I was running, I saw something I hope I'll never see again.

These poor saps were waiting for soup outside a temple, and this jerk comes by and throws rotten tomatoes at them. Can you believe that? I'm sorry, but it doesn't matter what you think of Jewish people, they don't deserve that. No one does. It just isn't right."

"But-," Tony started.

Donato put his hand up, instantly stopping Tony's speech. Calmly, the elder patriarch said, "Sit down, Danny. They're not worth fighting over. Sit down, have some wine."

Danny shook his head, "No thanks, Pop. I'm tired. I think I'll go to bed." He turned to his mother and said, "Thank you for another wonderful meal, Mamma."

Teresa nodded to her son and watched him climb the stairs.

CHAPTER FOUR
June 1935

Manny Kimmel watched his best fighter, Nate Rubin, spar with one of the club members, Rudy Schneider. The Central Ward Boxing Club had no pretense of prestige, but its history was evident in the peeling paint and chipped cement floors. Nate looked bored as he staved off Rudy's flurry of punches. Although they each hit their mark, the effect was minimal on Nate's physique. Sparring involved gloves after all, and Nate was accustomed to bare knuckle fighting.

Manny had been Nate's trainer for five years. Looking at Manny, one would have never known he had been a champion fighter in his day. Weighing in at just one hundred and fifteen pounds, he looked like a falling leaf could deliver him a knockout blow. Age hadn't treated him well, and his constant exposure to cigar and cigarette smoke didn't help.

What Manny lacked in good looks, he made up for in knowledge. Five years ago, when he had spotted Nate at the club, he immediately knew that if this fighter was trainable, that he'd be good. His hunch paid off. Nate was one of the hardest working fighters there, always working out, always eager to schedule another fight even if the venue was a smoker.

Manny remembered their first smoker like it was yesterday. He'd brought the kid there, wondering if he'd been doing the right thing.

Smokers were vicious fights, which often ended in brutal injuries, sometimes fatalities. The extreme violence drew large crowds.

Nate had been pitted against a brute of a Hawaiian named Jerry Jamison. He'd no sooner stepped into the ring than Jamison threw a powerful right, sending his protégé literally flying across the ring. Bouncing off the ropes, Nate fell forward onto the mat. Not missing a beat, the boy picked himself up off the floor, spit out some blood and sneered, "Is that all you got?"

Pulling himself out of his revere, Manny rasped, "Okay, that's enough." He coughed violently for a half a minute.

Nate looked over to his trainer with concern. Nodding a dismissive acknowledge to his sparring partner, he walked over to the side of the ring. "You okay?" he asked.

"Yeah, yeah, don't worry yourself over me," Manny wheezed. "You just concentrate on that right cross."

"Don't worry about my right cross, old man," Nate said fondly. "I'll clobber that Limey bastard tomorrow."

"You'd better. You're undefeated. Better keep it that way if you want to continue eating," Manny said gruffly.

Nate nodded dully, a cloud of concern washing over his expression. Failure wasn't an option. He shared a small place with his father and thus far had managed to pay the bills and keep them fed, but he could only afford to continue if he kept getting booked for fights. The second he loses his appeal, he'd be on the streets.

Manny winced as he watched his young charge. He could see the weight of responsibility descend upon him. It was one thing to take a fight seriously and another to be motivated by fear. Fear was a distraction that could kill one in the ring.

"Don't worry, kid. You'll do fine," he said. "You're 'Light's Out'!"

Nate grinned and relaxed. "Yeah."

"Just do your thing tomorrow, and the poor sap won't know what hit him."

"How much's the take?"

"Don't know," Manny replied. "I'm thinking a couple hundred."

"Can't we get more?"

"Kid, I don't know," Manny said with a sigh. "You know how it is. Times are rough, and I don't know how easy it will be to find someone to put in the ring with you."

"Why?"

"They'll want some chance of winning. Look at you! You're in great shape and have a perfect record."

"Maybe I should throw a few fights then."

Manny cuffed him on the side of the head. "I don't want to ever hear you say that again. You hear me?"

"Ow! Whatcha do that for?" Nate rubbed his head with his fingertips.

"The money we get for you is because you're undefeated. If you go and lose fights, you'll be just like the other poor saps that show up looking for a fight. You've seen them right? They get $20 because they don't have the reputation you have. You want to be like them?"

"No. Of course not. I was just thinking that…"

"Don't go and do any thinking. You're a fighter not a manager. Let me do all the thinking for us both, okay?"

Nate nodded and grinned. "Okay."

Nate and Manny approached the wharf at Port Newark at a brisk pace. It was a cold and rainy night; one that didn't inspire a stroll. Nate looked over at the large and expensive Packards, Lincolns, and Dusenbergs parked conspicuously by the side of the road. Large men in black suits leaned against them, staring down anyone who got too close.

"Looks like the Social Register of New York showed up to see you clobber Eric Collins tonight," Manny said, glancing at Nate.

"Somehow I don't think that's the outcome they'll be hoping for," Nate muttered.

"No?" Manny asked sarcastically.

"I'm thinking they'll be wanting to get their money back from the last time."

"Serves them right for betting against you!"

Nate grinned. "Couldn't agree more."

Port Newark, with its piers that stretched out into the cold misty Newark Bay, was the eerie setting for this event. The cold and icy wind raced along the broken wooden slats of the warehouses that lined the wharf. Most of the buildings, that were once filled with goods earmarked for the American public,were now empty and abandoned. Only one was buzzing with activity. This warehouse, once used by the Army Corp of Engineers, was now a hot spot for the wealthy and poor residents of Newark. The one thing they had in common was an enthusiasm for illegal fights that didn't follow the fistic rules of Marquis of Queensbury.

Nate had been fighting in smokers since he was fifteen. He remembered his first fight with pride. The match had been the typical no-weight-limit fight, which was especially tough since his opponent had thirty pounds as well as five years on him. He had been a 6 to 1 underdog.

His Uncle Reuben had brought twenty dollars to wager for that fight. Nate had placed the bet himself with Fat Jack, who smirked, promising the boy eight to one if he won. Nate stunned the crowd when he broke his opponent's jaw in a single blow within five minutes.

The common man rooted for Nate with a passion. He was their representative, and they loved him.The dark cold depression was upon everyone but Nate made most poor men forget about their troubles and perhaps if Nate were to win they too, had a chance of winning.

The elite, represented by their dark suited well dressed drivers however, looked down their noses at Nate as he entered the smoke-filled arena.

The haze and smoke, coming from the coal burning stoves adjacent to the pier, was overwhelming and Manny did his best to cover his cough. The smoke stung Nate's eyes, but he didn't blink. He was being watched by the majority of the onlookers. To Nate It was important to show strength at all times.

"Go home, Jew boy," snarled a tall blond man with a strong German accent on his left.

"Hans, leave the poor kike alone," a squat man with a long handlebar mustache said, his voice condescendingly sweet. "After tonight he'll realize his mistake."

Nate gave them both what he hoped passed as bored look. "We'll see. I hope you brought your money." He casually mentioned.

"I've got plenty of money, you filthy money-grubbing kike, don't you worry. You'll never see a dime of it though," Hans spat. He made a lunge for Nate and the other man held him back.

"Let it go," the second German said. "He'll get his in the end."

Hans stopped struggling and straightened his suit jacket. "Ja, Herr Held. You're right, of course."

Nate stared at them both and wondered about their poor veiled threat. He opened his mouth to ask them what they meant when Manny prodded him along.

"Don't get into it with those two," Manny whispered.

Nate craned his neck around to look back at them as he allowed Manny to push him forward. The one Hans had referred to as Mr. Held continue to stare at him with a self-satisfied look of victory. "Who the hell do they think they are?"

"Nazis," Manny whispered.

Nate's head whipped around to look at his trainer. "Really? Nazis? Here?"

Manny rolled his eyes. "Why not here? They're everywhere."

Nate looked back at the two one last time and then turned his attention to a man in front of him. His face was weathered and his jacket torn in two places.

"You're gonna get him, right? You're gonna clobber him, aren't you?" The man's eyes shone with hope.

Nate put a reassuring hand on his shoulder. "You betcha. Count on it."

"I put two dollars on ya," the man said proudly. His grin revealed two rotted teeth. "I know you'll win. I just know it."

Other men approached them, each holding up the dollar bills they planned to wager on him. Nate looked around at them and nodded an acknowledgement to each one. "It's a good bet."

They all cheered as Nate walked to the ring. Nate's attention quickly shifted to his opponent, Eric Collins. Manny patted him on the back. "Good, focus on Collins. He's got a vicious left hook, that one."

Nate scoffed. "You worried?"

"I'm not worried. Just watch yourself, okay?"

Nate laughed. "I'll watch out for that hook, but I doubt he'll get a chance to land one on me."

"Don't get too cocky, kid," Manny muttered. "Collin's no green rookie."

"I know. Don't worry so much."

"I said I'm not worried."

"Whatever you say."

Manny shook his head at his young charge. Confidence was a good thing as long as it was warranted. Over confidence could get Nate killed.

Nate was no longer paying any attention to Manny. He was sizing up his competition and looking around the ring at the throng of onlookers. As usual, they were divided down the middle. On the right were the street people, the dock workers, the real men of Newark. They shouted words of encouragement to him, and he nodded to them with a small confident smile.

On the left were the not-so-friendly high society people. They were downright hostile. The promoter was volleying back and forth between the two sides, collecting bets and encouraging more. Nate was always the favorite, being that he was undefeated and an experienced brawler. By the looks of it, he was two to one on this match. He was accustomed to being three or four to one, but looking to his left he surmised that the wealthy were betting heavily against him. Prejudice delivered its own odds.

To the right, Nate saw the men, having no reservation, betting their last dollars, no doubt. It was as if they didn't even consider the thought that he might lose; they simply believed in him. It touched him deeply. He couldn't let them down.

With a renewed determination, Nate stepped into the ring, sizing the Irish fighter up and down. Collins did the same with him. Collins was brutish in appearance but no larger than Nate. Manny taught Nate to respect his opponents; it was dangerous not to. Looking at Collins, it was clear to Nate that Eric's trainer had not instilled that quality in him. The hatred and scorn that emanated from the fighter's blue eyes gave Nate pause. He was used to anger but not this pure loathing.

The promoter was still collecting bets as the referee recited the rules of the match amidst the cheers and jeers of the crowd. No rounds, no restrictions in blows, just a fight to the end. As was customary, they tapped their bare knuckles against one another and retreated to opposite corners for a last- minute conference with their trainers.

"Watch for that hook. Okay?" Manny said.

"I know," Nate said nodding his head.

"He'll throw it at any angle, so watch out for it."

"Yeah."

"He'll try to grab you and then push you back and then-"

Nate interrupted, "He'll throw a left hook."

"If you're prepared for it, it won't kill you."

"You worry too much."

"I'm not worried."

They looked at one another and both grinned.

Nate turned to study Collins from across the ring, waiting for the bell to sound. There would be no break, no chance to regroup, no opportunity to come to the corner and hear Manny's words of encouragement. He had to knock this guy out quickly and just be done with it.

The bell rang and the crowd erupted into a cacophony of cheers. Nate could hear numerous derogatory names shouted at him amidst the constant reassuring call of "Lights Out". He circled around Collins, waiting to see what he would do. He could hear Manny's warning, "Watch out for that left hook!" echoing through his mind.

Nate jabbed a quick test shot at Collin's right cheek. Collins replied with a jab of his own to his left side. They both pulled back to reassess. Suddenly, Collins came at him with a flurry of punches to his torso, forcing Nate back against the ropes. When Collins stopped, Nate landed a powerful right cross to his jaw, sending Collins back a few feet. Nate bounced off the ropes, watching his opponent carefully, waiting for the next onslaught.

He didn't have to wait long. Collins came at him again with a set of jabs to his face. Left, right, left, right and then it came. A powerful left hook, which sent Nate flying three feet back. Nate concentrated on keeping his feet under him as his head spun. Collins approached again with an intense menacing look. Nate knew he was going in for the kill. Collins wouldn't stop at a victory; he wanted to end Nate's career then and there.

Nate could hear the rush of blood in his ears, but beyond that he could hear the chant of "Lights Out, Lights Out". Just when Collins pulled back his left hand, Nate twisted to the right, thrust his right hand upward and delivered a powerful uppercut.

As his fist connected with the Irish brute's jaw, he saw the look of utter bewilderment cross Collin's face. It was clear that he had grossly underestimated Nate.

The uppercut was so powerful it lifted Collin's body up into the air. Nate then delivered a left hook that knocked Collins unconscious midair. His limp body fell onto the canvas with a sickening thud. When Collin's manager threw in the towel with disgust, the cheering from the right made up for the stony silence from the left.

"Lights Out! Lights Out!" The chant grew in intensity. Nate looked over at the two Germans, both beet red with anger, and grinned at them. Realizing there was nothing they could do, the two men turned and walked away.

Still grinning Nate turned to Manny, who beamed with pride at him. He joined in the ongoing cry, "Lights Out!"

CHAPTER FIVE

Willie Greene looked around the East Ward Boxing Club with pride. The few white hairs surrounding his domelike head were hardly ever seen. The faded blue New York Giants baseball cap was almost always crammed down tight over his brow. He tugged on that cap as he watched his young charge, Danny Petrucelli, pummel the punching bag.

Willie had been instrumental in turning the huge abandoned warehouse, which used to be a motor pool depot for old abandoned cars and busses, into a sanctuary for the local teenagers and adults. He figured if they had a place to come and get out their aggressions, they wouldn't resort to crime.

Willie wasn't immune to the dream of every fight promoter: to discover new budding talent. Danny Petrucelli made his heart race. Working on the docks, combined with his discipline to run every day, made Danny lean and strong. But even beyond that, he was light on his feet. He watched Danny's intricate footwork, musing that he could very well wind up with the handle "Dancing Man".

Danny stopped hitting the bag and turned to Willie. He was hardly winded. "You think I have a chance against La Roma tomorrow?"

A puzzled look crossed Willie's face. "Of course you do, kid. What are you talking about?"

"He's got a reputation that's all."

Willie scoffed. "La Roma's good. You're better though. The thing with him is he tires pretty quick. He don't have your stamina, your youth. Trust me, you'll do fine."

Danny nodded. "Yeah, I know. I'm just nervous, that's all."

"Good!" Willie exclaimed approvingly. When Danny looked confused, he laughed and added. "It keeps that adrenaline going."

"I guess."

"Just make sure to eat a good meal three hours before the fight and drink lots of water throughout the day. Eat something light about a half an hour before you step in the ring." Willie continued to tell Danny about what he needed to do to prepare for his bout the next day.

Danny nodded patiently to his coach. He's heard his coach's instructions on how to prepare for a fight many times and was itching to just jump rope. The adrenaline was already pumping, and it was difficult to stand still and listen patiently.

Willie saw that he had lost the interest of his protégé and rolled his eyes and gave him a nod. "Go on." He knew where Danny was headed.

With a grateful grin, Danny dashed off to the far corner. He was an expert at the rope and found it more relaxing than any other form of exercise.

There were two teenagers jumping rope in the corner. When they saw Danny approach, they immediately stopped, dropping their ropes in eager anticipation of what was to come.

Danny shot them a grin. "Hello, Jason. Hey there, George."

"Hiya, Mr. Petrucelli. How's it going?" George replied. He was a seventeen- year- old Italian boy.

"Great, just great," Danny replied. He bent down to pick up the rope.

"Here you go," Jason said excitedly, handling Danny his rope. "Take mine."

"Thank you," Danny said.

The boys backed up a few steps, giving Danny room. A few of the older members stopped what they were doing to look on.

Danny started out with a basic jump and as he picked up speed, the room was filled with the high- pitched whirring sound of the rope. Never missing a stride, Danny alternated between running in place and jumping straight up.

As he continued his workout, the gym faded out of view. He was in harmony with his body and the rope as he continued to increase the speed. He felt light and free when he was doing this cardio workout.

The rope started passing two or three times under his feet between jumps. Sometimes he would cross the rope in front of him while jumping, still alternating between straight jumping and running in place. After twenty minutes, he finally stopped, completely out of breath. Looking around he was startled to noticed that the entire gym had gathered around. They burst into spontaneous applause, causing him to grin sheepishly and blush.

Willie suppressed a grin. "Show's over," he said in a mock gruff tone, fooling no one. It was clear was as proud as could be.

"Jeepers, Danny," George said. "That was incredible!"

"Yeah," Jason agreed, awe infusing his voice. "Amazing!"

"Thanks,' Danny said with a quick nod. He turned Willie. "What now?"

"Go home and rest," Willie said. "You've done enough for today. Get up in the morning and go for good run and be here an hour before the fight. Got it?"

"Yeah," Danny said with a grin. "I got it."

By mid-afternoon the East Ward Gym was filled in anticipation of the four- round exhibition between Danny Petrucelli and Stanley La Roma, an up and comer , who impressed many of the onlookers in New York at the last amateur Golden Gloves tournament. La Roma was from the Bronx and like so many Bronx Italians, he was tough, which gave him tremendous crowd appeal.

Danny watched La Roma punch the air dramatically for show. He then winked at a few of the ladies clapping enthusiastically nearby;

they were obviously drawn to his good looks and self-confidence. Although he was pushing thirty years old, his wavy black hair and piercing blue eyes made him very popular with the women.

Danny leaned into Willie, whispering in his ear. "Why's he here? He could have his pick of fights."

"He's here for you," Willie said simply.

'Me?"

"Don't be dense, kid. Your name's getting around."

"Really?"

"Don't let it go to your head," Willie said rolling his eyes. The truth was Willie was a little nervous. He knew La Roma's management had been sandbagging their fighter for years, saving him for the right time when they could bring him out for the better fighters and therefore better purses. Willie hoped that Danny's age advantage and dexterity in the ring was enough to keep his kid alive.

Willie also had another ace in the hole, something the scouts for La Roma probably didn't know. Danny trained with Ernie Monaco, a fitness specialist, someone with cutting edge training concepts designed to sculpt Danny's muscles and give him an edge with endurance.

In addition, the fights La Roma's scouts had witnessed were not representative of Danny's true abilities. Danny had been specifically asked to hold back enough to keep the match alive for four rounds. He would always win, but the victories were unimpressive and boring. To date, Danny had not been allowed to go all out. That is until this afternoon.

Danny stepped into the ring and joined La Roma in the center with the referee, who went over the rules of the fight. Danny's heart raced as La Roma attempted to intimidate him with an intense, unblinking stare. After the referee finished speaking, they touched gloves and went back to their corners, awaiting the bell's ring.

"Keep moving," Willie said as Danny waited to start. "Stay clear of his power punch and keep after him."

Danny nodded, never taking his eyes off his opponent. When the bell rang, the cheering erupted from the crowd. Danny didn't have a nickname yet, but his opponent obviously did. "Rooster,

Rooster!" was the predominant cry, which echoed through the large room.

Puzzled, Danny looked back at Willie and mouthed the word "Rooster" questioningly. Willie shrugged back, yelling at him pay attention on his opponent. Stanley threw a quick punch at Danny's head, trying to take advantage of his opponent's lapse in attention, which Danny dodged easily. As they circled each other Stanley's head bobbed in and out, much like a barnyard rooster. Danny grinned at the appropriate nickname for his opponent.

Danny's legwork was impressive. He was light on his toes as he danced around the ring. He and La Roma traded punches for the first two rounds, each sizing up the other's strengths and weaknesses. At the end of the second round, La Roma was tired and was favoring his right side.

Danny watched La Roma's manager patch him up as Willie pressed cold silver coins to his right eye. Wincing Danny said, "This guy's tough."

Willie flicked his eyes up at Danny's before going back to his work. "Yeah, he's not holding back, is he?"

"No. And I'm not either."

"No.

"His ribs seem to be hurting him."

"Good, you noticed that," Willie said with a smile. "I was about to point that out to you."

"Of course, I noticed that," Danny scoffed.

"So, what you gonna to do about that?"

"Go for his right side."

The bell rang, and Danny came out of his corner like a rocket, charging at his opponent fearlessly. La Roma stood his ground and shot out an uppercut when Danny was within range. Deftly avoiding the blow, Danny pummeled La Roma on his right ribs, pushing him back against the ropes.

Finally, La Roma was able to get a few good shots in, driving Danny back to the center of the ring. Exhausted Danny still moved with dexterity albeit, not as quickly. He avoided two more jabs from La Roma and wound back, delivering a powerful left hook. La Roma dropped to the canvas and struggled to get back on his feet. The referee pushed Danny back and began the ten-count.

La Roma was on his feet by seven but there was doubt of his injuries. Danny looked to the ref who nodded for them to continue and Danny delivered another blow, this time to his chin. The force of the blow was not great, as Danny did not want to permanently injure his opponent. It had the desired effect though and knocked him to the canvas for the full ten-count. The referee raised Danny's arm in victory as the crowd cheered Danny.

CHAPTER SIX
April 1936

The crisp April morning felt good as Tony pedaled hard to reach his destination. His palms itched in excitement. He knew where Guido's restaurant was as everyone did, but he'd never been inside. You only went in if you were invited and that invitation was approved by one of the captains of the Cantalupos. This was their headquarters.

When Demaio had given him the added task of delivering loaves to local business, he'd hoped that one day the Cantalupos would place an order and that he would be the one to deliver. Ever since the days on the soup lines when this family had fed his family, he'd secretly dreamt of being asked to join the family. He knew it was the only true financial security this world could offer.

He parked his bike and slung the bag of loaves over his shoulder. The oval sign on the front door claimed the restaurant was closed. Disappointment washed over Tony as he wondered what to do. To come all this way only to turn around not only dashed his hopes and dreams, but Demaio wouldn't be happy that Tony had wasted the trip. He might not give Tony another chance.

He walked tentatively over to the large window and cupped his hands over his brow and looked inside the dark building. A burly man peered back at him making him jump.

Big Guido opened the door with a slightly suppressed smug grin. "You from Larson's?" he asked. Big Guido had no relation to the restaurant name, but Cantalupo thought it funny to have him stationed there. He'd tease the round man that he should remember not to eat the restaurant in his next meal.

"Yeah," Tony breathed. "Where do you want these?"

Big Guido turned to the back of the large room and shouted, "Ralph!"

While they waited for Ralph to come to the front, Tony took the opportunity to look around the restaurant. The main room was deserted. Most of the tables were set up for the next service with checkered table cloths and plain white china set up for four. One table in the back had a half- eaten lasagna and cup of coffee next to an ashtray filled with cigarette butts. It was clear that Big Guido was here by himself today.

"You looking for someone?" Big Guido asked, his expression inscrutable.

Startled, Tony said, "I just wondered if Art Belle was here."

"You know Art?"

Tony shook his head, blushing slightly. "No." Arte Belle was Philip Cantalupo's right hand man. The media loved to plaster him all over their papers, making him a near celebrity in Newark.

Big Guido grinned knowingly. "I'll let him know he's got a fan."

Tony was about to respond when a wiry kid came out of the kitchen. His hands were covered in flour. "Did you call me?"

"Yeah. Ralph's your name, ain't it?"

Ralph nodded. Despite his young years, he wasn't intimidated by Big Guido's rough manner.

"Do something with this bread, will ya?" Big Guido said indicating Tony's bag.

"Sure thing," Ralph responded quickly.

Tony couldn't help feeling a flash of jealousy at Ralph's station. As he handed the loaves to Ralph, he asked, "You Marco Carpote's son?"

Ralph looked surprised. "Yeah. You know my Pop?"

"He worked at the bakery with my father," Tony replied. He extended his hand toward Ralph. "I'm Tony Petrucelli."

Ralph accepted Tony's handshake and grinned. "You Danny Petrucelli's brother or something?"

"Yeah," Tony said proudly, glancing over at Big Guido. Anything that got him noticed with one of Cantalupo's men was an asset.

Tony noticed the big man's instant recognition, as Big Guido's face split into a grin. "Really? He's your brother? He's something that one."

"Undefeated, right?" Ralph asked in admiration.

Tony stood up a bit taller and nodded, trying to look at ease with his new found fame by association. "Yeah, that's right. You two going to his fight on Saturday?"

"Who's he fightin'?" Big Guido asked.

Before Tony could reply, Ralph eagerly jumped in. "Vick Minola."

Tony grinned in pleasure. Ralph knowing the name of his brother's opponent was a true sign that he was a fan. "That's right. Should be a good fight."

Big Guido nodded. "I'll be there. Does Danny ever fight smokers?"

"Nah, not so far. He's thinking about it though. He and his trainer have been tossing it around."

"He should," Big Guido said.

Ralph looked eagerly at Tony, snapping his fingers. "You know, he should really fight Light's Out in a smoker! Now there'd be a fight worth paying for."

"Nah," Big Guido said. "I mean no offense, but the kid's not ready for Light's Out."

Tony's back stiffened and he muttered, "Yeah, well, he don't need to play in no smoker anyway," He didn't like the thought of his brother losing to some kike.

Ralph nodded in agreement. "Nah, let the mockies fight in those places. Danny's doing fine where he is."

Tony relaxed and grinned. "Yeah. Right! Look, I should go, but I'll see you at the fight Saturday?"

"Wouldn't miss it," Ralph said.

Friday night arrived and the smoker was packed. Nate stood grimacing in the middle of the ring, breathing hard. Some distance away, amid the smoke and noise, Mickey Brown laid on his back, the ref kneeling in to begin the count. To count him out, Nate prayed, please count him out.

The smoker had lived up to its billing, both fighters, pushing the action, taking punishment. His youth gave him added quickness and stamina, however, and Nate masterfully took control as the minutes passed. Now Brown, knocked to the canvas for the third time with numerous welts and blood dripping from a nose broken yet again, lay still.

This had to be it. Nate saw Mickey roll onto his side and initially felt relief. He was okay. But like some hellish wish up toy, Mickey got his elbow underneath him, planted his opposite foot and arose once more.

Nate took up his fighting posture again, but glanced around the ring for help.

"Fight!" snapped the ref from between the two men and backed away.

Mickey staggered heavily forward. Half beaten to pulp, the veteran's signature footwork and finesse were gone. Nate was painfully aware of what another solid blow from his fist or from the canvas for that matter, could mean to his opponent. He looked to Manny, who held out his hands and shook his head helplessly. Nate wheeled around to face Mickey's corner, easily avoiding a wild swing from Brown. The trainer scowled back at him, a short stub of a cigar sticking out of his old merciless face. "Throw in the towel! He's done!" Nate tried to will the trainer through telepathy, but the trainer's concern for his fighter was non- existent.

Nate found himself dancing away from his opponent for the first time in his career. Jeers and boos emanated from behind Mickey's corner, where sat many wealthy patrons and more than a few anti-Semites.

As Mickey Brown continued to come awkwardly at him, Nate realized that the Nazis movement would be fueled if he were to end up badly maiming or even killing his white opponent. It would outrage them. Besides, Nate had yet to kill an opponent in the ring and didn't want to start a new trend tonight.

He fended off a punch and moved inside tying Brown up. Finally, Nate saw his chance. He let Mickey's roundhouse right whiff by and leaned in.

As the exhausted fighter's head turned profile in the follow-through, Nate shot a careful jab into the point of his chin. It was a relatively gentle blow but because of his position and vulnerability, Mickey's head snapped around and he fell like a dead weight. Still worried that the fall to the mat might end the man, Nate caught the sweaty body and laid it on the mat.

Pieces of fruit and other articles flew at Nate from members of the audience whose bloodlust was left unsatisfied. "You gonna kiss him goodnight now, you faggot?" he heard someone yell.

But Manny smiled as he threw a towel around Nate's head and led him from the smoky arena. Manny ushered him into the dressing room and slammed and latched the door. "That was quick thinking, kid." He looked at Nate, beaten up, his lip fattened and split in two. Affection beamed from his eyes as he said, "Don't ever expect that kind of consideration from an opponent."

"I know, I just couldn't…," Nate looked up at his trainer. "You know."

"Yeah, kid. I know."

Anticipating the bell, Danny stared at his opponent across the ring, who glared back. Vick Minola had a strong following seated right behind him. A tumult of shouts and a flurry of waving arms and fists surrounded the fighter. Danny looked around at the crowd and found he had a few fans himself. His brother stood by Ralph Carpote, along with a few others from his neighborhood. They attempted to be as vocal as Minola's people, which made Danny grin.

"Remember, stay clean," Willie caution brought his attention back into the ring. "He'll let you land a punch to draw you in and then deliver his punishing blow. That's how he wins fights."

And win fights Vick Minola did. At 12-2, his only losses were to other brawlers. Vick's trainer, Scott Turino, had contacted Willie after Danny's first bout. Clearly, Turino felt that Danny possessed insufficient power to beat his fighter and that his dancing style would just fatigue him so that Vick's punch would knock him out after a few rounds. Willie accepted the challenge, knowing that Turino underestimated Danny's finesse and skill. He, like his fighter, looked for the power behind each blow and didn't value the mental aspect of the sport.

The bell sounded, and the two fighters popped up and, as if by agreement, immediately assumed their roles. Danny kept his feet moving, jabbing, and ducking in for a combination when he saw a chance. Minola doggedly plodded forward, left glove raised, and ready to shield, right arm cocked.

Midway through the round Danny learned about fighting a brawler. Vick caught him with a quick strong left, which pushed him off balance. Then, came the right cross Minola was known for. The crowd went wild as Danny barely managed to keep his feet. Dazed, he backed up. Minola showed surprising speed as he mercilessly pursued Danny into the ropes. Danny leaned back just beyond a sweeping right and used the opening to bounce off the ropes to his left and back into the center of the ring, landing a combination of his own as Vick turned.

Between rounds, Vick sat back and resumed his confident glare. He had no respect for his opponent and was surprised his trainer had set up the match. Petrucelli would tire himself out with all that fancy footwork, aided by whatever punishment he could inflict. Then he'd be a sitting duck. Six rounds is a long time. All he had to do was wait it out and the fight was his.

Willie turned Danny's head around to face him. "Hey! Quit starin' at that guy and listen up! What'd I tell you? You can't get careless like that again. You were lucky-"

Willie caught himself, realizing he needed to fill him with confidence, not tear him down. "Look, just stick with the game plan and you'll clobber the guy!" he blustered just as the bell rang.

Willie felt his stomach knot up as he watched his young fighter. He knew the strategy over in the Minola camp. But Danny had more stamina, more ability. Didn't he? Willie concealed a big nervous smile by pursung his lips. Doubts started to plague the old man as he watched Vick bide his time. One more punch like the last Danny sustained and it was all over.

The next two round went to Danny without question. He stayed out of serious trouble, avoiding the brunt of Vick's punches while barraging his face and ribs. Minola might have swayed the judges in round one with the near knockdown, but Danny won every round since.

In round five, Minola's style became more forceful and desperate. He walked steadily at Danny, who still danced nimbly just out of reach and darted in with quick blows whenever Vick left himself open. Willie saw that Danny was starting to look a bit cocky. "Watch yourself," Willie hissed into his ear. "Now's the time he's really gonna come at you. Keep your feet moving."

Vick Minola looked to his trainer, who stood directly in front of his fighter yelling and gesticulating. As soon as Turino moved out of the way, Vick threw a contemptuous glare across the ring at Danny. Danny held his gaze, realizing there was nothing behind the threatening look. His opponent was breaking down.

Back in the ring, Minola was still dangerous but was far too slow now. Danny added further punishment, easily avoiding the desperate swings. Near the end of the round, Minola lost his balance after another miss, leaving himself open to Danny's powerful left hook. The blow knocked him to his knees.

Minola regained his feet just as the bell sounded. He staggered to his corner and sat limply on his stool. It didn't take more than a moment for the trainer to throw in the towel causing the ref to wave the match over. He walked over to Danny and raised the fighter's arm victory.

Turning to face the audience, Danny saw his brother practically doing cartwheels. All his muscles hurt but despite the pain, he grinned broadly at him.

CHAPTER SEVEN
November 1937

The Petrucelli family was unusually quiet as they settled into their evening meal. The gnocchi with meat sauce had successfully captured their attention. For a good few minutes, all that could be heard was the reassuring sound of folks hitting the China and the occasional sighs of contentment. Teresa looked up and smiled at her family lovingly.

Catching her look, Maria squeezed her hand. "Mamma, you've outdone yourself again."

"I can teach you how to prepare this sometime," Teresa said fondly. "It really isn't difficult."

"Sounds good, Mamma,"

"And you can make it for your family when you get married."

Maria looked down at her plate and nodded in silence. Teresa looked her over and sighed. She still didn't have a boyfriend and it didn't look like she was moving in the direction of getting one in the near future. Her weekends were spent with girlfriends and family; she never went on dates. Teresa knew she shouldn't nag, but she couldn't help herself. Becoming an old maid wasn't an acceptable outcome for her only daughter. She was far too beautiful to let her prime years go to waste,

Noticing that Teresa was about to launch into a familiar one-sided dialogue that started with the importance of family and ended in her desire to have grandchildren, Danny stepped in, beating his mother to the punch. "So, Maria, how is your new job at the provision house?"

Maria's beautiful eyes lit with enthusiasm and gratitude. "I love working again," she said with a soft sigh. She turned to her father. "Thank you so much for arranging it for me."

Donato smiled with pride. "You're welcome, my daughter. One of the benefits of working in shipping and receiving is that I get to know all the drivers pretty well. Sam mentioned that his brother's boss was looking for a new secretary, so all I had to do was mention that my daughter was looking for work. He owed me. I've covered for him enough times."

Tony looked at her skeptically. "They treating you okay there, sis?"

"Yes, Tony. They are all very respectful."

"Good. You tell me if that changes okay?"

"It won't, but okay," Maria said with a smile. She loved that her brother was overly protective. Most of her girlfriends complained of their brothers and fathers suffocating them with protection, but she wasn't in any hurry to have gentlemen callers.

Having Tony on her side was a good deterrent, as was having an up- and- coming boxing celebrity for a brother. She turned to Danny and said with admiration, "I heard you clobbered Sanderson last night."

"Something like that!" Danny said sheepishly.

"Modest to the end," Donato said with a smile. "It wasn't something like that, it was exactly like that!"

Tony jumped up from his seat, giving the air a series of punches. "That dumb cluck didn't know what hit him!"

"Oh, I think he knew," Maria said with giggles. "My brother's fist was hard to miss."

They all laughed. As they continued to banner and extol Danny's prowess in the ring, Teresa studied her daughter. She wondered if Maria would ever know the happiness she felt at this moment. Having a family all gathered around the dinner table, talking and laughing freely about the week's events was an experience she hoped her daughter would share one day.

⊹ ⊹ ⊹

It was a few days later, and the provision house cafeteria was packed with workers of all levels. Most were seated already with sandwiches and containers of soup; the dull roar of chatter made conversation difficult. As Maria walked into the din, she leaned in toward her girlfriend to hear the latest gossip about a fellow secretary's engagement party. She feigned polite interest as the girl chattered away excitedly.

"The party was divine, "Sonya said, her hands clasped to her chest in angelic imitation. "The hors d' oeuvres were simple, but elegant. It was held in Larissa's family's home. Cramped quarters, jammed to the rafters with everyone they ever knew."

Maria smiled and nodded, stifling a bored yawn. Looking around she spotted a half empty table a few feet away.

"You brought your own lunch again?' Sonya asked.

Maria nodded. "I think mamma cooks too much each night on purpose. She wants to make sure I eat a good meal for lunch. Besides she'd consider it a personal insult if I were to buy my lunch at work. She barely tolerates my working as it is."

Sonya sighed. "I don't have any such luck. No mamma to cook for me." When it looked like Maria was about to launch into a sympathetic dialogue, Sonya shook her head. "It's okay. Really. Besides it gives me an excuse to bat my eyelashes at Gregory."

"The guy behind the sandwich counter?" Maria did her best to hide her revulsion at the idea.

Sonya didn't notice Maria's lack of support. "Of course, you silly goose! Who else would I be talking about?" With a grin, Sonya trotted away.

"Who else indeed," Maria muttered as she waved her friend away. She called after her. "I'll save you seat."

Sonya waved her hand carelessly over her shoulder in agreement as she hurried off to order a ham on rye. Maria trotted over to the partially empty table, concerned that it might not be there for long and sat down on the bench. She watched Sonya's antics with Gregory and wondered how she could be so overt with her affections. Even from her distance she could hear Sonya's playful giggles.

Shaking her head, she took out the meatball sandwich. The tomato sauce was oozing out appetizingly. She carefully laid out the forest green napkin her mother had provided and placed the slightly tarnished fork on top. Most people didn't carry linen to work with them, but Teresa Petrucelli made it clear that Maria wasn't most people. Maria grinned as she thought about her mother.

She continued to study her friend as she coyly thanked Gregory for the sandwich. Suddenly, she had an odd but familiar feeling that someone was watching her. She shivered as she looked around the room. She received attention from the opposite sex frequently but never really got used to it. She sincerely wished they would leave her alone. She refused to hide her beauty but was expert at putting up an impenetrable wall around her. The cold exterior made most men back away quickly.

Ready to repel the onlooker with a frosty look, she scanned the room. She wouldn't be able to enjoy her sandwich until he was taken care of. The majority of the occupants were men, but most were absorbed in their food. Time was limited for lunch. Finally, she spotted the eyes of her admirer. Prepared to send him her best don't- even- think- about- it glare, she was caught off guard by his dark good looks and smiling brown eyes.

In unchartered waters, she was mesmerized by him and could only stare. The rest of the room faded away as she found herself smiling and basking in the warmth of his return smile. She wondered what it would feel like to run her hands through his hair, touch her lips to his…

"It's about time!" Sonya's hushed voice cut across Maria's daydream, abruptly bringing her back to the noisy and unromantic lunch room.

Maria looked up dazedly at her friend. She wondered momentarily where she was and how she got there, "Why?"

Sonya gave her a knowing smile. "He's cute."

Maria's mouth dropped open, and she blushed furiously. "No, I…" She was at a loss as to what to say next.

Sitting down on the bench across from Maria, Sonya said gently, "I'm just saying it's about time you got yourself a boyfriend"

"Not interested," Maria said instinctively.

"Not interested my foot," Sonya scoffed, "There's no sense in denying it."

Maria shook her head. Getting irritated with her friend, she mumbled, "I don't know what you're talking about."

"There's nothing wrong with-"

"Drop it."

Sonya shrugged. "Whatever you say. Can I ask him out?"

Maria glared at her.

Sonya giggled. "Guess that's a no."

Three tables away, Nate Rubin frowned at the bowed head of the gorgeous brunette. If someone had asked him if he believed in love at first sight yesterday, he would have said no. He knew better now. The way their eyes had locked, and the depth he'd seen within her being, even from that distance, was amazing. She was incredible, and he just had to find a way to talk to her.

She had held his gaze for what seemed like... well, time had simple frozen. When her friend had joined, she had been startled away from their connection and now she wouldn't look at him at all. He silently willed her to look at him just one more time. As he continued to watch her, her averted features became increasingly angry. He found himself wondering if he had imagined what they had shared across the lunch room. He laughed at himself, realizing how silly he was acting. They hadn't even met!

"What's funny?" his father asked.

"Nothing, Pop," he replied, not wanting to share his musings.

Nate had come to the provision house to spend some time with his father over lunch. He tried come out on a regular basis. With all the training he did, he didn't see his father very often, and he instinctively knew that Jules needed Nate. He was all his father had in life.

"You fighting another smoker soon?" Jules asked.

"Yeah, next week."

"Good! That's good."

Jules kept his voice low and his head bowed. He looked like he was trying to blend in with the bench he was sitting on.

Nate watched his father with a puzzled expression. "Who do you normally eat with?"

Jules looked up at his son. "No one. Why?"

"No one?"

"I eat alone. It's better that way."

Nate just stared at his father, who resumed eating, staring at the food in front of him. He opened his mouth to ask more questions, but decided against it. Instead, he looked over at the dark-haired beauty and sighed. If only she would look at him again. That's all it would take for him to be able to drum up the courage to go over and ask her out.

CHAPTER EIGHT

Danny loved running each day. It was so much better than loading heavy crates onto trucks with his brother for Larson. He was grateful for the work and prayed each day that he would continue to receive pay but he dreamed of earning a living through boxing.

He let his legs carry him through the neighborhoods of Newark. He usually stayed within the bounds of the Italian community but sometimes he got bored of the familiar surroundings and ventured off new areas. Today, he decided to run the length of Walnut Street and back. It was a long stretch with many shops and tantalizing smells.

He slowed down as he approached the Walnut Street Athletic Club. Outside a few of the members were smoking cigarettes. Although he didn't recognize the thin man or the fat one, he did remember the Argentinean one in the middle. Chills ran down Danny's spine as he remembered that black Packard on that cold day by the Jewish soup line two and half years ago.

"Hey, kid!" Nick Martens cried out jovially.

Danny wanted to just continue running. He looked over at the group of men and realized with a sigh that he needed to confront them. Flashes of rotten tomatoes hitting the men on the soup line flooded his mind.

"That's Danny Petrucelli," said a large man with a big belly admiringly. "Not bad."

"Not bad?" Nick said, motioning Danny to come closer. "Herb, are you kidding? This kid's a legend in the making."

Danny felt nauseous at their admiration. "I don't know about that," he said uneasily.

"Modest," Nick said smoothly. "An odd trait for a boxing champion."

"Yeah well, I owe it all to my trainer."

Nick's casual friendliness frosted a little. "Willie Greene. You're talking about Willie, aren't you?"

"Yes," Danny said, looking him directly in the eye. "He's the best."

Nick's voice became strained. "I would disagree, of course."

The thin man muttered, "Kike lover."

Nick put out a placating hand to his friend. "Walter, I'm thinking he just don't know better. We all make mistakes." He turned back to Danny. "However this is your lucky day!"

"How so?" Danny's voice became uncharacteristically clipped.

Nick stared hard at him. "I'm giving you a chance of a lifetime, kid. Don't go blowing it with attitude."

Danny continued to hold Nick's gaze. Keeping his voice neutral he asked, "Chance of a lifetime?"

Nick allowed himself to smile again. "I'm going to allow you came here and train at the best facility in town."

Danny looked down and remained silent as he fought to control his anger. Nick mistook this as a possible change of heart and became excited at the thought of capturing one of Newark's most promising boxers. "Think about it, kid. We have state of the art facilities here, the best trainers, the best equipment. Anything you'd want."

"I'm happy where I'm at," Danny said, his voice deceptively quiet. His fists clenched and unclenched at his side. He looked at the three men, calculating that he could probably knock Herb and Walter out with one punch. Nick, on the other hand, would be harder. It might take few minutes to knock him unconscious, and he'd probably take a few punches in the process. It wasn't worth the chance of injury, and added time for recovery cost him purses.

"Are you happy with the money?" Nick asked slyly.

"What do you mean?"

"You sure old Willie's giving you your fair share?"

Herb nodded. "When it comes to Kikes you can only be sure of one thing. They'll be taking your money whenever they can."

"You got that right, Herb. Run while you can, kid. They're all the same. Having a Sheeny for a manager is like having a Limey watching over your beer for you while you take a piss. It ain't going to be there when you get back," Walter said, laughing loudly at his own joke.

The other two joined in with raucous laughter until they notice that Danny wasn't joining in. Danny's face had turned bright red as he backed away from the men; he didn't trust himself to not strike out at them if they were in range.

"I remember you, you know. From that day on the soup lines by the Temple," Danny gritted out. "I wouldn't join your club if my life depended on it. You and your men can go to hell for all I care." He took off down the road, continuing his run, his anger spurring him on faster.

The three men watched Danny run away, each experiencing different emotions. Herb and Walter were shocked by Danny's word and refusal of Nick's offer. Nick was furious. How dare that little punk talk to him that way? He stormed into his club, his stumping footsteps echoing through the building. Herb and Walter followed tentatively, knowing it was best to stay quiet when their boss was in this mood.

An olive-skinned kid in his mid-twenties ran up to Nick. "What happened? You look pissed."

"A filthy little Kike lover just told me to go to hell!" Nick shouted.

Although Herb and Walter looked like they wanted to melt into the walls, the kid looked unaffected. He turned to Herb and asked, "Who's he talking about?"

Herb whispered back, not wanting to draw attention to himself, "The Italian fighter, you know, Johnny, that kid. What's his name?" Herb looked to Walter for help.

"Danny Petrucelli," Walter answered.

"No," Johnny whispered in disbelief. "I thought he was okay."

Nick gestured wildly around the room. "I offered him a place here. Who wouldn't want that? I gave him a chance to get out from under Willie Greene."

Johnny shrugged. "He'll get his in the end."

"That's right," Herb agreed.

"Yeah," Walter said, nodding.

"They all will. After the Fuhrer's ultimate victory, they don't stand a chance," Nick said scathingly. "In the meantime, we just have to bide our time."

"In the meantime, maybe I can mess with him a bit," Johnny said with a grin.

Nick looked at him, his mood lightening as he sensed his little brother had a plan. "What do you have in mind?"

"That delicious little tasty morsel of a sister he has. I fucked her once, you know. Long time ago," Johnny said.

"Really?" Herb asked, enthralled. "Was she hot?"

"A real little slut," Johnny replied.

"Wonder if he knows," Herb said.

"Doubt it," Johnny answered, still grinning. "They're Catholic. They all think she's a good girl."

"Was she?" Nick asked, leering. "Good I mean?"

"Yeah, real good."

The four men laughed. Johnny licked his lips in anticipation of revisiting Maria. Nick slapped him on the back, his good mood returning.

"Okay, okay. Let's talk about that at the next meeting," Nick said.

"It's in a week, right?" Walter said.

Nick nodded. "Yeah. Make sure to bring new blood. We need recruits."

Herb looked uneasy. "How we supposed to do that?"

"Just invite worthy men, young people, next week," Nick said. "We'll do the rest."

"I heard that Albert Held's going to be there," Walter said. "Is that true?"

"Yeah," Nick confirmed. "So, I want a good showing."

"We need manpower and money," Johnny added. "We need more backing if we're going carry out our mission here."

"Let's show Mr. Held what we can do. Let's show him just how committed the Walnut Street Club really is. Let's fill this room!" Nick's voice boomed loud and clear.

"Yeah!" The other three shouted. They all pumped their fists into the air and cheered. "Sieg…Heil! Seig…Heil! Sieg…Heil!"

A few days later Tony and Danny were working side by side on the docks, loading the bread trucks for delivery. They didn't always get the same shift or area at Larson's, but Mike Demaio did his best to put them together. It wasn't that Demaio was particularly fond of the brothers, but he learned long ago that they were far more productive when paired together. Demaio was acutely aware that his job was as expendable as the next man's. It was important that he increase production whenever possible.

"You ever been to the Kosher Bakery?" Danny asked his brother.

Tony shuddered. "No, and I'd be happy to never set foot in there. Why you asking?"

Danny shrugged. "No reason. Just curious is all."

"I've heard it's filthy."

"I'm sure it's fine."

"Jews don't bathe you know. They're not clean," Tony said matter-of-factly.

Danny rolled his eyes. "Where'd you get that idea?"

"Tommy and Sam from shipping were telling me about these Jews they saw the other day. They smelled bad and their clothes look like they hadn't been washed in days. Sam said it was because they were so cheap, they didn't want to shell out for the soap," Tony replied. He was proud to have knowledge his brother didn't seem to have. Usually, Danny was the one teaching him, so it was nice to know more about something for once. "Jews only really care about money, you know."

Danny kept loading boxes as he listened to his brother prattle on. Keeping his voice carefully neutral, he asked. "And how many Jews have you met?"

"None. It don't matter though. They're all the same."

Danny's voice took on a hard edge. "All the same? Are you kidding me? You sound like those guys at the Walnut Street Club." Danny glared at Tony's back as he loaded a heavy box onto the truck.

Tony didn't catch his brother's tone. "Which guys?" he asked curiously.

"Nick Martens and his crew," Danny said with disgust. "They're a bunch of creeps."

Tony turned to look at his brother. "Why? What'd they say?"

Danny motioned to the boxes in front of Tony. "Keep going. We can't afford to take a break."

Tony walked over to the next box and picked it up, waiting for Danny to continue. When he didn't. Tony asked impatiently, "You gonna tell me what happened?"

Danny felt the anger from the previous day well up inside him. His workouts provided him some release but not enough to handle the utter frustration he felt. "Nothing. It's over."

"Walnut Street's a decent club, you know," Tony said blithely. "Better than the one we go to. Maybe you could make nice with Martens and step- up notch."

Danny's face turned red. "You don't know what you're talking about," he burst out. He looked around, realizing that people were staring at him. Danny rarely raised his voice.

Startled, Tony said, "What's gotten into you?"

Danny closed his eyes and counted to three. "Sorry," he offered. "It's just that Nick Marten's a jerk. Okay, you want to know what happened? I'll tell you." Danny told him about his first encounter with Nick and Nate at the soup lines at the Temple. As his older brother, Danny felt an obligation to educate Tony about the world they lived in. Sheltering him forever wouldn't do him any favors in the long run. As he told the story, he looked away from his kid brother, choosing to focus on the truck's contents instead.

After he finished the story, he looked back at Tony, expecting him to be appalled and sickened. Instead, he found Tony grinning ear to ear. "Rotten tomatoes probably improved the Kike's smell," was all he said.

Danny stared at him for a moment before he backed away from his brother. Shaking his head, he said in low, menacing voice, "Get out of here. Get out of here before I knock you silly!" The last was shouted. He had to shout to compete with the roar of blood that sounded through his ears.

Tony's grin vanished as he recognized the fury in his brother's face, something he had never seen before. He stammered for a moment before turning around and running off.

A few days later, Tony found himself walking in the direction of the Walnut Street Athletic Club. After the big blow up he'd had with his brother, he was acutely curious about Nick and his club. Perhaps he belonged there more than the East Ward Club.

As he approached the building his gait was halting, reflecting his uncertainly. He slowed his pace and considered turning back. Joining this club would cement the conflict he'd had with Danny, possibly destroying any chance of reconciliation. Although, he reasoned to himself, there was no harm in just walking inside and looking around. He moved forward and opened the front door to the club, holding his breath.

Tony immediate recognized the large figure of Nick Martens, being familiar with the Argentinean's triumphs in the soccer world. Back in 1930, Nick had scored one of the two goals in the first half of the World Cup held in Uruguay. Argentina was then up 2-1 against Uruguay, and it looked like they were going to carry home the victory.

There had been a controversy about which ball to use and since neither team could agree, they compromised by switching balls at half time. Many felt that the Uruguay's leather football cursed Argentina's team, who didn't score another goal the rest of the game.

To say that the loss didn't sit well with Nick was a gross understatement. He cursed the Uruguay team so loudly that even his own teammates tried to quiet him. When he received a verbal warning from one of the referees, it sent him over the edge. Nick punched the referee in the mouth, breaking two teeth. Before he was forcibly dragged from the field, he had injured two of the Uruguayan players in his fit rage.

Nick was suspended for a year for ungentlemanly conduct. As a result of his behavior, he lost the majority of his fan base. By the time the suspension was lifted he had dropped out of the sport and seemingly off the face of the Earth, only to resurface recently in Newark, New Jersey.

Tony understood Nick's frustration. Although Nick had overreacted, the officials had been quick to censure him. He certainly deserved a reprimand but after all, Nick was a great center forward, and his absence was a loss to the game.

Nick squinted across the room at Tony. Excusing himself from the two men he was talking to, he walked over to greet Tony. "Hello!" he called out with a charming smile. Their organization needed new recruits- young men eager to help the cause. Perhaps, this was one such prospect.

Tony wiped his hands on his pants. "Hi!"

"What can I do for you?" asked cordially, noting Tony's nervousness.

"Oh, nothing," Tony said, feeling awkward. "I just thought I'd come by and see what your club looked like from the inside. Sorry to bother you."

"No bother," Nick said, extending his right hand. "I'm Nick Martens. Glad to meet you."

"Yes, sir. I know who you are," Tony replied, shaking his hand vigorously. "I followed all your games on the radio. You were an amazing player. The best."

Nick grinned. "Really! That's nice of you to say. Say, you look familiar. Do I know you?"

"No, sir, I don't think so."

"What's your name?"

"Tony Petrucelli. It is an honor to meet you."

Nick's smile faltered as he studied Tony. "Petrucelli, huh? Any relation to Danny Petrucelli? Yes, of course you are. You're the spitting image of him. Is he your brother?"

Tony nodded. "Yeah, look I know you two had words the other day…"

Nick barked out a laugh. "That's an understatement."

Tony looked down at his loafers. "I should go." Without looking up, he turned for the door.

"No!" Nick barked. When Tony jumped, he realized he frightened the young man. He forced himself to calm down, placing a congenial smile back on his face. "What I mean is you don't need to go. Just because Danny and I don't see aye on everything, doesn't mean you and I can't be friends."

Tony hadn't realized that he'd been holding his breath until he let it out. "Danny and I don't exactly see eye to eye either," he replied shakily.

"What brother does?" Nick said putting an arm around Tony's shoulder. Can I show you around?"

"Yeah," Tony said with a smile.

Nick toured Tony around the club, introducing various members to him as he showed him the facility. He stopped at the boxing ring, and they watched two boxers spar for a while. A few other club members gathered around the ring to watch the combatants. Nick studied Tony and asked, "So what do you two argue about?"

"Huh?" Tony asked.

"You and your brother. You said you don't see eye to eye. I just wondered what about."

"Oh, nothing much," Tony said nervously, looking back at the boxers.

Nick leaned into him and whispered, "It's okay. You can tell me. Maybe I can help."

Tony looked him in the eye, pausing to consider how to tell Nick. Finally, he realized that honesty was probably the best approach. "You. We argued about you."

Nick nodded and grinned, looking back up at the sparring match. "Really?"

"Yeah. Danny was upset because you threw tomatoes at a bunch of Kikes."

Nick noted the use of the term 'Kikes' "And what did you say?"

Tony looked around at the other members who were waiting for his response. Finally, he grinned and replied, "That you probably improved their smell."

Nick laughed loud and long, which sparked similar laughter with the other men. "That's a good one," Nick said after he could catch his breath. "You belong here, you know."

"I do?" Tony asked, his eyes shining with excitement. Here was his idol giving him all this attention, asking him to be a part of his group.

"You bet," one of the other men chimed in. "Anyone that understands how foul smelling a Jew is fits right in."

Tony nodded and said, "I might just think about that."

Nick's smile remained although his demeanor got more serious. "You know there is a growing movement to handle the problem."

"Yeah, I know. In Germany."

Nick nodded. "Yes, but also here."

"Here?"

"Yes."

Tony looked around at the gathering, which was slowly increasingly in number. Now, a dozen men stood there, looking at him with interest. He suddenly felt important, like his ideas mattered. Danny wasn't here to try to rule his thoughts, his ideas. These men looked at him with respect.

Nick put his arm back around Tony's shoulder. "We're having a meeting in two days. It'll be here. Think you can come?"

Tony smiled. "Sure! What's it about?"

"It's meeting of the Friends of the New Germany. We're about cleaning up the filth, if you know what I mean." Nick nodded knowingly to Tony.

"I think I do," Tony replied. "When is it?"

"8:00pm."

"I'll be here!"

"Good," Nick said releasing him. "And bring any like- minded young men you might know. We can use all the help we can get!"

CHAPTER NINE

Two days later, Tony walked briskly down Walnut Street in eager anticipation of the Friends of the New Germany meeting. He hadn't told his family where he was going. He hadn't lied, Tony reasoned, but they didn't need to know his every movement. Although Donato was always preaching about the virtues of Mussolini, he didn't approve of the Nazi movement. Since Mussolini had just visited Hitler in Germany in September, it was clear that the two would be allies. For this reason, Donato wouldn't speak out against the German leader, but he also was not his advocate.

Donato truly believed that Mussolini would bring about a peace and harmony to a nation torn by class structure. That is what Il Duce promised in his speeches. Joining forces with Hitler gave Mussolini access to Germany's brawn to support their common Fascist ideals.

As Tony approached the Walnut Street Athletic Club, his enthusiasm waned. If he wasn't comfortable telling his family where he was going, was this the right thing to do? Yes, he told himself, he was going in to find out more about the movement. He hadn't agreed to join and besides didn't this group align with his basic beliefs? The Jews were a menace. They were slowly taking over all the power in America. If someone didn't do something about it, they would dominate the world. They needed to be controlled.

With a new resolve, he opened the door and saw a small group of young men surrounded by veteran members. He only recognized a few faces. One was Ralph Carpote from Guido's. Nick was deep in conversation with him, and the boy was obviously entranced by the soccer star.

A portly man with a long mustache was talking to a small group of young men, none of whom Tony knew. He couldn't distinguish the man's words, as he was too far away, but he detected a strong German accent. Tony approached them and listened carefully.

"But aren't Jews human beings?" one boy asked, "I mean, don't they deserve some respect?"

The man nodded indulgently to him. "You bring up a good point, Michael. Who says young people can't think for themselves, I ask you?" He paused, looking pointedly at the gathered veteran members. As if on cue, they all murmured their agreement. He then addressed the other young men. "I bet your parents don't appreciate you, do they?" They all shook their head. "No, of course not."

"Michael, going back to your excellent comment. Yes, Jews are human beings. But now you would say that fleas are animals, wouldn't you?"

Michael blushed with importance at being selected out. "Yes, sir," he responded immediately.

"Not very pleasant animals, though, right?"

The other boys standing there looked a little annoyed that Michael was getting all the attention. Before Michael could respond, he jumped in saying, "No, they're damned annoying!"

"That's right! Stewart, is it?" the portly German asked. When the boy nodded vigorously, he continued. "So, I ask you, is it your duty to aid the flea in its quest to bite us as we sleep?"

"No!" the three boys cried in unison.

The man smiled. "Exactly. Same with the Jews. We have a duty to rid the world of their annoyance." He turned and extended his hand out to Tony. "I'm Albert Held. And you are?"

"Tony Petrucelli," a voice said from behind Tony. Nick Martens placed his hand on Tony's right shoulder. "This is the young man I was telling you about."

"Right!" Albert said. "I remember. Glad you could make it."

Tony shook his hand and grinned. "Thank you for inviting me," he said politely.

"And do you know everyone else here?" Albert asked.

"No," Tony replied. "Well, I know Ralph and Nick, but that's about it."

"Well, allow me to make the introductions!" Albert exclaimed. He proceeded to introduce all the young men to one another.

A tall blond man came out from the shadows with a serene smile. "We're very glad to have all of you here. You can all be of great help to us. We need young blood in our organization." The man's voice resonated through the hall, causing everyone to turn toward him.

"Ja, Ja," Albert replied. "Have you all met Hans Ruether?" They'll took turns shaking his hand as they were individually introduced to him.

"Shall we begin?" Hans asked. They all sat down in the chairs, which were set up in a circle. There were nine guests in attendance, all between the ages of eighteen and twenty- five.

After everyone had found their seats, he started in without preamble. "Are your parents wealthy?" he asked looking around at each of the boys expectantly. They all immediately shook their heads. "No, of course not! Aren't you tired of being a second- class citizen here in this free country called America?"

A few nodded their heads, but Tony hesitated. He never felt like a second- class citizen. His father did, but he couldn't say that he did.

"Aren't you tired of working at the docks lifting heavy boxes?"

To that Tony could honestly nod heartily. He could definitely agree with that.

"Do you want this sort of life for your children?"

More joined in to agree with Hans. "No!"

"Exactly! It's the Jews that are taking the good jobs. It's the Jews that are making money at the expense of the real Americans, the workers.

"They call themselves a *religion*. What a joke! The only reason that they call themselves a religion to preserve the Jewish race. It's their clever little lie," Hans said. He looked around at the group to judge their response. They were thoughtfully considering his words.

Nick sat forward in his chair. His voice was low as he asked, "How many of you have gone to a Jew because he has better prices?"

A few raised their hands and looked embarrassed about it.

"No," Nick said with a smile. "It's okay. I understand. But think about this, anyone can sell junk, right?" He waited for them to nod. "Jews know how to sell things, how to make things look appealing, but what about the true quality of the product? And if you manage to get quality product from a Jew, you can be sure that he's bargained down the price from someone. Hard working laborers he's exploiting on a daily basis!" His voice rose as he felt the audience's agreement.

"Those Jews have ripped me off enough times!" one person shouted.

"Yeah, me too!" another cried.

Hans smiled broadly, glancing over at Nick, taking back the reigns of the conversation with a nod. "Good! Should America be owned by Jews?"

"No!" the group all shouted.

"Will you join our cause and help us return America to the hardworking people?"

"Yes!"

Tony nodded with them throughout the rest of the meeting. He hated the way his family struggled for money to put food on the dinner table, while Jewish people ate like royalty. His father and mother deserved better. So did his sister. Even Danny. They all did.

The next evening, Tony sat quietly eating his dinner. The family was chatting away happily about the day's events. Danny avoided direct eye contact with his brother, choosing instead to converse with Maria about her work. She was regaling him with the antics of Sonja, who was now dating Gregory from the cafeteria but had eyes for a man in the accounting department, who was in turn in love with someone in Sonya's department. Maria suspected that the minute the man turned his attention to Sonya she'd lose interest and find someone else to entice.

Teresa, noticing Tony's reticence, leaned in toward him and whispered, "Is everything all right?"

Looking up at his mother Tony forced a smile. "Sure, Mamma, why wouldn't it be?"

Danny's eyes flickered over to his mother and brother. He felt guilty. Over the last few days, he had distanced himself from Tony and was pretty sure that was the cause of his brother's sullenness. He opened his mouth wanting to remedy the situation, but the closed it again. There really wasn't much to say.

Teresa glanced around the table and noticed Danny's eyes flick away. "Is something going on between the two of you?"

"It's fine," Danny mumbled. 'Don't worry about it."

Teresa's brow furrowed as she studied Danny. "I'm still your Mamma. If I want to worry about my sons, it's my God- given right!" Her voice rose in volume, letting her family know that she was more than mildly displeased.

Danny sighed and reached out his hands, placing it over his mother's. "Tony and I had an argument at work. More like disagreement. We'll be fine."

Teresa grunted an acknowledgement to her son. She turned her attention to Tony, who still looked unhappy. Her family's happiness and harmony were her highest priority. Having Danny's cooperation, she felt halfway there. "All right, Tony, your turn. What is it? You can tell me."

Tony looked from her to Danny and back again to Teresa. Was this the right time to announce his new affiliation? He knew Danny wouldn't agree and would probably get angry with him again, but maybe he could sway Donato.

Tony gave his mother a tentative smile and then turned to look at Donato. "Pappa?"

"Yes, son," Donato said, concern etched his brow.

"I want you know that I've listened to you all these years. Mussolini is a great man with great ideas."

Donato beamed with pleasure. "You're a good son! And you couldn't be more right. Mussolini will lead our mother country to greatness. Someday, we will return as kings of our own land."

Tony nodded nervously, his heart racing in his chest. "Yes, Pappa. And Mussolini has chosen a very strong ally with power. Someone who can aid him in his quest for equality for Italy."

Donato looked confused. "What are you saying?"

"Pappa, Hitler is a great man too. Together, he and Mussolini will do great things, not only for Italy but for American as well!"

"What?" Danny shouted. "How can you say that?"

Tony glared at Danny. "I can say that because it's true! Hitler will change things for the better. Aren't you tired of the Jews getting all the breaks? Aren't you tired of working so hard for so little?" He felt a surge of adrenaline he had experienced the night before. If he could only get his family to see the light, to understand how powerful their message was.

Maria's soft voice cut into the stunned silence that had permeated the room. "Tony,'what's going on with you?"

Tony looked over at her. "I joined a group last night. A group that's actually doing something about the problem." He looked around the table at the blank faces of his family. "They're the good guys."

"Tony." Maria said, her voice shaking with concern and fear. "What group did you join? You didn't join the..." he voice trailed off as she stared at him. Drumming up her courage, she continued her though. "You didn't join the Nazis ,did you?"

"Friends of the New Germany," Tony said proudly.

Danny jumped up and yelled. "That's Nick Marten's gang. Those are *Nazis*! Are you crazy?"

Tony stood up, facing his brother. "Don't you call me crazy. They're good people."

Teresa arose from her chair and walked over to Danny. She pushed gently on his shoulder, encouraging him to sit back down. Imploring him with her eyes to calm down.

Danny complied, taking a deep breath before he spoke. "They're using you," he said, struggling to keep his voice even. "It's all part of their plan."

"Tony," Maria said, her voice imploring. "Don't do this. You know what the Nazis are doing in Europe."

"Exaggerations," Tony replied. His voice was sincere as he looked into his sister's eyes. "The Jews are spreading false rumors on a daily basis to discredit them. It's not as bad as you think."

"That's not true," Donato said gently. He motioned for Tony to sit back down, who ignored the request. "Our German cousin wrote us a letter last week. She paints a very ugly picture."

Maria gasped, covering her mouth with her hand. "Gerty?" She asked. "Is she alright?"

"Yes, yes," Donato said reassuringly. "Gertrude's fine. But she has some friends that are under scrutiny right now. And one girl just disappeared. I'm sure she'll turn up, but…"

"But she might not," Danny supplied with a finality in his voice. He turned back to Tony. "Your friends are monsters, little brother. Pure and simple."

"Monsters?" He was stunned by his family's response. He looked around the room at them all with unshed tears in his eyes. "Is what you think of me? You think I'm monster?"

Danny looked hard at Tony, his voice filled with disgust. "Are you a Nazi?"

Tony looked away from his brother and into the disappointed eyes of his mother. He backed up toward the front door.

"Tony!" Donato commanded. "Come back here. Let's talk this over more. Of course, we don't think you're a monster."

Tony shook his head. "I've got to get out of here." he said before he turned his back and ran out the door.

The slam of the front door made Maria jump. Danny stood back up to go after him, but Teresa motioned for him to stay. "He'll come back," she said. "He needs some time to cool off. Tony's a good boy. He'll make the right decision."

Maria turned to her father. "What else did Gerty say?"

"Daughter, I don't want to worry you, "Donato said gently. "She'll be okay. She's not Jewish, after all. No harm will come to her."

Maria shook her head. "What makes you think they'll stop at the Jews?"

Donato harrumphed. "That's all Hitler's interested in."

Maria held gaze. "Hitler's not going to stop until he has world domination. Someone has to take a stand. Someone has to do something to stop him before it's too late."

Donato waved his hands dismissively. "You're overreacting."

Danny reached out and gasped his sister's arm, shaking it in support. "You're right, and don't let anyone convince you otherwise. Hitler's a menace, and I don't think Mussolini is too far off either." The last he directed as his father.

Donto's mouth drew into a thin line. "Don't ever let me hear you say that about our leader in this house again. Do you hear me? Never!"

Danny stood up slowly and though about his next words carefully. "Father, I'm sorry, but you're wrong about him."

Teresa and Maria gasped at his boldness. Donato turned a shade of red that none of them had ever seen. "Get out," he shouted fiercely. "Get out, and don't come back until you can keep a civil tongue in your mouth!"

Danny nodded and walked out the door, careful to not slam it as his brother had. He sat down on the second step right outside the door and stared off into space, wondering if his family would ever be the same. He heard the door creak open behind him, but he didn't look back.

His mother sat down next to him and looked out onto the quiet street. After a few moments, she said softly, "Give your brother time. He'll come around, but he needs his big brother. He needs you."

Danny sighed and looked back at her. With disgust, he said, "But he's become a Nazi!"

"No," Teresa said gently. "No, he hasn't. He may think he has, but he's still my son. I know him."

Danny nodded. He looked back out at the street. "I hope you're right."

Teresa touched his arm, drawing his attention back to her, "You must make it safe for him to talk to you, safe to admit his error, admit he was wrong. Don't be too angry."

"I don't know," he replied honestly. "Will that be enough?"

"Love is always enough. Love is always stronger than hate. Remember that."

Danny looked into her eyes and grinned. "When did you get so smart, Mamma?"

Teresa returned the smile. "I'm the same person I've always been. You're just coming around to realize that I might know a thing or two. Children always think their parents don't know anything until they realize that they've known what they've been talking about all long."

Danny grinned at his mother and let her wrap him into her embrace. "You really think Tony will come around?" He wanted to be reassured on last time.

"Yes," Teresa said. "I know it in my heart. I know my son."

CHAPTER TEN

The next day, Tony and Danny worked side by side in silence at the loading dock. Mike Demaio observed the brothers from his office, perched two stories above the workers below. Frowning, he stroked his nonexistent beard, the one he had shaved off two weeks earlier at his wife's insistence. She had the crazy idea that old man Larson might promote him if he were clean shaven. Although to him it was a laughable idea that he might earn more if he didn't have a beard, he cared more for his wife than he did his beard.

Mike pulled on a warm wool coat over his wiry frame and the tan woolen cap his wife had just knitted him onto his graying hair. He clanked down the metal stairs, wincing as the cold wind hit his cheek. He went over to the pallet where the brothers were loading a shipment onto an outgoing truck. The tension between the two was palpable.

"How's it going, Danny?" he asked tentatively.

"Fine, Mr. Demaio," Danny replied without breaking stride. If he were to stay on target, he couldn't afford to stop working even to talk to his boss.

"And you, Tony?"

"Fine, sir," Tony replied.

"Good," Mike said, unconvinced. Sighing, he pointed at another truck one hundred yards away. "Tony, would you help Rocco? I'd like to talk to your brother for a few moments."

Fear washed over Danny and spilled onto Tony. They momentarily forgot their feud. "Sure thing, Mr. Demaio," Tony replied quickly. "Anything you need, you just ask." He glanced nervously to Danny, who nodded back to him in what he hoped was a reassuring manner.

Danny heart and mind raced equally. What would their family do if he lost this job? He couldn't bear the soup lines again. Maybe the provision house had an opening. Maria could put in a good word. What had he done wrong?

Mike caught Danny's look of stark fear and groaned inwardly. "Oh God, Danny, no. I'm not firing you. Sorry, I shouldn't have been so mysterious. No, it is just that I need your help with something. Can we go back up to my office? It's freezing out here."

Danny let out the pent-up air in one big gust, relaxing his shoulders to a point where he nearly sank to the ground. Smiling he said, "Thank God! Thank you, Mr. Demaio. I'd be happy to help you in any way I can." He looked around for Tony and gave him a wave and a smile. Tony waved back with a relieved smile, immediately understanding that his brother was out of danger.

Danny climbed the steps, relishing the thought of the warm confines of the eagle's nest, as the workers referred to the boss's office.

Walking into the small office, he sighed with pleasure at the warmth enveloping him from the potbelly stove. The heat was channeled from this office into the neighboring spaces of other administrative staff, a clever system developed by Stephen Larson's father. The old man had passed away a few years ago, leaving his baking empire to his son.

"Nice, isn't it?" Mike commented.

"Heavenly," Danny said with a grin. "Old man Ian Larson was an amazing man."

"Yes, he was. God rest his soul," Mike replied. 'Can't say the same for his son."

Danny was taken aback by his boss's open disrespect of the owner. "Yes, sir," he said awkwardly, staring at the floor. He couldn't agree more, but was fearful of voicing anything concrete against the current owner. It was too easy to cross the line.

"It's okay, Danny. He's kind of an idiot, isn't he?"

Danny nodded. "I've never met him personally, but yes sir, I'd say that's about right. Things just don't run as smoothly as they did before. He's using his bakers on the docks when they're still needed in the kitchen."

"Like your dad," Mike commented. "I know. When we were able to rehire him, I tried to get him back in the kitchen, but Stephen had other ideas. Never understood the logic."

"Yeah, well, we're all grateful for the work," Danny said. "Just would have been nice for him to be out of the cold, hard labor of the docks."

"Speaking of which," Mike said motioning for Danny to sit down, while he took his seat behind his cluttered desk. "I have an idea for you."

Danny sat down as directed. "Me?"

Demiao give him a smile. "Yeah, you. You're a good worker, and I'm thinking you're looking for a change."

Danny sighed with relief. "It would be nice, but honestly I'll take anything that can keep my family fed."

Mike put his hand up. "I know, I know. And if you don't want this change, it ain't an order. You can go back to the loading bay. I just…" His voice trailed off as he looked out the window.

Danny waited for him to continue, studying his worried face. "What is it?" he asked after a few moments passed.

Mike leaned back in his chair and looked him in the eye. "You know there are two bakeries, right?"

Danny nodded slowly. "Sure. Everyone knows that."

"Right," Mike said absently. "Of course, they do. What do you know of the other bakery?"

Danny shrugged. "It's Jewish. Kosher. Actually, I don't know how much about it. Why?"

Mike leaned back in his chair. "You don't sound afraid of it."

Confusion crossed his face. "Afraid? Why would I be afraid?"

"You'd be surprised at how many of my men won't go near that place. I have to admit, I'm not too crazy about it either. Gives me the heebie-jeebies."

Danny was truly puzzled. "Why?"

"Those weird men coming and going with those long beards. It's just…anyway, it don't matter. The point is you're okay with it, right?"

"Yeah."

"Good because Larson wants the books for the entire company to be done under the same roof, this roof. He don't trust the Jews in the other bakery to do the weekly audit right, so he wants it done here. Problem is we need someone to run back and forth between the two places bringing receipts, bank statement, you know everything our accountants will need."

"You need a runner?" Danny couldn't believe his luck. Not only could he get his daily runs in during work hours and get paid for it, but he could get out of the confines of this place.

Mike nodded. "Basically. I mean you don't need to run all the way or anything. Just make decent time."

"I'm the right man for the job!" Danny exclaimed. "Actually, I need to run as much as I can. Right now, I have to squeeze it in before work. It'd be nice to sleep in."

That's right!" Mike said hitting the table. "You're a champion boxer. Yeah, this might work for you."

"I don't know about champion, but yes, sir, I love boxing."

"Good, then you'll do it?"

"Yeah, sure!"

Mike sighed in relief. "I have to tell you this is a load off my mind. I figured you'd probably do it, but I'm glad to know you're actually happy with the assignment. I felt a little guilty asking."

Danny studied him for a moment. "I'm curious, sir, if you don't mind my asking, why did you ask me? I mean, out of all the men here that you could have offered this to, why me?"

Mike shrugged. "I saw you the other day with that Darkie. I figured anyone that'd stand up for a nigger might just be willing to deal with a Kike or two."

Danny couldn't mask his stunned expression. He sat back in his chair and looked out at the loading dock. A few weeks ago, a man from Calcutta had wandered out near Johnny Gouza's station looking for work. He had arrived as a manservant for a wealthy Englishman, but the man died of a heart attack on the boat just as they were arriving into America. Abandoned in a foreign land, he was referred to Mr. Demaio for work by a few kind Catholic missionaries.

Johnny immediately started heckling the terrified man. A few other men gathered around to join in the fun, and soon they were taking turns pushing the Indian man between them in a circle. When Johnny kicked him in the butt, causing him to fall on his hands and knees, Danny stepped in. Being that he was out-numbered, Danny knew he had to handle the situation decisively. He yanked Johnny up by the collar, saying, "Knock it off, will you?"

"What's it to you Petrucelli?" Johnny snarled.

"Just leave him alone." Danny stared him directly in the eye, willing him to back down. Although he knew he could flatten Johnny easily, he didn't relish the thought. Brawling at the work place could get you fired.

"But this nigger's dirtying up the place, trying to steal work from our people."

Danny looked over at the cowering man. "What are you doing here?"

The man trembled violently, "I'm here to see Mr. Demaio. He's expecting me."

Danny looked up at the eagle's nest and saw Mr. Demaio looking down at them. They all watched him put on his coat and trudge reluctantly down the stairs. When he was in front of the man, he asked, "You the guy Father Minion sent over?"

Relief flooded the man as he pushed himself up. "Yes, sir, that's me."

Mr. Demaio looked around at the assembled group. "Fine, follow me. It won't be said that Larson's ain't charitable." The men had grumbled before going back to their work.

"Danny," Mr. Demaio said sharply. "You still with me?"

Danny started in his chair. Realizing where he was, he nodded. "Yeah, I was just wondering if you gave that guy a job,"

Mr. Demaio grinned. "I sure did. He's cleaning out the toilets for half the pay. Mr. Larson though it was funny."

Danny stood up, masking his disgust. "When do you want me to start?"

"Now. Run over there and pick up the ledger for me, okay?"

"Sure thing," Danny replied. He was anxious to leave the office. The warmth had suddenly become suffocating, and he was looking forward to the brisk air and change of environment.

He trotted down the steps and ran out the front gates. He looked up at the sky and groaned. It looked like it would rain. He sped up and hoped he would make it to the other bakery before the sky opened up on him.

It was forty blocks from one bakery to the other. Danny marveled at the sameness of the small wood framed homes that lined South Street. He smiled at the cheerful sounds of children playing inside the houses.

When he arrived at the bakery, he stopped outside the six-story brick building to catch his breath. It had been a good run. The building spanned the entire block and looked deserted. Danny climbed the stairs to the large steel encased door on the second floor.

He tried the door, but it was locked. He looked around the door and found a small off- white button, which he pressed twice. He waited and tried not to fidget, wondering what the inside of this mysterious building held. He saw the movement behind the peephole and smiled to the person in what he hoped passed as an affable manner. The great door opened, and he found himself speechless. He had expected an old man with a long beard, but instead found a pretty young woman in a plain brown smock dress looking up at him inquisitively.

"May I help you?" she asked after he didn't say anything.

"Um, yes, er, I mean…" he trailed off trying to remember why he was there and what his mission was. She had the most beautiful cheekbones and full around lips. Her large brown eyes spoke of an inner beauty. She was innocent and sweet; he was sure of that.

"Are you from the other bakery?" she asked with a hint of a smile on her lips.

"Yes!" Danny nearly shouted. "That's it. I'm from the other Larson bakery."

"Yes, we've been expecting you. You're here for the ledgers, right?"

"Yeah, that's right," he agreed, nodding his head for emphasis.

"Well, come in then," she said, stepping away from the door allowing him to enter. "I'm Sarah Greenberg, Mr. Neftalis's personal secretary."

He took a step into the hallway, pausing for a moment to allow his eyes to adjust to the dim lighting. Looking around, he saw that the place was very clean but sparse in decoration. Realizing he hadn't acknowledged her introduction, he stammered, "I'm Danny Petrucelli. Nice to meet you." He thrust his hand out awkwardly to her.

She giggled softly and took his hands. "Nice to meet you, Mr. Petrucelli."

He had the distinct impression she was teasing him but didn't mind, especially when his hands touched hers. He gasped at its softness, which sent shivers down his spine.

She pulled her hand away and said, "Come with me. I'll introduce you to the controller, my boss."

He followed her though the maze of corridors. He wondered what lay behind each of the doors he passed. He thought about asking her but then realized it really wasn't any of his business; he couldn't bear saying the wrong thing and possibly offending Sarah.

Finally, they came to a door that was ajar. Pushing it open, Sarah said, "Sir? Danny Petrucelli from the other bakery is here."

"Send him in," Danny heard a deep voice reply.

He found it interesting that they referred to his bakery as the "other" bakery, almost as if it were less desirable. He grinned realizing they did the same thing at his bakery.

Danny entered the small anteroom to Mr. Neftalis's office, taking in all the knickknacks that crowded the space. His heart quickened at Sarah's desk. There was a small bowl with scented potpourri, giving the room a fresh smell. Her desk was very organized with multiple stacks of papers and ledgers.

He followed Sarah into her boss's office and couldn't help but gape at the old man behind the desk. He had a long beard and shabby clothes that didn't fit his frail frame well. The various mismatched patches all over his pants and jacket gave Danny the impression that these clothes dated back before the turn of the century.

He peered at Danny over his half- moon glasses, which were perched at the end of his nose. "So, you're here to help me with my accounting, are you?" The word "help" was spoken with derision.

"Yes, sir, I mean no, sir, I mean…"

"Now, Meyer," Sarah said with a soft but firm voice. "We've been over this. Stephen Larson has every right-"

"Yes, he does," bit out the old man. "But I don't have to like it, do I?"

"No, you don't. But don't take it out on the messenger," Sarah chided.

He squinted at Danny. "You know what they used to do with messengers who brought bad news, don't you?"

Danny shook his head. "No, sir."

He made a motion of slitting his throat. "Immediate execution. No one wants to hear bad news. It can get you killed."

"Don't be so melodramatic!" Sarah exclaimed with mock seriousness. She gave him an engaging smile, hoping to lighten his mood.

Meyer was not immune to her charm. He immediately softened, saying with a dismissive wave of the hand. "Give him what he needs. Did you offer him tea?"

"No," Sarah said. She turned to Danny. "Would you like some tea?"

"Yes," Danny said eagerly. Any chance to talk to her, to be in her presence was valuable to him. "I'd love some tea."

The old man glared at Danny. "You watch yourself, young man! Sarah's like a daughter to me. You understand?"

"Yes!" Danny replied, taking an immediate step away from Sarah.

Sarah hid a smile behind her hand. "Okay, we'll get some tea and then I'll give you all the papers we've gathered together for Mr. Demaio."

Danny followed her out of the office, bowing briefly to the old man who just continued to glare at him. They went down another series of corridors before entering a kitchen area. Although the equipment in the kitchen was antiquated, the room was inviting. There was a large wooden table with matching chairs to the right.

"Where is everyone?" he asked.

Sarah's brow furrowed in confusion at the question. "Working," she answered slowly as if expecting it to be trick question.

"But don't your bakers bake the bread in here?"

"In this kitchen?" she asked, giggling at the thought until she realized he was serious. Her laughter ended abruptly with a cough. "No, Danny, this is the executive lunch room. It's where management eats lunch each day."

"Oh," Danny replied, blushing because he knew she thought he was being silly. He still didn't understand why there was a kitchen for their lunchroom.

"Don't you have a staff kitchen?"

"No," Danny said. "We've got a large cafeteria. Personally, I eat outside in the summer and in the warehouse when it's cold. That's where all the loaders eat, pretty much, but the indoor workers and management share the cafeteria."

"Really? But who cooks?"

"People bring things from home. And there's premade sandwiches available, usually. No one cooks though, not at least that I know of."

"Oh," Sarah said softly, her voice sounding a little sad. "That's too bad."

"Why'd you say that?"

She looked at him for a moment before replying. "We're all family here. I guess I just can't imagine things any other way."

Danny nodded, not knowing what to say to that.

Sarah smiled and motioned for him to take a seat. "How do you take your tea?"

"Honey. Thanks."

"No milk?"

"No."

"Okay," she said. "I'll put the water up."

Danny settled into his chair and watched her put the kettle on the stove. Her long brown hair fell down her back, almost touching her waist. Smiling he pictured her making dinner for him each night, wearing a plain white apron, maybe with a little lace around the edges. "Do you cook Italian?" he asked in a faraway voice.

Puzzled, she turned around, certain she hadn't heard him correctly. "Pardon me?"

Danny caught himself and sat up straight in his chair. "I mean, does your bakery cook Italian bread?" He silently prayed that she didn't guess his true thoughts or pick up on the fact that his heart was beating twice its usual speed.

"Oh," she said accepting the explanation. "No, we produce the strictly Kosher breads here. Your bakery handles Italian loaves, doesn't it?"

Danny nodded, realizing that his apparent question was not very intelligent. Of course, they wouldn't bake Italian bread in a Kosher bakery. Sarah, being the sweet well- mannered girl though didn't allude to his stupidity but rather took the question in stride.

"Is this your first time here?" she asked.

"Yes," he replied. "I don't think anyone I know has ever stepped foot inside this building."

"You make it sound like we're cursed," Sarah said stiffly. She was used to people looking at her a little differently, but it still stung.

"No, no," Danny rushed to say. "Not at all. I just meant that I don't know anything about Kosher bakeries. That's all."

"Forgive me," Sarah said, bowing her head. "I'm a little too sensitive. Your questions are fair and valid. If you'd like I can show you around and teach you a little about us."

Danny's face lit up. "Really? That'd be great!"

Sarah laughed in surprise. "I didn't expect you to be so eager to learn. That's refreshing."

The kettle's whistling brought her attention back to the tea. She poured the boiling water into a small blue and white teapot. "Is there anything I can answer for you while I prepare tea?"

Danny sat back and relaxed again. "I know very little, but I do know that you need to keep separate kitchens for dairy and one for non-dairy."

"They don't need to be separate rooms, but the equipment needs to be different."

"But why? I know the rule but don't really understand it."

Sarah put the teapot and cups onto a small wooden tray and brought it to the table. "It's simple. Meat and dairy don't mix." She put his cup in front of him.

"Why!"

"Because the Torah says so."

"But…," Danny let his question die. "Never mind. Thanks for answering my questions." He poured a spoonful of honey into his tea and stirred it.

"No, please ask."

Danny looked up at her. "I just wonder why you can't mix dairy and meat. It just doesn't make much sense to me."

"I appreciate your honesty," Sarah said sitting down, taking a sip of her tea. " And I can understand how you wouldn't necessarily understand. Tell me, you're Catholic, right?"

"Yes.

"Can you tell me why getting baptized is important?"

"Sure, it's the only way to reach salvation. You can't get into heaven unless you're baptized."

"But why?"

Danny stared at her and thought about it. He knew it was vitally important to be baptized, but there was really no other answer to why other than because that's what his church instructed their parishioners to do. It was in the Bible. He nodded. "I see your point."

"Thank you," Sarah said.

"For what?"

"For listening. And being open to a different viewpoint."

Danny shook his head. "You shouldn't have to thank me for that."

"It's rare," Sarah said with a sad smile. "You've no idea how rare."

Danny nodded. "I know. The other guys at my bakery…" Danny blushed as he realized there was no polite way to end that sentence.

Sarah covered his hands with hers. "Danny, you've got to learn to trust me a little. Tell me what's on your mind. Don't worry so much about offending me."

Sarah's cool hand had an electric effect on Danny's skin. He felt safe with her, like he could tell her anything. "Well, the other guys kind of talk badly about this place," he said looking around. "In fact, my boss, Mr. Demaio, didn't have anyone else willing to come here."

Sarah looked at him, her eyes shining. "But you didn't mind. You came."

"Yeah, I was curious. Interested," he said, correcting himself.

"It's fine to be curious."

"Okay," he said sheepishly. "I was curious. I wondered what it looked like in here. What went on behind the doors? Who the men were with the long beards?"

"Well, I can't answer everything today, but I can at least show you what we do here. When you're finished with your tea, I'll take you on the grand tour."

"Do you really have the time?"

"No," she said grinning.

Danny stood up too. "I shouldn't be bothering you."

Sarah stood up too. "I was teasing you. I mean I'm always really busy around here, but Mr. Neftalis asked me to offer you tea, didn't he? He's a wise man. I think he knew you might have questions."

"Oh," Danny said with a smile. "Well then, I guess we should take that grand tour."

Tony finished his shift and looked around for Danny. He knew where his brother must be. That damn Kosher bakery Demaio had somehow tricked him into servicing. Grunting, he shoved his hands into his coat pocket and started for the front gate.

Katherine, Demaio's gorgeous personal secretary, brushed past him, causing his heart to race. He knew her long chestnut hair must be like silk to touch. She wore a bulky woolen coat, but it didn't hide her slender perfect hourglass figure and slender ankles. Tony considered what words he could utter to interest her in him. As always, the answer was the same. None. Katherine worked in the eagle's nest with the managers, and he was just a dock worker.

"Tony!" a familiar voice called out, pulling him out of his sullen introspection.

Tony turned to see Ralph propped up against the gate. "Ralph!" he exclaimed with a smile. It was good to see a friendly face. "What brings you here to Larsons?"

"I thought I'd buy you a beer," Ralph said. "Anything the matter? You don't look too happy."

"No, I'm okay."

Ralph let it go and led him to a local tavern. Sitting down at a barstool, he ordered two beers on tap and waited for Tony to settle in. After he drained the first, Ralph ordered another and said, "So you going to tell me?"

Tony drank half the glass and wiped his mouth. "It's just Danny."

Ralph nodded. "He's running for the Kikes, ain't he?"

Tony's back straightened. "How the hell did you know that?" He asked angrily.

"We have some members at Larson's, you know. No need to be embarrassed. I don't think anything less of you." Ralph said, pushing the glass toward Tony. "I just thought you might need a friend. I know if my brother was running around with those types, I'd be pissed."

"Damn straight," he said draining his mug. Ralph signaled for another and Tony continued. "I don't know him anymore."

"Hopefully, he'll come to his senses. Soon," Ralph said meaningfully.

"I sure hope so," Tony agreed.

"So, you coming to the next meeting?"

"Sure. When is it?"

"Next Tuesday."

Tony nodded. "I'll be there. Hey, how long have you been a member?"

Ralph shrugged. "A while now. Months."

"You still work for Cantalupo?"

Ralph shook his head. "Nah. They're bunch of Kike lovers over there."

Tony's world immediately tilted at an odd angle. "What?" he asked, wondering if the spinning feeling was from drinking two beers on an empty stomach or the fact that his idols were siding with the enemy. "That can't be right."

"That's what Nick said, so I left them."

"They let you leave?" Tony had always heard that you didn't leave the Cantalupo family business alive.

"I wasn't anyone of significance. Just a kid no one listened to," Ralph said, his voice tinged with hurt. "It's not the same with Nick and the others. They care what I think."

Tony nodded, still dazed by the knowledge that Art Belle and the others were all Jew lovers. Maybe Nick and Ralph had it wrong. Still, Nick would know, wouldn't he? Wanting to push the unpleasant thoughts far away he took a long drink of the third mug and asked, "So how did you find out about the Friends anyway?"

Ralph shrugged. "I was at a smoker and that fucking Nate Rubin had won another fight. I was cursing him out when this pimply kid came up to me. Introduced himself as Alfred. You met him the other night, right?"

Tony shrugged. "Don't know, maybe."

"Yeah, well you'll get to know him. He's been around longer than me. Anyway, he asked me to come to a meeting, so I did. Never looked back."

Tony nodded. "Sounds good to me."

Ralph smiled and relaxed. Nick would be pleased. For some reason, Ralph didn't understand why Tony was important to him. He felt a tinge of jealousy, but he let it pass. After all, Nick had selected him out to meet up with Tony and secure him for the next meeting.

CHAPTER ELEVEN

Jules and Nate sat at their small kitchen table eating dinner. The cold wind was barely shielded by the thin walls. They couldn't afford much in the way of heat, so they each wore multiple layers of sweaters and warmed themselves with cheap red wine.

Jules had partaken of the wine far more than Nate, a seemingly common pattern over the few weeks. Nate's worried eyes studied his father's rosy cheeks and blood shot eyes.

"Father?" Nate began. "Are you alright?"

Jules jerked his head up to look at his son, losing his balance, causing him to tip back in the chair, nearly falling to the floor. Nate quickly grabbed his father's arm, righting him back onto the chair. "Sure," he said. "Why'd you ask?"

"You don't look so good," Nate replied bluntly.

Jules laughed loudly as if his son had just told a hilarious joke and continued until he forgot why he had started laughing, whereupon his laughter died as suddenly as it had started. "What were we talking about?"

"Nothing, Father," Nate said with a sad smile.

Jules reached out and grasped his shoulder. "You remind me of my mother," he said softly. "You're good boy."

Nate smiled at him. "I don't know much about her. Can you tell me about my grandmother?"

Jules eyes welled up with tears. "I wish I could tell you more. She died when I was only five years old. She was a beautiful woman. Wait! I have a picture I can show you," he said, jumping out of his chair, knocking it over backwards. He stumbled precariously over to his small bedroom just off the kitchen. Nate followed him in and sat on the bed, waiting for him to finish rummaging through the closet. Finally, Jules pulled out the treasured photo, one that Nate had seen many times growing up.

Nate pretended, as he always did, that he had never seen the picture before. He felt his father's intent eyes on him as he waited for his reaction to the photo. Nate didn't disappoint him. "She was incredible," he said admiringly. "I can tell she was a kind woman."

"Very," Jules said, sitting beside his son. He seemed to have sobered up a little. "I miss her so much, even today."

"What can you remember about her?" Nate asked.

Jules closed his eyes and sighed. "Lilacs."

"Lilacs?"

"Yes, she smelled of Lilacs and soap. So sweet, so clean. Perfect."

"What about grandfather?"

Jules' eyes opened. It was as if someone had poured a bucket of water on him, starling him out of a beautiful dream. "Not much to say about him," he said shortly.

"You never talk about him," Nate said gently. "I'd like to know more about your father. Please tell me."

Jules looked at his son and nodded. "You have the right to know. All right, but I'm going to need more wine." He stood up and walked back to the table. He poured himself and Nate a glass and sat down, crossing one leg over the other. "My father hated my mother."

Appalled, Nate asked, "What? Why would you say that?"

"Because it's true," Jules said taking a long sip of his wine, hoping to lose himself once more in the fog of oblivion.

"But what makes you think that he would hate his own wife? Such a beautiful sweet woman."

"Growing up, he would curse her constantly to me. Anytime I won an award or did well at school, the first words out of his mouth were that I had gotten my brains from him, not my mother. If I disagreed, he's sock me one in the jaw."

Nate's mouth hung open. How could he not have known this about his family? "Oh, God, Father, I'm so sorry. You don't have to talk about this if you don't want to. I didn't realize."

"No, no," Jules said pouring himself another glass. "I want to tell you. I should tell you."

"Okay, but just go easy on the wine, okay?"

Jules stopped pouring and put the bottle down. He nodded and pushed the glass away. "Okay."

Nate remained silent for a few moments and then asked, "Why do you think he was so mean about her?"

"I didn't know for the longest time but finally, one of my uncles took me aside and told me the story. Apparently, my mother worked two jobs to help put food on the table. She'd teach kids piano in the evening. One of the kids' fathers tried to rape her. Came close too, but she fought him off and ran away."

Nate gasped. "That's horrible."

"Yeah, I know. But that wasn't the worst part. My father blamed her for the incident. Even when she came home covered in bruises from her ordeal, he'd told her that she must have asked for it.

"I was only four then, but I remember him screaming at her. I hid in the bedroom wishing I had the courage to come out and defend her. But I couldn't. I was just too little. The next day, I assumed he'd beaten her because of all the black and blue marks on her face and arms. I never dreamed that she'd been attacked," Jules whispered, tears streaming down his face.

Nate went over to him and pulled him into his arms, letting him weep into his arms. "It wasn't your fault," he reassured him. "You were only four!"

His face was buried in his son's chest. "I know, but I wish I could have done something. Protected her in some way. He made her life miserable after that. And then, she was gone," he said, his voice muffled.

Nate thought about whether he should let the conversation die but realized that this was probably his last chance to learn all that he could about his grandmother. After tonight, he vowed to never bring up this subject again. His voice was barely audible. "How did she die?"

"I never knew the details," Jules said, pulling himself up. He wiped his eyes. "It was work related. She worked in a mill, and there was some automated machine that malfunctioned. She was gone in a matter of minutes."

"That's horrible," Nate said. "So tragic. And your father? What happened to him?

Jules shrugged. "I left the house when I was seventeen. Struck it out on my own. Dad never tried to find me, and I stopped visiting him as soon as I realized he just didn't care about me. I heard later than he died of tuberculosis. Alone in his house." There was little pity in Jules's voice.

Nate nodded. "Sounds like the ending he deserved." He covered his father's hand with his. "Father?"

"Yes, son?"

"I love you."

Jules looked into Nate's eyes and smiled. "I love you, too. So much, Nate of mine. I wish I could have done more for you."

"You've done a lot for me. You were always there for me, loved me unconditionally. Now that I know the true story of your father, I'm amazed that you were able to be such a good father to me. Even when Mom left, you never wavered," Nate said.

"Your mother was a good woman, you know. She just couldn't take the pressure of raising a family," Jules said, answering the unspoken question about his mother's absence.

Nate put his hand up. "Don't defend her. She's not worth it. She left. That's the end of that. You're the one that stuck by me. You're all that I need."

A few days later, Nate chose to run through the Italian neighborhood. It was an unusually warm weekend day and many people were out strolling, making decent exercise difficult. Realizing his error, he turned around, hoping to find a more deserted area for his run when he saw the dark-haired beauty from the provision house on the other side of the street. He stopped abruptly and just stared at her.

It had been over a month since he'd last seen her. He had visited his father a few more times after that but never saw her again. It was a large company and therefore not surprising that their paths didn't cross again. Since he didn't know her name and his father really had no connection there, he didn't know how to find her again. He'd kicked himself repetitively over the last month for not having approached her that day in the cafeteria.

For such an innocent meeting, it had stayed with him, lingering in his mind. Although he often received interest from different woman, he couldn't picture himself have a lasting relationship with any of them. He dated occasionally but until he saw this woman, he had never considered marriage. He could marry this dark-haired beauty.

Crossing the street, he vowed not to make the same mistake twice. She could slap him in the face, but he was going to ask her out on a date. As he approached her, he wondered what he should say. His heart sped up as he got closer. She appeared to be alone, examining the large loaves of Italian bread poking out of a large brown wicker basket outside a local market.

"Hello!" he called out, not thinking of anything else more ingenious to say.

Maria Petrucelli, sensing the greeting was meant for her, lifted her eyes to meet the chocolate brown ones of Nate. Excitement laced with relief flooded though her. He had found her. Her mystery man from the cafeteria wasn't lost to her after all.

Her full lips softened as she looked into his eyes. She lowered her gaze to his lips and wondered what they would feel like against hers. She had little experience in such things but instinctively knew it would be a great kiss.

"Hello," Nate said, repeating his earlier greeting. He realized that he wasn't the only one flustered by their meeting. She looked as dazed as he felt.

"Hi!" Maria said, guiltily shifting her eyes back to his. "I saw you before at the provision house, didn't I?"

Nate grinned with relief. "Yes, you remember! I've thought a lot about you since then- wondered how you were, who you were. Please tell me your name."

Maria hesitated before answering. Should she answer? Then, she realized what little harm could come by giving him her name. "Maria Petrucelli."

"Maria Petrucelli," he repeated softly. "Beautiful name for a beautiful woman."

"And your name, please?" she asked in a mock serious tone.

"Oh, right! Strange man on a street corner asks you your name. Not terribly proper, is it? Nate Rubin, ma'am," he replied, tipping his imaginary hat. "It is a pleasure to make your acquaintance." He bowed before her with great flourish.

Maria giggled. "Mr. Rubin, it's nice to meet you."

"Nate. Please."

"I'll consider it."

"And would you consider going on a date with me?" Nate asked. His confidence dropped a notch as his heart started to hammer in his chest, and his palms suddenly became itchy. "You would do me a great honor if you accept my invitation to dinner."

"I…" Suddenly Maria felt out of her depth. She backed up away from Nate and shook her head. "I can't. Please leave me alone."

Nate stared at her and wondered at the sudden change. What had he done? What had gone wrong? "But -"

Maria took one last look at him before she dashed down the street back home. Nate watched her in stunned silence and wondered if his being Jewish was the reason for her departure. Although he knew he should be incensed, he found himself wanting to explain that he and his father don't practice Judaism to any real extent. He certainly wasn't orthodox. As she disappeared around the corner, he wondered if he'd ever see her again.

Tony pushed open the doors of the Walnut Club and grinned as a few of the members called out to him with a jovial, "Hello, Tony!" He cheerfully responded in kind.

Nick glanced over and gave him a broad smile. He broke away from the client and walked over to him. "Good to see you!" he greeted him with a hearty slap on the back.

"Thanks," Tony said feeling happier than he had in a long time. He felt that he really belonged here and was a part something important. He was needed and respected.

"What did you think of last Tuesday's meeting?" Nick asked casually.

"Great!" Tony replied enthusiastically. "Thanks for letting me come."

"Of course," Nick replied. "We need you."

"Thanks," Tony replied. He couldn't believe that Nick Martens, the Argentinean soccer superstar was actually telling him that he needed him. "I am honored to be a part of your group."

Nick motioned for Tony to follow him across the large floor to one of the rings. "Keep that right glove up, Terry!" he called to the large blond in the ring. He nodded when Terry promptly complied. He turned to study Tony for a moment. "Are you ready to join?"

"Sure!" Tony replied. "What do I need to do?"

"Not much." Nick said with a quick laugh. "It's not like we're going to haze you or anything. We just like people to prove themselves a little before we bring them into the fold."

"Makes sense," Tony said feeling a little nervous. "So, what kind of thing should I do?"

"Surprise me," he said with a wink. "Make it good!"

Tony nodded and realized after a moment Nick meant now, so he turned around and walked to the door. What should he do? Ralph Carpote had mentioned that he and some friends liked to wait until an egg was really rotten and then toss them at a Jew's store front. If you threw it just right it would ooze down the window and reek to the heavens.

Tony pushed open the door and walked outside, deep in thought. It was Saturday, which meant the Jews were all in synagogue. The stores were all closed, so they'd be easy targets. He though briefly of calling Ralph but realized it would be more impressive if he did this job on his own.

Where would he get rotten eggs? In his family, no food went to waste. He walked around the outside of the Walnut Club looking for inspiration. Just outside one of the back doors sat a crate of old, rotting tomatoes. He wrinkled his nose to see if they smelled, but it appeared the tomatoes didn't stink the way eggs did. Shrugging, he picked it up and walked down Walnut Street.

Nick looked out a window at his young charge and smiled. He had hoped that Tony would discover the crate. He signaled for one of the club members to follow Tony and see if he carried out the assignment. Once a person committed to the cause with some action against the Jewish plague, Nick and the rest could count on them to stick it out. Unfortunately, not everyone had the stomach to really give Kikes what they deserved.

Tony took a few turns and found himself in the unfamiliar territory of the Jews. As predicted, the shops were closed, and the streets were fairly deserted. He found a Kosher Deli and decided that would be his best bet. There was a certain irony in throwing rotten vegetables at a store purporting to supply godly food above the common food he and his friends ate.

Rage burned inside him as he picked up the tomato and let it fly. It fell a little short, hitting the brick wall instead of the window front Tony was aiming for. No matter, there were dozens more. Tomato after tomato flew through the air and splattered satisfactorily on the walls and window, making a large mess.

When the last tomato hit the wall, he threw the crate in front of the door and turned to walk away. He stopped short when he saw a little boy, maybe eight years old, staring at him with wide eyes. The look of fear he saw in the boy's eyes startled him.

As the boy ran off, Tony suppressed twinges of guilt that quickly surface. He started to walk home when he noticed a man from the club leaning against the wall. The man tipped his hat to Tony in a silent salute before jogging away. Tony knew that if he was going to join the Friends and earn the respect of the group and Nick, he needed to get his hands dirty. It was the correct thing to do. But then why did that little boy's eyes bore into his soul?

CHAPTER TWELVE

Nate sat in the corner of the ring, catching his breath at the end of round five. His opponent didn't look good, but he wouldn't go down, despite the potentially lethal uppercut Nate had delivered. Surprised the Irishman hadn't even stumbled, Nate had nearly lost the round, having lost his concentration. A boxer cannot afford to be off his game for even a moment.

The Central War Boxing Club was filled with people. Although Nate still fought in smokers now and then, he had successfully switched over to Club fighting. It paid better and was much safer. A few of his past opponents from the smokers never resurfaced and rumor had it that there were five fight related deaths in the last year from the one location. Manny reassured him that none of his opponents had died, but Nate knew that some were permanently injured. It didn't set well with him. Club matches were much more regulated and much less dangerous.

Looking over at the other corner, Andy McBride was being treated for two cuts under his left eye. Just as he was making a mental note of that weakness, Manny whispered, "That eye's bound to be sensitive."

Nate grinned. "I was just thinking that."

"His ribs look a little tender on the left side as well."

"Okay."

"Just deliver a few more blows like the one you gave last round, and we'll be home for dinner."

Nate looked at him. "Didn't seem to have much effect."

"You don't think so?" Manny asked. "Just 'cause he didn't go down, don't mean it didn't hurt."

Nate nodded. The bell rang, and he stood up a little quicker than his opponent, which made him smile. Maybe Manny was right, and McBride was just hiding his pain more.

They danced around each other for a few moments, each looking for an opening. Nate purposefully left his left side open, encouraging McBride to deliver some right crosses. It worked and when McBride overreached, Nate slammed him with three solid punches to the already bruised ribcage. McBride sank to his knees in pain.

The referee pulled Nate back and waited until McBride stood. Seeing that he was ready to continue to fight, the referee blew his whistle again. The fight continued another six rounds, but McBride never recovered fully after that. Nate purposely didn't knock him out, knowing the match would be more valuable and popular to the onlookers if it went the full twelve rounds.

After the match, Manny rubbed Nate down in the dressing room. "You did good, kid," Manny said happily. "You keep going like this, and we'll make the big time."

"Yeah," Nate said. He was too tired to keep his eyes open. "Madison Square Garden."

"That'll be the start. World tours."

Nate grinned. "Yeah, right! Maybe we can hit Germany on the way around the world."

Manny laughed gruffly. "I guess not the world, at least for a while, but someday."

"Yeah, someday."

"Nate?" Manny asked with some amount of eagerness.

"Yeah, boss?" Nate enjoyed the friendship he had with trainer. It was unusual to find someone you trusted so completely in this industry. "What's on your mind?"

"I've been thinking. Maybe it's time to think about a real big fight. Something with meat, something that'll bring press."

Nate's eyes popped open. "What do you have in mind?"

"There's a kid I keep hearing about. He's rising up the ranks. Doing pretty darn well over on the East Side. Italian. Name's Danny Petrucelli."

Nate swiveled to face Manny. "Petrucelli, huh? I think I met him few years ago." As he thought about that day on line at the soup kitchen his face burned red. "He didn't exactly see me at my best." Nate explained what happened with Nick Martens and how he had chased the kid off out of embarrassment.

"Don't sweat it," Manny said. "From what I hear, the kid's a good egg. He'd understand."

"Yeah, I supposed," Nate said. He suddenly started, realizing that last name sounded familiar from a different place. "Shit. Does this kid have a sister?"

Manny frowned. "Probably, why?"

"No reason," Nate said, feeling cursed.

Danny walked into his familiar gym and was greeted with a round of cheers. He smiled back at the people as he headed for the lockers. Willie was waiting for him, scowling.

"You're late," he said without preamble.

"No, I'm not."

Willie looked at his watch. "One o'clock means one o'clock. Not a quarter past."

"Go easy on me, okay? Mom needed help with the upper cupboards in the kitchen." He started changing into his boxing gear.

"Oh well then," Willie said sarcastically, exaggerating his arm movements. "If your mother needed help with her housecleaning then by all means I understand why you're late to a boxing match. I'm so sorry to have inconvenienced you! Are you sure it's okay for me to be keeping you today?"

Danny looked contrite. "Don't be like that. I'm sorry."

Willie nodded, seemingly satisfied. "Come here, let me get you ready."

Johnny Martinez walked in with fresh towels. He nodded a hello to Willie and Danny. Johnny had been working at East Side for two years and although he never stepped foot in the ring, he was a big fan of the sport.

"Has Fists arrived yet?" Danny asked Johnny.

"He was early," Willie answered before Johnny could reply.

Danny looked up and noticed a trace of a smile cross Willie's lips. "Yeah, yeah, I get the message."

"You're prepped on him?" Willie asked.

"You told me everything yesterday."

Johnny looked at them both and said, "So you know to go for his right side, right? He got hit pretty hard in his ribs last month. Hasn't really recovered yet. Probably shouldn't be in the ring."

Danny paused as he put on his robe. He looked at Willie. "You didn't mention that. Is he okay to fight?"

Willie shrugged. "I didn't hear anything about it."

"You want the official answer?" Willie asked.

"I want the real answer," Danny said seriously. Is he too hurt to fight?"

"I don't know," Willie said, pulling Danny over to the bench to work on his muscles. Kneading his left arm, he said, "Who are we to say?"

"Oh, come on," Danny said with irritation. "If not you, who?"

"He'll be okay." Willie said. "Johnny you can go."

Johnny nodded. "Sure thing. Hey, I'm sorry if I said something I shouldn't have. I was just trying to help."

"Thanks, Johnny," Danny said. "I appreciate the information."

Danny allowed Willie to work on his shoulders. After a few minutes, he popped off the bench. "I want to see him."

"What? Before the fight?" Willie asked, started. "That's unheard of!"

"I don't care. I want to see him," Danny said stubbornly. He closed the belt on his robe and walked out in search of his opponent.

It didn't take long to find him. He went to a neighboring dressing room and approached the man in the gold robe. "I hear you're injured. Is that true?"

The man was shorter than Danny, and his face wore a permanent scowl. His eyebrows joined to form one brow, giving him an intense look. "Get out here!" he muttered, looking away. He turned to his trainer. "Jerry, tell him to mind his own business, will ya?"

Danny turned to the trainer, a wiry man who looked to be in his forties. "Can I speak to you for a second?" he asked.

The man nodded, walking around the bench to go outside with Danny. "Look kid, just go out in the ring and fight. He's ready for action."

"But is he hurt?"

Jerry looked back at his boxer and sighed. "Look, I tried to get him to postpone the match another month, but the guy's got to eat. He's adamant. If not you, he'll fight someone else."

"But I don't want -" Danny began.

Willie pulled him away, putting his hand up. "It's okay, Jerry. We'll meet you out there, okay?

"But-," Danny started.

Again, Willie put his hand up and told him to get ready. He brought Danny back into the dressing room. "He's a grown man. He can make his own decisions. Look, you heard his trainer. If he don't fight you, he'll fight someone else."

Danny felt ill. The last thing he ever wanted to do was permanently injure someone. Fighting someone who was already hurt was dangerous. He understood his opponent's need to put food on the table, but it wasn't smart to fight with bruised ribs. He didn't want to be responsible for putting the guy in the hospital. "What if I don't go out there?"

"You'll forfeit. He'll win, and you'll get your first loss. You want that?"

Danny sighed, "No."

"You've got a big heart, kid. Just go out there and win."

Danny nodded and followed Willie out to the ring, feeling depressed for the first time since he began boxing. He stepped into the ring and traded punches with the un browed man, holding back on his intensity. In stark contrast, Fists was going all out, trying to pound Danny into the ground.

After a few rounds, Danny sat in his corner, staring off into space. He looked over at Fists, who was looking out into the crowd with self- satisfied smile. Danny followed his line of vision and noticed that Johnny was smiling back at him. Confused, Danny looked up at Willie.

"What is it?" Willie asked.

"I think I've been had," Danny said. Quiet anger boiled up inside him.

"What do you mean?"

Danny nodded over at Johnny, who still wore a smug smile. "How well do you know Johnny anyway?"

"Not well," Willie said. "Why?"

The bell rang. Danny said, "I'll tell you later," and stood up with a resolve to end this match. Now that he thought about it, Fists didn't react to punches like an injured man. Danny circled around him, dancing with a new lightness of step. Fists threw a couple of punches that Danny dodged easily.

Danny's eyes flashed with anger as he threw a series of punches at Fists' chest and ribs. The crowd cheered loudly, spurring Danny on further. He deftly avoided a right cross and gave him an uppercut to the right ribs. He heard a distinct crack and saw the intense pain reflected pain reflected in Fists' eyes. Fists fell to his knees and threw up onto the canvas before passing out on the mat.

Danny nodded at the inanimate form of his opponent but felt no joy in the victory. He searched the crowd for Johnny, who cowered under the scrutiny, scuttling back into the dressing room. Danny followed him, Willie close on his heels.

"Why the fuck would you do that?" Danny shouted. "You're scum, you know that?"

Johnny trembled as he stood in front of Danny, praying that he wasn't going to die tonight. "I'm sorry, please forgive me."

Willie looked from Danny to Johnny and back to Danny. His confusion was apparent. "What's going on?"

Danny continued to stare at Johnny. "Why don't you tell him? Confession's good for the soul. Isn't that what they say?"

Johnny nodded, relieved to be still standing there and not splattered on the floor. "I...made a mistake," he answered lamely.

"What kind of mistake?" Willie asked, still trying to decipher what was going on.

"Fists' manager Jerry offered me a piece of the purse if I'd feed Danny here information," Johnny said.

Willie closed his eyes and groaned. "Fists wasn't hurt, was he?"

"No," Johnny said quietly.

"But why would you say that?" Willie asked.

"So that I'd go easy on him," Danny supplied. "Isn't that it? Because I'm a sap or something, right? Do I have it right?"

Johnny nodded and then said, "No, I mean, yes, I mean. You're not a sap, but you care. You care about people. I figured you might just throw the fight to save the guy."

Danny nodded. "And it almost worked. If you two hadn't been so cocky..."

"I'm sorry, Danny. Really, I am."

Willie's face was slowly turning red as comprehension dawned on him. Without warning his right hand shot out and popped Johnny in the face.

"Ow!" Johnny said, surprised to get the punch from the old man to his right.

"You deserved that," Danny said quietly. "Now you know better than to show your face here again, right?"

Johnny nodded, holding the right side of his face gingerly. "Yeah and just so you know, I really am sorry. I needed the money. I know that's not a good reason for doing what I did, but I just want you to know that I'm sorry."

Danny nodded and watched him walk out the door. "Jesus," he muttered. "I can't believe that."

Willie nodded. "I know. But you showed that scumbag of an opponent, didn't you? You plugged him good. He might not have had a broken rib before the fight, but he sure as hell does now."

Danny looked up at him. "That's not how I want to fight. I don't like fighting angry like that. It just isn't my style."

"I know, kid. He had it coming though. Kind of justice, if you ask me," Willie said quietly.

"Nice right cross you've got there, old friend," Manny said from the door.

Willie spun around and smiled sheepishly. "Yeah, I only bring that out when I have to. Shit my knuckles are sore." He rubbed them for effect.

"You don't fool me," Manny said. He walked into the room and nodded to Danny. "Nice fight."

"You think so?" Danny asked gruffly, still angered by the betrayal.

Manny studied him. "I don't know what that was all about, but when you decided to fight, you were good."

Danny's anger evaporated, and he grinned. "You saw that."

"I see everything," Manny commented. He turned to Willie. "I'd like to talk to you about a match between your fighter and mine."

Willie stood up right and smiled. "That's great. Sure, let's talk about that."

Danny perked up as well. "Who's that?"

"Danny," Willie said patiently. "This is Manny Kimmel. He represents Nate Rubin."

"Lights Out," Danny breathed. "No, shit. Really?"

"You bet, kid," Manny said. "Listen why don't you shower up, and I'll have a talk here with your manager? We'll figure something out."

Willie and Manny walked out. As Willie walked through the club, he was patted on the back by a number of club members. He smiled and accepted the compliments about Danny.

"Let's go outside," Manny suggested. "Can I buy you lunch?"

"Sure, I didn't get a chance to eat before the fights," Willie said cheerfully. "I'm famished."

They walked a few blocks down to deli and sat at a table, pulling out the menus. "So, you've had your eye on Danny," Willie said matter-of-factly.

Manny chuckled. "Yeah, yeah. Don't let it get to your head."

Willie grinned. "It's hard not to. He's good. How long have we been in this business anyway?"

"Seems like forever. Twenty years?"

"Yeah, sounds right. And we've finally got two champions. Nate and Danny. They've both got promise. You still fighting in those smokers?"

"Nah," Manny said, motioning to the passing waitress to pour him some coffee. "Nate's been out of those for six months now. He hates them. Me too, for that matter."

"Danny's never fought there, never seen the seedy side of the business."

Manny nodded. "You going to tell me what happened today?"

Willie briefed him on what Fists was trying to do. "He's got a good heart that kid. Probably too good for this sport."

"He'll learn," Manny reassured him. "This will toughen him up a bit."

"So, you're serious about putting a match together for Nate and Danny?"

"Yeah. They're both getting a name for themselves. A big match could really help them both."

Willie nodded. "I agree. Where do you want to have it?"

"Your club," Manny said without hesitation. "It's much nicer, and you've put so much into it. Plus, it's more centrally located. Better for press."

"Great!" Willie said. He was proud of his club. He'd come in a years ago and put a lot into rebuilding that place. He had plans for the future and a big match would help him build the club up even further. Finding investors would be easy. "When were you thinking?"

"March."

"That soon?"

"Why not?" Manny asked. "They're ready. It'll give us time to put a buzz out."

Willie grinned. "March it is!"

CHAPTER THIRTEEN

Nate came after his training to find his father sitting on the sofa. Jules looked up quickly and with an overly bright smile said, "Hello, Nate! What brings you back so soon? You're early." He stuffed a small book in between the seat cushion.

Nate frowned. It was obvious his father didn't want him to see what he was reading, so he didn't say anything. "I'm done training."

"But you have that big match with that Italian kid…," his voice trailed off as he tried to remember the name.

"Danny Petrucelli," Nate supplied. "Don't worry, I'll be ready. I still have two months!"

"Yes, but word's already getting around. I'm proud of you, son."

"Thank you, Father," Nate said. He sat down next to Jules and started when he saw his father's face. "Father!"

Jules frowned. "What is it?"

"Your face!"

"My what?" Jules asked perplexed. His hand went up to his bruised cheek and blushed. "Oh, that."

"Oh, that? What's *that*?" Nate shouted the last word, his voice reaching a panicked level. "Why do you have a bruise on your right cheek?"

"I, uh, tripped. It's slippery these days," Jules supplied, knowing that his explanation was weak. It sounded false even to his own ears.

His best tactic was to change the conversation to something more neutral. "I made chicken soup. Would you like some?"

"Later," Nate said curtly. Seeing that his father looked inordinately uncomfortable, he softened his tone. "Father, please talk to me."

Jules looked up and sighed. "There's some guys at work," he began.

Nate waited for him to continue but when he didn't, Nate asked, "Which guys? What did they do?"

Jules shrugged looking away. "We got into a fight's all."

"A fight? You?"

"It wasn't important."

"What was the fight about?"

"What's it ever about?"

"Because you're Jewish?"

Jules nodded. "Look, can we talk about something else? Anything will do."

Nate sighed and stood up. He walked into the kitchen and inhaled deeply. "The soup does smell good. Can I pour you a bowl?"

"I had some already. You have it."

Nate complied, ladling himself a bowl. "Thanks, Father. It looks good."

"So, tell me more about the fight you have planned with Petrucelli. What's he like?"

"They call him Dancing Man," Nate answered. "He's supposed to be very light on his feet."

"Kind of the opposite of you," Jules said teasingly.

Nate grinned, happy to see that his father's mood was improving. "Yeah, kind of like. I've never been accused of being a dancer in the ring."

"Should make for a good match," Jules observed. "That's what the word on the street is. Plus, there's the fact that you're a Jewish boxer fighting an Italian Catholic. That's going to make good press."

"I'd rather it didn't," Nate said curtly. "That's not what I want the focus to be about."

"You can't do much about that," Jules said heavily. "We can't choose our race. We're just stuck with it."

"Stuck with it?" Nate repeated. "I've never heard you talk like that. Does this have anything to do with those guys at work?"

Jules shrugged. "I don't want to talk about it."

"Okay," Nate said reluctantly. He sat down with his father, and they talked about various things until it got late. Jules finally went to bed, pulling the book he had stuffed into the cushion with him. Nate pretended not to notice, but watched his father tuck the book into his sweater pocket, which was draped on the chair by his bed.

Nate waited for Jules to start snoring before he snuck into the room and carefully extracted the light brown book. It was well worn and dog-eared and written in German. On the cover were the words, *Deutscher National-Katechismus* and written next to it in his father's lettering was "The German Catachism." There were many notes in the margins, also written in his father's handwriting.

Jules rolled over, and Nate froze. He crept out of the bedroom and went back to the living room. He sat on the sofa and paged through the book. It was filled with questions and answers about the Jewish people, why the Nazis are at war with them, and why they are bad for the Fatherland.

Nate flipped through the book, anger and shock building within him with each word he read. "How does the Jew subjugate the German people?" The answer written in the margin in his father's hand was, "By loaning the German people money. Thousands of good, hard working German people were destroyed by borrowing money from the Jews. Farmers, who have owned their debts, couldn't pay the interest."

It went on to describe "racial defilement" as training the blood of the German people by marrying a Jew. If a German marries a Jew, they are no longer a part of the German community. It ended with a call to loyalty of all German people, to preserve the sanctity of the German way of life.

Nate closed the book at started off into space. What the hell was his father doing with this book, and why would he be taking notes? He had to find a way to talk to Jules about this. He crept back into the room and slipped the book back into its previous hiding place. Sighing, Nate closed the door to his father's room and went to bed. He prayed Jules would find the courage to talk to him about this. In the meantime, Nate planned to watch his father carefully.

Donato wiped the corner of his mouth with his napkin. The empty plates, adorned with bits of sauce and breadcrumbs were a testament to another well enjoyed meal. "Delicious," he said, nodding to his wife. "As always."

"Thank you," Teresa said with a smile.

"It will help fuel my practice tonight," Danny said.

"You have to go again?" Teresa asked with a scowl. "I hardly ever see you these days."

"He has a big match, Mamma," Maria said. "He's fighting Nate Rubin."

Tony snorted. He had pointedly ignored his brother through the entire meal and had planned to avoid the subject of the upcoming fight, but now that Maria mentioned it, it was hard to keep quiet. "I can't believe my own brother's fighting a Kike."

Danny glared at him. "And I can't believe my own brother's a Nazi."

"He's not a Nazi." Teresa said sharply.

"What if I am" Tony asked defiantly. His voice lost some of its confidence.

""You're not," Donato said quietly. "No son of mine is."

Tony looked at Donato, his eyes reflecting his surprise. "But Pappa, Mussolini's banded with Adolf Hitler. How can you be against his party?"

"Benito Mussolini's a great man. He's just trying to save Italy and restore her to her people. Adolf Hitler has his own agenda. Mussolini will make use of Hitler's temporary power because he's a brilliant strategist, but never make the mistake of thinking that those two men are the same. They're not," Donato explained patiently.

"I can't believe I'm hearing this. But Father, you can't really tell me you approve of Danny fighting a Kike, can you?" Tony asked.

Donato sighed. "I don't trust Jews. You know that. But I don't hate Jews with the passion that the Nazis do. I don't hate anyone with that kind of vengeance. It is wrong and goes against the teaching of Jesus."

"Jesus was persecuted by the Jews!" Tony shouted. "They nailed him up onto a cross and killed him. It was barbaric."

Teresa shook her head firmly at her son. "Your father's right, Tony. Even if you're right, Jesus would be the first to forgive." She looked imploring to her son, silently willing him to see reason.

"You don't understand," Tony said. He stood up abruptly, causing his chair to tip over, clattering loudly to the floor. "I can't believe my own family members are Jew lovers . I hope for your sake, you see the truth sooner than later. The Jews are taking over. Can't you see that? Is that what you want?"

Teresa's eyes welled with tears. "Tony, listen to yourself. This isn't you."

Tony waved his arms wildly and backed away from the table. He looked around at the stunned expressions on the faces of each family member. His mouth opened to say something, but he just shook his head. "There's no talking to you, is there? I'm going out. I don't know when I'll be back."

Tony spun around and ran to the door. He expected someone, maybe his mother to call him back, but they all remained silent. He opened the door, gave one last look at his family before he grunted, slamming the door with a satisfying loud bang.

He smiled a smug smile until he realized that the air was colder than he had anticipated and his sweater wasn't going to provide much protection. He thought momentarily about going back inside but realized that there was no way to do that without looking foolish, so he just ran down to the Walnut Street Athletic Club.

He was late for the meeting but hoped they'd understand. Not everyone could always be there on time. The meetings weren't exactly a secret, but they weren't publicly announced. The subject of the Nazi movement was politely ignored for the most part by the community. They neither embraced nor shunned the group.

Tony made it to the building within 10 minutes. He rubbed his hands briskly as he leapt up the three steps to the closed door. Opening it, he sighed with contentment as the warm air welcomed him. Off in the distance he could hear the group gathered in the main hall, so he followed the voices.

"Tony!" Nick Martens said jovially. He had interrupted Hans Reuther, who looked annoyed. "Good that you came!" Nick walked over to greet Tony effusively.

"Sorry, I'm late," Tony muttered.

"You okay?" Nick asked, concerned.

Tony looked around at the dozens of men assembled. This chapter of the Friends of the New German was expanding rapidly. "Yeah, I'm fine. Just pissed off, that's all."

Hans's irritation vanished quickly when he saw Tony's expression. He came around to usher Tony inside. "Let me guess. A Jew's behind this, isn't he?"

Tony nodded with a slight smile. "Of course!"

The group laughed, and Tony felt better. Here was a group that would understand him and understand why it was wrong that his brother was fighting Rubin. He settled into his chair and told the group about the argument he just had with his family. As he spoke, he looked around at the sympathetic faces of the group and felt emboldened to continue. "It's my father I'm most disappointed in," he said with a sigh. "He's not making any sense."

Nick and Hans exchanged a look, and Hans leaned into Tony, "You're right. He's not making sense but that's what the Jews are good at. They confuse people, make them lose all reason, their ability to think for themselves. That's their plan."

"And that brother of yours," Nick grumbled. "It's not exactly helping to have a Jew lover in the house."

An instinctively wave of anger washed over Tony at Nick's attack on his family. Danny was still his brother. Sighing, Tony had to admit that Nick was correct, though. Danny had sided with the enemy. It was hard to defend that. "Yeah, it isn't," Tony agreed.

Hans observed Tony's internal battle and said gently, "It's okay that you love him, Tony. He's your brother."

Tony sighed in relief. "Yes! You understand!"

Hans smiled and nodded. "Of course, I do. Hopefully Danny will come around."

"He might not," Tony said.

"Then he won't," Hans replied with a casual shrug.

Tony smiled in relief. He looked over at Nick, who looked less agreeable. "He'll come around," Tony said assuring him.

Nick gave him a weak smile. The tension in the corners of his mouth belayed his true feeling. "It doesn't really matter either way. The important thing is that you're here."

Tony, not noticing Nick's tension, returned the smile with a relieved sigh. He looked around at the rest of the young men, who were silently listening to the exchange. "So, what were you discussing before I came in?"

Hans sat back in his chair. "As a matter of fact, we were talking about your brother's upcoming fight."

"Really," Tony said. He felt an uneasiness creep over him. "What about it?"

"He's fighting that Jew," Nick said, his voice laced with anger.

"I know," Tony said, looking at Hans in confusion. "I told you that's what I was fighting with my family about."

Hans looked reproachfully at Nick. "Nick knows that you're on our side. We're just concerned about the publicity. That's all."

"What do you mean?" Tony asked.

"The fight's getting a lot of press," Hans replied. The others in the room nodded.

"So?" Tony asked looking around. He noticed a few of the men roll their eyes.

"Press for Jews isn't a good thing," Hans said patiently. "It's never good for the enemy to get publicity."

Tony blushed, feeling stupid. "Oh. I get it now. So, what's the plan?"

"That's what we were talking about," Nick said. He was struggling to remain calm.

Nick worked hard to keep his voice even, but his cheeks were splotched with red. "It's important that we take a stand at this fight. Send message." A few of the men in the room cheered. Nick grinned in response. He leaned close to Tony and said in a low menacing voice, "You get my meaning?"

A thrill of fear shot painfully up Tony's spine. He struggled to conceal a wince. He needed to be careful, very careful not wear his emotion on his sleeve. "What kind of message?" He inwardly cringed at the reedy quality of his voice. He cleared his throat and spoke with a husky tone. "What are you going to do?"

Hans put his hands up and shook his head at Nick. "Nothing for you to worry about now. We're still in the planning phase anyway. We'll let you know what you need to do but don't worry, no harm will come to your brother. I promise."

Tony's mouth went dry and the room spun counterclockwise. They were talking about violence, something that had never been mentioned before. The way Hans promised Tony that his brother wouldn't be hurt made him realize just the opposite was true. In that moment, he knew this group had deadly plans and if allowed to continue, Danny would most certainly get hurt.

Hans looked like he was expecting some sort of response. Mechanically, Tony nodded. "Okay. Just let me know what you want me to do. I'm in." He needed a chance to get away, to think things through. Until then, it was vital that these people believe that he was still a part of their group. He hoped the shock he was feeling wasn't obvious to the others. Those few classes of drama in high school seemed to be paying off. No one looked at him askance.

Hans sighed in relief. "Good. We'll keep you informed with the rest of the group. Now, let's talk about another matter. Greenberg's Deli. How did it go this week with the flyers and pickets?"

Tony listened to the group discuss how they targeted Saul Greenberg's business for a small demonstration, trying to discourage the non-Jewish patronage. Two of the new recruits talked excitedly about how they got a few people to not go into the store. They gave them coupons for another store in a different neighborhood, in the hopes that they would continue shopping in the new location. When they were finished, they had thrown rocks in the store window, shattering the glass all over the sidewalk. The group laughed raucously. Tony tried to mimic the laughter, but felt sick to his stomach.

As the group continued to talk, Tony kept hearing the words of his father over and over in his head, "*I don't hate Jews with the passion that the Nazis do. I don't hate anyone with that kind of vengeance.*" These people really did hate with a passion. Tony wished he could leave but knew that would draw suspicion. He needed portray the same enthusiasm as when he had walked in. He prayed that he could figure out a way to get out of this mess that he had created.

CHAPTER FOURTEEN

Tony jumped when the horn sounded for lunch the next day. He had arrived home late the previous night after the meeting and had crept into bed. He wasn't eager to run into his family, especially Danny. Fortunately, they were all in bed. He tossed and turned the whole night, wondering how he could get back to his old way of life, the one where he was blissfully unaware of the Nazi's true intentions.

The sun was barely rising when he left the house. The cold air helped to keep him awake. He went to work early and started unloading with the night shift. They looked at him askance, but were grateful for the help. Tony just wanted to keep busy, doing anything but thinking about what he had almost done.

He looked up from his pallet, squinting at the sun and wiped his hands. He grabbed his brown bag of lunch that Teresa had left out for him. Even when they weren't speaking, his mother wanted to see him well fed. He brushed away a stray tear that threatened to freeze on his face. It must be the lack of sleep that made him so sentimental.

He walked over to the lunch room and stopped dead in his tracks. Arte Bella, Philip Cantalupo's right hand man, was casually leaning up against a brick wall staring him down. His large, bulky form and dark expression would make any man tremble with fear. Tony turned around to see if the monster was maybe looking at someone else, but it was painfully clear that the look was intended for him.

Slowly turning back, Tony thought briefly about running, but where would he go? He needed this job and would show up every day. Grimacing, he realized the only thing he could do was face the man, see why he was here, and what Tony had done to anger him so.

Moving like lead weights were attached to his legs, Tony slogged his way over to Arte, who didn't move an inch but waited patiently for him to arrive. His expression never shifted. Tony was certain that the man never blinked.

"Mr. Bella?" he croaked. Tony coughed and tried his voice again. "Mr. Bella, is there something I can do for you?"

Arte looked him up and down. "Why don't you come for a ride with me? Bring your lunch with you if you like. Just don't make a mess in my car."

"Okay," Tony said, his voice still shaking. "Whatever you say, sir."

Arte turned and walked out to the street, heading straight for a large black Packard. A large, fat man sat behind the wheel and a tall skinny one occupied the backseat. Arte opened the back door and barked, "Move over!" The skinny man instantly scooted to the far side.

Arte looked back at Tony and raised an eyebrow as he held the door open.. Tony got into the car and briefly wondered if he'd make it out alive. Arte squeezed in next to him and closed the door. The driver took off like a shot.

"You going to eat or not?" he asked gruffly.

The last thing Tony felt like doing was eating. "I'm not hungry," he said. Drumming up his courage, he realized nothing could be worse than not knowing why he was here. "Look, did I do something?"

Arte nodded his head slowly. "You were at the Walnut Club last night."

Tony's mouth gaped open. "How did you know that?" he asked without thinking. "I mean, yes, sir, I was."

Arte's mouth formed at thin line. "We've been watching those Nazi scum since they arrived in Newark," he said. "You've gone to four of the meetings, haven't you?"

"Yes, sir," Tony said, still digesting the news that his movements had caught the notice of the largest mob boss in Newark.

"I know your family," Arte continued. "Good people. Why would you do something so stupid?"

Tony looked at his hands, which were shaking in his lap. "I don't know, sir. I…I don't…I wasn't thinking," he finished lamely.

Arte nodded. "Yeah, well good thing you came to your senses."

Tony looked at him in surprise. "Huh?"

Arte's look softened a bit. "I could tell you were a little spooked after the meeting. You ran out of there like you'd seen a ghost. That's why we're talking. Otherwise, you'd be on the list."

"What list?" Tony wasn't sure he wanted to know.

Arte looked at him like he was a simpleton. "You really need to ask?"

"No…no, sir," Tony though about the other new recruits, the boys from his neighborhood that had fallen prey to Nick, Hans, and the other Nazi leaders. "I just thought that maybe…the others, you know…"

Arte shrugged. "The others deserve what they get. And we're still wondering about you." The look he gave Tony made him want to throw up.

Tony glanced at the guy to his left and shuddered. His cold brown eyes burrowed a hole into his soul. He then caught the glare of the driver and quickly returned his eyes to Arte's. "I made a mistake," Tony whispered. "I thought… I didn't realize… I just… I don't know what I was thinking," he finished lamely.

Arte nodded. "I believe you," he said quietly. "And more importantly, Philip Cantalupo believes you."

Tony's eyes widened. "You mean Philip Cantalupo knows who I am?"

"Mr. Cantalupo's very familiar with everyone on the list," he said ominously. "Everyone."

"Right." Tony's mouth went dry again.

"So, you want to make it right?"

Tony felt the first ray of hope, since this car ride had begun. "How?"

"Are you sure about this, Mr. Bella," the man from Tony's right asked gruffy. "I mean, what do we know about this kid?"

"You questioning me?" Arte bellowed across Tony to the man.

The man shook his head and looked contrite. "No, boss."

Arte put his attention back on Tony. "You doublecross us, kid and you're going to wish you were dead."

Tony nodded vigorously. "I know. I would never do that. What can I do? You said I could make things right."

"There's a group," Arte began. The man to Tony's right coughed in what seemed to be disagreement. When Arte glared at him, he mumbled an apology. "A group of men doing something about the problem. We're meetin' in three days. Be there."

"Where is it?"

"Elizabeth. Yeshiva Hall. Look, this thing's on the down low, got it? Tell no one."

Again, Tony nodded vigorously. "Got it."

The car pulled back up to the bakery, right where they had picked him up. Arte opened the door, and Tony jumped out. Arte gave him a small smile. "You still got three minutes to eat. Chewing's for wimps, right?"

Tony laughed nervously. "Right," he said as he bounded into the loading bay. He looked back and watched the Packard leave. He pulled out the sandwich and took a large bite. Danny came up to him and whispered, "You really know how to pick your friends. Now you're hanging with the mob?"

Tony couldn't answer because his mouth was filled with food. In a way, it was a mixed blessing because he didn't know what he'd say to his brother. He'd promised to keep quiet about the meeting, and the last thing he wanted to do was break his word within five minutes of making it.

Danny shook his head in disgust and walked away. The sandwich lost all taste, and Tony found it hard to swallow. He hoped that someday his brother would understand and forgive him for his past stupidity. Actions speak louder than words, his father always said. Let his actions prove his repentance.

✢ ✢ ✢

Tony had no trouble finding Yeshiva Hall in Elizabeth. Two Jewish men with yamakas strolled by, nodding to him politely. Tony just stared at them as they passed, feeling foolish after. He climbed the steps to the old building and opened the door.

It was dark inside. Tony waited for his eyes to adjust. He briefly wondered if any of the Friends of the New Germany members had followed him here. Realizing that was a possibility, as he had not taken a direct route to the building. Looking over his shoulder frequently, he was relieved to have been quiet alone in his journey.

When the door opened a few seconds later, Tony jumped. The man was also startled to find Tony camped out by the door.

He looked up at the large figure of a man. It was impossible to make out any feature in his face, it was just too dark. "I'm not sure where I'm going," he stammered by way of explanation. "It's a big building."

Skeptical the man remained silent and lit a match. Tony immediately recognized him as Big Guido, one of Cantalupo's men. Sighing in relief, he said, "Arte Bella sent me"

"Did he now?" the man scoffed. "You'd better be on the up and up."

"I…I am!" Tony stammered.

The man grunted. "Follow me. I'll show you where we're going."

Tony nodded gratefully, "I'm Tony Petrucelli," he said, feeling more confident.

"I know."

"You know?" Tony asked in disbelief.

Big Guido didn't offer any explanation as to how or why he knew who Tony was. Tony realized that he should probably keep his mouth shut and just follow him as instructed.

After walking down a long corridor, turning right and then quickly left in almost pitch black darkness, they finally descended three flights of stairs into the basement. The staircase opened to a large cavernous room with cold stone walls. The room was lit with candles and lanterns and held a few hundred people. Tony gasped as he looked around at the sea of unfamiliar faces.

Many of the people assembled were Jewish, but there were a lot of Italian people there too. Some from his neighborhood. Tony recognized Nate Rubin in the group. Nate looked him up and down before turning his back to him.

After a few moments, the attendees found chairs where they could. The rest stood. Tony leaned up against the wall and waited to see what would happen. It didn't take long before short man wearing a Yamaka walked to the front of the assembly.

"Good evening," he called to the group. They all immediately fell silent. "Thank you for coming. Some of you are new to us, so let me introduce myself. I am Abraham Goldberg, and I am the leader of the New Jersey Minutemen."

The Minutemen were named because on a minute's notice they would group and fight the Nazi menace.

The crowd murmured approvingly, which made Abraham smile. "Whoever invited you tonight can answer all your questions, so please do not interrupt the proceedings. We are on a strict timeline and must get through our agenda."

Abraham Goldberg went over the events since the last meeting. Various subgroups had met and formulated plans for the big rally. Others were working on finding people in the community willing to fight against the Nazis. There was screening process before they were invited into this this meeting. Abraham made it clear that everyone there tonight had been approved by the executive council and that they should all feel fortunate.

As Abraham continued to speak, it became clear to Tony that none of them had been able to infiltrate the Nazi meetings. The best they could do was watch from outside the Walnut Club and the other half dozen or so meeting places around Newark. The Minutemen knew when and where they met but could not discover the exact plans of the group. The Friends of The New Germany were unaware of the Minutemen's existence, and it was vital it stayed that way.

"Nick Martens and Hans Reuther have recruited twelve new members this month. They're working toward expanding their ranks, building toward something big. We don't know what it is, but let me assure you it's big. Philip Cantalupo here has something to report. Philip?"

A murmur went through the crowd as the man slowly made his way to the front of the room. Tony had never met the man personally and was eager to see what he looked like. When he turned to face the audience, Tony stifled a gasp. The man approaching the podium, the powerful mob boss that he had idolized all his life, was old and frail.

When Philip reached the front of the room, he looked over the crowd for a moment until his eyes settled on Tony. Adrenaline spike through him as he realized that Cantalupo had been looking for him. Suddenly, Tony realized that he had been invited here for a reason, one that could change the course of his life as he knew it. As Cantalupo continued to stare at Tony, the other occupants turned to see what had caught his eye. They all looked Tony up and down, trying to decipher what had captured this powerful man's attention.

Finally, Philip Cantalupo spoke. His voice had all the virility of a man in his twenties. "Tonight, I bring with me hope. Hope for the future of Newark, hope for the future of our great nation. I bring to you a member, one of the latest recruits of the Friends of the New Germany. Tony Petrucelli."

The entire room turned in unison to look at Tony. There was no doubt in anyone's mind that he was the one Cantalupo was referring to. Tony's face turned beet red as he looked around at the people glaring at him, disgust and revulsion palpable in their eyes. Although they remained silent, Tony felt their curses pierce him with their stares. Tony felt new levels of shame for his prior alliance and bowed his head against the anger of the group.

"No, no my friends," Cantalupo said enthusiastically. "Do you not see the great opportunity this brings? Tony can be our eyes and ears of the Nazis. He and he alone can feed us with the much-needed information we need to end their reign. With knowledge, we can defeat them before they start!"

Although skeptical, many of the audience members turned back to look at Cantalupo, their anger at Tony lessening. Some continued to stare Tony down, but Tony's attention turned to his stomach, which was attempting to turn inside out. Cantalupo wanted him to be a spy? He had thought he would come tonight and help out where he could.

Tony had hoped he could somehow slip out of the Friends of the New Germany group without being noticed and help the Minutemen.

As if reading his mind, Cantalupo said, "Of course it will take great bravery on the part of our friends here. No one would debate how dangerous the Nazis are."

There was a murmur of agreement in the group, and some of the glances Tony was receiving were more favorable, some even held a measure of respect. As the meeting continued, various people stood up and shared stories. A few of the older Jewish men told stories of persecution from history and how they can defeat the Nazis if they stick together and hold strong.

By the end of the meeting, Tony felt proud to be a part of the Minutemen. Although he was still terrified about his new role, he knew he was doing the right thing and that was a strong comfort. When the meeting ended, the members took turns leaving, so as not to draw attention to anyone who might be outside. It was vital than their existence stay a secret. There were various exits to the building, and they took turns leaving.

As the group dispersed, Philip Cantalupo sought Tony out. Brushing his hands against his pants, Tony greeted the old man. "Hello, sir."

"Hello, Tony," Cantalupo replied. "What did you think?"

"Um," Tony began, trying to think of the words to describe the complicated emotions coursing through him. "I…wow!"

Cantalupo laughed. "Wow sums it up pretty well, I'd say. So, we have some time while this place empties out. Come talk to me."

Tony followed him over to a corner where Abraham stood with a few of Cantalupo's men. Abraham greeted him with a cautious smile and firm handshake. "It is good to have you on board," he said.

Tony nodded, wondering at the faith this man seemed to have in him. "Thank you, sir."

Canatlupo asked, "So, Tony, what can you tell us about the Nazi plans? What do you know?"

"Not a whole lot," Tony replied. "Hans and Nick are planning something around the big fight between Nate Rubin and my brother."

The men gathered around Tony were instantly alert. "The match scheduled for March?" Abraham asked.

"Yeah," Tony said. "They're really pissed off about it."

"Can't stand to see a Jew be good at anything," one of the nearby men muttered.

"What are they planning?" Cantalupo asked Tony.

Tony shrugged. "I don't know. I don't think they have anything specific in mind yet. But whatever they're planning it sounded…" Tony shivered, letting his voice trail off.

Cantalupo put his arm around him comfortingly. "Don't worry. We won't let anything happen to Danny."

Tony nodded. He took a deep breath in an effort to calm his anxiety. He hated the feeling of fear that threatened to overwhelm him. "Thank you."

Cantalupo smiled at him and said, "So, you'll keep going to their meetings?"

"Yeah. How should I get the information to you?"

"If you have anything to report, just find me or one of my men. Make sure the Nazis aren't tailing you. The good news is that they don't know about us, and they're cocky sons of bitches. They probably haven't even considered that someone might be here to stop them."

Abraham grasped Tony by the arm and looked deep into his eyes. "Send word as soon as you can. We're counting on you."

Tony felt emboldened by the man's confidence in him. "I'll do whatever I can," he said softly, searching the man's eyes. How could he forgive him so easily? How could they trust him? "I…," Tony began, trying to formulate the words to ask the questions that burned through his mind.

Abraham met Tony's gaze with open honesty. "You want to know how I can trust you after you allied yourself with the Nazis. Is that right?"

Tony nodded in relief. He glanced at the others who looked to their leader to answer. Turning his attention back to Abraham, he replied, "Yes. How can you forgive me?"

"It is simple," Abraham said. "We all make mistakes. What a man does when he realizes he's made a mistake is the mark of who he is."

"But -," Tony began.

Abraham cut him off. "We need to trust you as you are our best hope for victory."

Tony nodded and replied. "I won't let you down."

Abraham nodded. "I believe you."

Tony turned to Cantalupo. "I'll come to you after each meeting and tell you exactly what they did and said."

"Try to buddy up with Nick as well."

Tony nodded and gulped at the thought. "Okay." The thrill of fear shot through him again.

"You'll do fine, kid. And remember, tell no one. Not even Danny, okay? We can't risk them finding out."

Tony left the meeting hall twenty minutes later. It was late and no one was on the streets as he left. His mind was swimming with all the events of the evening and with his new espionage status with the group. He wished he could at least talk to his family about it, let them know that he had turned over a new leaf, but he knew better. Any risk of the Friends of the New Germany finding out about his role in their organization would be unacceptable.

As he walked in the door, he notices his brother reading a book on the sofa. He closed the door quietly, hoping that he wouldn't draw attention to himself. He crept up the first few steps on his room when Danny called out, "Late night?"

Tony sighed and turned around. "Yeah. You reading?" He closed his eyes against the stupidity of the question.

Danny grinned. "Nah, just marveling at the typeset."

Tony grinned back at the banter. It reminded him of the way things used to be between them. "Yeah, yeah."

"So, where were you?" Danny asked. He immediately wished he hadn't. He didn't particularly want to know what his brother was up to. Whether it was meeting with the Nazis or the mob, neither was any good. "Never mind. I don't want to know." He put his face back into the book, the pleasant mood gone.

Tony sat down and tried to think of something he could tell his brother. Something that would let him know that he was a different man. He wasn't that same stupid kid that had left the house in a rage during dinner to meet with Nazis.

"Danny?"

Danny sighed and looked up. "Yeah?"

"I…" He searched for something to say. "Never mind" He stood up and stretched. "See you in the morning."

Danny watched his brother climbed the stairs. Something was different about him. He looked happier, lighter. He closed his eyes and prayed that Tony was on a better track. Any track that didn't involve cold-blooded killers would be welcome.

CHAPTER FIFTEEN

It had been weeks since Danny had seen Sarah. He kept missing her at the office when he did his runs. He didn't want to be conspicuous in his interest, so he never asked about her whereabouts. He missed her and found himself looking longingly at her empty chair with disappointment whenever he would pick up the receipt from her boss. He wondered how she was.

After his shift was over, he jogged over to the Kosher bakery and waited outside the building, hoping to catch a glimpse of her leaving. He rubbed his hands against the cold and looked up at the sky. It was fast growing dark, and he debated how long he should wait. Perhaps, she had left before he arrived or maybe she was staying late into the night. It was Wednesday, so his mother was making lasagna. His mouth watered at the thought, but he stayed rooted to his spot. She had to come out eventually.

An hour later, she did emerge, along with a few other workers. She pulled her coat close to her and ran down the stairs. Danny's heart skipped a beat as he watched her. After a split-second moment of hesitation, he chased after her down the road; if he didn't seize this opportunity, he might never see her.

"Sarah!" he called, oblivious to the other onlookers, who turned to stare at him.

Sarah turned around, looking startled and a little afraid. When she saw it was him, she closed her eyes in relief. "Danny," she breathed. "Thank God! I heard the footsteps and thought…"

"Sorry," Danny said, blushing. "I didn't think. I should have done a better job of announcing myself." He paused for a moment and then said, "You shouldn't be walking around here by yourself. It isn't safe."

Sarah smiled. "My father would agree with you. He's always telling me that young ladies shouldn't walk alone on the streets especially Jewish women and especially at night. Too much of a target."

"He's right."

"I don't usually walk at night, but I had some extra paperwork to go through, which couldn't wait 'til morning."

"Next time, call me. I'll come and get you."

She blushed and looked down at her feet. "That's very sweet of you."

"In fact, I'll come by each afternoon and walk you home."

"You don't have to do that!" Sarah exclaimed; her eyes alive with pleasure. The thought pleased her. She would never have asked him but now that he offered, she felt a calming sense of relief.

"It would be my pleasure. We'll start today!"

"Thank you," she said, putting her hand in the crook of his arm. They strolled down the street together, engendering stares from neighbors and passersby.

"I think we've been noticed," he whispered.

She sighed sadly. "They probably assume we're dating."

An old woman with a slight hunch in her back gave him a decided frown as they passed. Frowning, Danny asked, "Is that a problem?"

Sarah looked up at him. "Jewish women are supposed to marry Jewish men."

Danny laughed. "But I'm just walking you home. I haven't proposed yet."

Sarah giggled. "Yet?"

"I like that sound," he whispered into her ear. "You should laugh more often."

Sarah smiled and moved in closer to Danny, relishing the warmth of his body next to hers. She tried to ignore the stern looks that accosted her. People that knew her father were passing her on their way home. None looked pleased with her choice of escort. Her father would be livid to discover a Gentile had caught her interest. He would lecture her for days on the importance of pure bloodlines.

After a couple blocks of silence, Danny stopped and turned her around to face him. "I'd like to meet your father."

Sarah gasped. Blushing, she realized how insulting her shocked expression would be to Danny. She closed her eyes to settle her nerves. "I don't think -"

"It's important," Danny interrupted. "Don't say no."

Sarah looked up at him, touching a greenish bruise under his left eye. "Does that hurt?" she asked absently.

"No," Danny said. He loved the feel of her soft fingertips on his skin. "You have a healing touch." Lost in the moment, he slowly lowered his lips towards hers. How he longed to feel the velvety texture of her lips.

Sarah's eyes opened wide. She stepped back away from him as if he were suddenly made of molten lava. "Danny!" she exclaimed in a stage whisper. "What are you thinking?"

Danny quickly looked around to see if anyone had noticed. Fortunately, the number of pedestrians had thinned out to just a few, who seemed more interested in getting out of the cold than their near kiss. "I'm sorry," he said with what he hoped was a charming smile. "You make me forget the rest of the world exists."

Sarah was speechless. A moment ago, she was upset with him for his bold attempt, but now she was just as enamored of him as she was when he first appeared at her bakery's doorstep.

Danny saw her indecision and took opportunity to move closer. When she looked like she would back off again, he stopped. "I won't try to kiss you again. I can control myself."

Sarah felt an indescribable disappointment at his promise. She should have felt relieved but instead, she found herself staring at his lips, which responded with a cocky grin. Her eyes shot up to his, and she blushed for the fifth time that night. "Good," she said, her voice coming out more like a croak.

"I'd still like to meet your father though."

Sarah sighed. "I'll try."

Danny nodded, feeling an overwhelming disappointment. "Why does it have to be so hard?"

Sarah shrugged. "I wish it didn't have to be. My father is very traditional, and I just don't see him allowing you in. I…" her voice trailed off and she stared at the pavement.

"Yes?" he asked when she didn't complete her thought.

Her eyes shot up, glistening with unshed tears. "I wish it didn't have to be this way. I have to go."

"Let me walk you the rest of the way," he said.

She nodded over to a small house across the street from where they stood. "That's my house." She ran across the street. When she reached the porch, she turned around to see if he was still there. He was right where she had just left him. He gave her a small wave. She returned the wave and disappeared into her house.

Danny continued to stare at the house for another twenty minutes. He just couldn't leave. He debated just walking to the house, ringing the doorbell and insisting that her father let him in. He knew that was crazy; it would make him look demented, but he just wanted to convince him that he was suitable for his daughter. Or at least he would know where he stood and maybe find out what he might need to do to become suitable in his eyes.

Although Tony was three years younger than Danny, he was far more experienced when it came to love. Danny had been on dates with various women but never had he felt anything close to the way he felt about Sarah. He leaned back against a storefront wall and rubbed his hands together. He really should get home. His family would be seated by now, and they probably wondered where he was. He could see his mother doling out the lasagna.

Just a few more minutes, Danny thought as he continued to stare at the house. His attention was drawn to a beat up old brown Ford roadster pulling up just under the street lamp in front of the house. Two young men sat in the front and two more sat in the rumble seat.

A shiny black Packard pulled up a few car lengths behind it, turning off its lights. No one emerged. The hairs on the back of Danny's neck stood on end, having nothing to do with the cold.

A tall skinny boy jumped from the passenger seat. "See you tomorrow!"

"Goodbye, Anton!" a chorus of young men replied.

The driver shouted, "Don't forget to get your sister to send along some of that Rugula tomorrow."

The boy pushed his glasses back on his face. "Sure thing. Sarah loves to bake."

Danny's heart skipped a beat. This must be Sarah's brother. Danny looked back nervously at the Packard, which hung back motionless like a panther ready to strike. He knew that car and thought it would be an odd coincidence for Nick Marten's car to be in their neighborhood.

He watched the brown car pull away and silently willed Anton to grow wings and fly into his house. Instead, he puttered around, looking inside his briefcase.

Like a bad dream the Packard car doors opened and three men emerged. The boy was oblivious to the intrusion on his street; he was still pouring over his notes. The men walked over to him, slowly and deliberately. One walked a little ahead of the others, the obvious leader.

"Hey, Jew boy!" he called out.

Danny closed his eyes in frustration. *Run*, he screamed in his mind. Why didn't he at least try to make a dash for his house?

Anton looked up at the men and froze. Danny could tell that he had just noticed them. How had Anton not have seen them before? Now they were completely surrounding him. Three he counted, closing his eyes against the fear.

"Jew boy," the other taunted. "What's your name, Jew boy?"

"Anton Greenberg," he said, his voice shaking as badly as his legs. "You want money? I don't have any."

One of the men punched him in the head before Anton could defend himself. He immediately dropped to the ground like a sack of flour. He tried to get up, but one of the men stepped on his back, pushing him back onto the pavement. "Going somewhere, Kike?" he said, spitting onto the back of Anton's head.

Another man unzipped his pants. "I think some nice Anglo piss might help your smell. What do you think?"

Danny was on top of the man before he could pull out his cock. He slammed the man with his fist, knocking him unconscious. He felt the battery of fists hit his back and legs and kicked straight back like a donkey, causing one of the men to grunt and fall backwards.

Two against one, not an unfair fight considering Danny's prowess. He looked them in the eye and said, "You know who I am?"

"Sure," one of them said. "You're that filthy Kike lover fighting that Jew in March. You're Tony's brother."

Danny felt his heart lurch at the mention of his brother's name. He fought back the depression that threatened to resurface. His brother ran with these men, for all he knew maybe Tony was a part of this attack. He shook himself. He didn't have time to think about any of this now. He positioned himself in front of the two men and waited for them to make their move.

It didn't take long. Both men lunged awkwardly at him. They were obviously attempting to take advantage of their strength in numbers but had no fighting skills. Danny ducked and shifted his weight to his foot, allowing them to overreach their target. His fist struck fast and hard on the back of the head of the nearest man, who fell instantly to the ground unconscious.

The other recovered quickly but looked less than eager to continue. It was clear Danny would wipe the pavement with him. He started backing up slowly and then ran down the street, away from his car, leaving his two comrades lying on the street.

Anton stood up brushed himself off. The front door opened, and Sarah came running out. She jumped into Danny's arms. "Thank you!"

She pulled away and went to her brother. "Are you okay? I can't believe they did this to you. Why?"

"Yes, I'm all right, thanks to my new friend here," Anton replied, rubbing the back of his head.

"We should get you to a doctor," Danny said. "You could have a concussion."

Anton grinned. "No need to go very far. I'm a doctor."

"Really?" Danny gave a low whistle. "Impressive. You look so young. How old are you?"

"Twenty," he said. "I'm in my residency."

"Shit, that's amazing!" Danny exclaimed. He stared at the bodies prone in front of him. The fact that these men tried to harm a young genius who had the purpose in life to save lives made him livid.

Anton noticed Danny's face turn red with anger as he continued to stare at the men lying on the street. Sighing, he said, "To these men and the ones who sent them here, it doesn't matter who I am. I'm a Jew, and that's all. Someone to be terminated.

Danny looked up into Anton's eyes. "Terminated?" He knew the Nazis hated the Jews, but that sounded harsh even for them. Anton was probably suffering from shock still and was exaggerating the incident.

"Yeah," Anton said tightly. "Terminated! Killed. What word would you use? Don't look at me like that."

Danny looked away. "I…," he began and stopped, not knowing what to say.

Anton sighed and closed his eyes, praying for the patience. Of course, Danny wouldn't understand the significance of tonight. He probably didn't even understand that he had saved a life tonight. Gentiles lived in a different word.

"I'm sorry, my friend. I shouldn't jump down your throat like that," Anton said quietly. "Forgive me."

Danny looked relieved. "No need."

"We should get out of the cold. Won't you come into the house?" Anton asked.

"No," Danny answered nervously. "I should really get going. Mother has dinner ready for me at home."

"Father isn't home," Sarah supplied not quite meeting his eye. "He's at a prayer meeting. I could whip up a snack to tide you over."

Danny tried not to look too relieved. He didn't want to meet Sarah's father tonight, but he was dying to see her home. "I guess I could come in for a few minutes. To be completely honest, I'm starved!"

"Well then, by all means. Come in!" Anton said walking up the path to the front door. "Sarah, bring him inside and I'll call the cops, so they can take these men away."

They entered the home and Anton turned to look Danny. "I'm an idiot! I don't even know your name."

"Danny. Danny Petrucelli," he supplied, extending his hands to Anton.

Anton took his hand firmly in his. "Anton Greenberg. A pleasure to meet you."

"Same here," Danny said.

"What brought you here to this corner at this time of night?" Anton asked, studying Danny carefully.

Danny looked to Sarah and wished he had time to confer with her. He didn't know how much she wanted Anton to know. He lifted his chin and replied, "I was walking your sister home."

Anton took a moment to digest that piece of information before he nodded. "I see. Okay, I'm going to make that phone call. Sarah, why don't you take Danny into the other room?"

Sarah nodded. "Follow me."

Danny looked around at the house. It was a small home, but warm and inviting. Handmade quilts and pillow adorned the sofa and chairs and books filled every bit of available space on the shelves around the walls.

"Have a seat. I'll come back with something to eat," Sarah said, indicating the most comfortable chair in the room. She hurried off to the kitchen.

Instead of sitting down, he went to the bookshelves and looked at the worn books crammed into the shelves, sometimes two layers deep. He was browsing an older encyclopedia when Sarah came in with a small tray of food and tea.

"The cops are on their way," Anton said, walking into the room. He sat on the sofa. "So, how long have you two been seeing each other?"

"We aren't!" Sarah cried, looking appalled at her brother.

Anton raised an eyebrow. "He walked you home, didn't he?"

"Yes, but we aren't dating," Sarah said, her voice calm.

Unconvinced, Anton looked to Danny.

Danny shrugged. "I'd like to date your sister."

"Danny!" Sarah cried, blushing furiously. "This isn't…"

"I'm not going to lie!" Danny replied firmly.

Sarah was rattled. "But–"

Anton raised his hand. "It's okay. It's not me you two need to convince."

Sarah nodded. "Will you tell him?"

Danny let out an exasperated sigh. "Tell who? And tell him what exactly? I just walked you home."

"That means a lot to some," Anton said cryptically.

"Who are you worried about?" Danny asked Sarah. "Is it your father?"

"Of course," Sarah answered. "He won't approve. I can promise you that."

"Even after tonight?" Danny asked.

Anton shook his head. "I'll try to help. But Danny, I have to be honest, it's an uphill battle."

"I'd appreciate any help I can get," Danny replied.

They all remained silent for a few moments, each lost in their own thoughts. Finally, Anton snapped his fingers and looked up at Danny with some excitement. "Tony Petrucelli's your brother, isn't he? That's the Tony that one goon was referring to."

"Yeah," Danny said, utterly stunned by the news that Anton knew Tony. "How do you know my brother?"

Anton grinned. "I'll tell you next Friday night. That is if you want to come to a special meeting. Are you interested in clobbering more Nazis?"

"You bet!" Danny said without hesitation. "What's this meeting about?"

"You'll find out when you get there. It's secret, so don't tell anyone, okay?"

Danny looked confused. "What would I tell them? I don't know anything."

"Good man," Anton replied. "Meet me outside my house after work next Friday, and I'll take you over there."

CHAPTER SIXTEEN

Danny's heart beat quickly in his chest as he and Anton walked to Yeshiva Hall. He glanced over at Anton, who gave him a reassuring smile. What was this meeting all about? He had tried to ply Anton for information during the car ride but didn't get anywhere. Anton maintained that it was easiest for him to just wait and see.

As they entered the building, Danny could hear the hushed voices of people up ahead down the long dark corridor. When the corridor opened up into the large lit room, Danny's breath caught in his throat. Two hundred people were milling around waiting for the meeting to start. Danny had expected maybe a few dozen men.

Anton was equally surprised. "Wow," he murmured. "It's never been this full!"

Danny looked around at the sea of unfamiliar faces. He spotted Nate, who shot him a grin. Still dazed from all people, Danny nodded his head distractedly to him.

"You know him?" Anton asked.

"Yeah, we fight in March."

"Really? You're a boxer?"

"Yeah," Danny said. "You follow the fights?"

Anton shook his head. "No, not really, but we're proud of Nate. I mean boxing isn't exactly a favorite sport of our people, but I respect greatness in pretty much any endeavor."

Danny nodded thoughtfully. "If your home is anything typical for the Jewish people, I can tell you are an intellectual group."

Anton grinned. "You saw our library."

Danny gave a low whistle. "Yeah. And they all looked very used."

"They've been read many times. In fact, father's working on making copies in his spare time. He wants to preserve them for future generations."

"Your father copies books by hand? That sounds so…" Danny searched for the right word, so as not to offend.

"Tedious?" Anton supplied.

"Yeah."

"It is. It's kind of a hobby for him though. He says it helps him to learn the knowledge contained in the books."

Danny continued to look around at the group, wondering if he might recognize anyone. Suddenly, his heart lurched in his chest. There standing with some men in Yamakas was someone who looked a lot like his brother. Danny squinted and shook his head. "That can't be," he said shaking his head with a rough laugh.

"What?" Anton asked.

"That looks like Tony. My brother."

Anton looked in the direction that Danny was indicating. Anton nodded. "Hey, that's right! Tony's been coming here for a few meetings now."

"You mean that's really Tony?" Danny's voice rose an octave, causing various people in the room to turn their heads, including Tony.

"Danny!" he shouted, forgetting the three men standing next to him. "I can't believe you're here!" he shouted. "Are you kidding me?"

The rest of the onlookers smiled to themselves before going back to their conversations. Anton backed away giving them an opportunity to get reacquainted.

Danny pulled away from Tony and shook his head. "How long have you…?" Danny began to ask, but he didn't know what he or Tony were involved in yet.

"Just a few weeks now," Tony answered. "I couldn't tell you. I wanted to, but I couldn't. We have to keep these meetings a secret. Keep this group's purpose a secret."

Danny nodded, still dazed. "Yeah, I know. I could tell something was up the other day. You seemed…different."

"Yeah," Tony said. He looked down at the floor. He doubted Danny would ever understand or be able to forgive him for his past tirades. Looking back, he blushed at all the things he'd said to Danny. All the prejudices he once held, which seemed so foreign to him now. "I'm sorry about all that. I was a complete ass. I'm so sorry. I'm trying to make it up now, but I know I never can. All I can do is take it one step at a time."

Danny stared at his brother in disbelief. "You're my brother, Tony. That will never change."

Tony looked up at Danny, vulnerability shining in his eyes. "You mean…," he didn't dare utter the words in case he had misunderstood Danny.

"Let me be completely clear," Danny said looking Tony directly in the eye. He spoke with sincerity and a strong intention to get his meaning across. "I love you and always will. Nothing you can do will ever change that. I can see that you've changed, and I couldn't be happier. Tony, I'm so proud of you."

Tony flew into his arms for the second time and hugged him so tightly Danny was sure he had bruises. Danny returned the embrace until he felt Tony's grip lessen.

The men in the hall began taking their seats, so Tony and Danny found some toward the back. Danny listened to the Minutemen talk about their plans for rallies and the past week's activities. Mostly, the group was focused on recruiting, which had been observably successful.

When Tony was asked to stand up and give a report, Danny's mouth dropped open. As his brother began to speak, Danny realized just how brave Tony was. By continuing to attend the Nazi meetings, he was risking a lot to make sure the group got up to date intelligence.

"There seems to be a financial backer," Tony explained. "I don't know the name, but he's someone local here in Newark, someone with money and someone who hates Jews."

A murmur of disappointment went through the crown. Money gave any group more power and reach. Tony continued to share with everyone all that he knew. When he sat down, he looked over at Danny who beamed with pride. Tony grinned and shrugged. "I had to do something."

⁜ ⁜ ⁜

The next morning, Tony stopped short as he entered the loading bay at Larson's. Arte Bella and two of his men stood at the gate waiting for him.

"Come with me," Arte said gruffly.

"But, my shift," Tony protested.

"I've got it covered. Don't worry."

Seeing that he had no choice, Tony allowed himself to be ushered once again into the black Packard. This time the backseat was empty. He slid over to the other side. The driver greeted him with a friendly smile. "Hello, Mr. Petrucelli. How are you this morning?"

"Fine," Tony answered hesitantly. The man looked very different now that he'd lost his scowl. The harsh lines in his face were gone, and he looked downright jovial.

Arte slipped in and shut the door. "Just drive, Frank," he said waving his hand his hand carelessly in front of him. The car sped off immediately.

"Mr. Cantalupo is impressed with you," Arte said without preamble. 'He wants to know if you're in love with your job or if you might like a new position. One with the family."

Tony couldn't contain his grin. "I don't like loading cargo, Mr. Belle. I just didn't have a choice. What does Mr. Cantalupo need help with?"

Arte shrugged. "He needs a few more runners. Interested?"

Tony nodded. "Numbers?"

Arte rolled his eyes. "No, toilet paper. Of course, numbers."

"Yes, sir. Sure, I'm interested."

"Good, Sal will show you the ropes. You'll be working under him. You know Sal Ruggio?"

Tony shook his head. "I don't really know anyone."

"It's okay. You will. Come by the restaurant at noon, okay?"

"Sure," Tony said. Everyone knew where the Cantalupo family hung out. The small Italian place with the red and white checkered table cloths across from Independence Park. It wasn't a place one normally wanted to be invited to; it usually meant the boss was displeased or wanted something from you. This was an expectation.

Nate couldn't get Maria out of his mind. He had been prepared to try to forget her after their last encounter. Not many women ran away from him. However, her beautiful eyes haunted his sleep. He had to try to see her again.

Every chance he could, he walked by the spot where he had last met her. It seemed an impossible goal and each day she wasn't there, he realized how foolish his plan was. He considered approaching Tony to see if he could talk to his sister on Nate's behalf but couldn't drum up the courage. It was one thing to defend the rights of the Jewish people, but it was another to approve of interfaith dating. Interfaith dating with his sister. He doubted if Tony or Danny would approve.

Just when he was about to chide himself for wasting his time, he saw her. He rushed over to her, hoping that see wouldn't run away again. "Maria," he said, his voice breathless with anticipation. "Please don't go."

Maria frowned at him and at herself. Although she firmly wished he would leave her alone, she was inexplicably relieved that he was standing there in front of her. "You," was all she could muster.

"Not a big fan of Jewish men?" he asked, failing to keep the hurt from his voice,

Maria's shocked expression surprised Nate. "What?" she asked, stunned by the question.

"You ran away last time. When I asked you out," he reasoned. "I just figured -"

She glared at him. "You figured wrong."

"Then why?"

"I don't owe you can explanation. Please leave me alone."

Nate stared at her, willing her to change her mind. If only he could share with her that he and her two brothers were working together, battling an enemy that threatened them all. Maybe, she would see him as a hero.

"Do you hate me?" he asked, his voice a whisper.

Maria's brows drew together in confusion. "No," she said. "Why would you think that?"

"Why won't you tell me what's wrong then?"

Maria searched for some reason, something that would divert her from the truth. She didn't date anyone. She didn't trust men and didn't want to get into an explanation about that on the streets of her neighborhood with someone that made her heartbeat too fast. It was too embarrassing, too humiliating.

"You're fighting by brother," she said after a few moments. "It wouldn't be right to see you."

Nate nodded, stunned. "You think it would be somehow disloyal," he said matter-of-factly. "I guess I can understand that."

Maria felt a sudden relief that he was accepting her pitiful explanation. She couldn't understand why that relief was accompanied by an anxious, gnawing disappointment. She nodded. "Exactly. It would be disloyal."

"I don't care."

"What?" She felt like laughing, but coughed instead and looked away.

"I don't care," he repeated. "He'll come around."

"Yes, but-"

"Just don't say no, okay?" Nate looked at her with hopeful eyes. "Please?"

Maria couldn't resist a smile. She shook her head, feeling like she was in the middle of a perfect dream. "Okay." Suddenly, she realized what she had said and the implied agreement. Her eyes hardened "I've got to go."

"Wait!" Nate felt panic well up inside of him. "How… When can I see you again?"

"I don't know," she said, backing away quickly. She felt helpless. What she wanted and what she could have were two different things.

"Meet me here next week."

"No."

"Please?"

"I can't."

"It isn't a date."

"Then what is it?"

"Nothing. I just have to see you."

"Maybe," she said before she took off running down the street.

Nate couldn't help grinning from ear to ear. She hadn't said no.

Tony felt bile rise to his throat and worked hard to tamp it down. He had to maintain a sense of agreement and loyalty with the Friends of The New Germany. If he were discovered to be a spy, that thought was unthinkable.

The group had grown. Tony estimated twenty new members in the last month. The leaders were sharing reports of their latest victories. Various Jewish store owners were being terrorized at home and at their business. Mostly it was the same thing, meeting after meeting.

Hans smiled at the group and turned to a young blond man. "Alfred, give me a report on my pet project. I think it is time to share the details of this little experiment."

The boy in question stood up. Tony was hard pressed not to roll his eyes at the boy's posture. He was obviously proud to be singled out by Hans Ruether. He couldn't be more than eighteen years old, still battling acne. His chest puffed out as he spoke, "As you directed, Herr Reuther, we have been teaching some of the Jews the right way of thinking. We have ten students of the German Nation Catechism." He held up a copy of the booklet.

"And how is their instruction going?" Hans was obviously amused.

Alfred grinned. "Good. I have to say this is the most fun I've had in a long time. It's fun hearing them finally speak the truth about their filthy race."

A few of the others chucked with Alfred. It was clear that they were working together on this "project".

"You'll like this, Tony," Hans said. He sat back in his chair and waves his hand to Alfred. "Tell Tony who you've been working over at the Provision House,"

Tony blood turned ice cold. That's where his sister worked. Would they have reason to harm Maria? He held his breath as he waited for their answer.

Alfred turned to Tony. "Jules Rubin. The father of that Kike opponent your brother's fighting. That's who. We've had fun making him recite different parts of the catechism to us each week. Given him some black eyes in the process."

Hans' grin broadened. "How else can you teach a Kike? Got to beat the smarts into him. It's the only way."

Tony did his best to hide his disgust. It was getting harder and harder each meeting, but he knew his life depended on it. Eyes were trained on him, waiting for a response. He laughed with the group, doing his best to keep it sounding natural. "That's too funny. But how do you do that? I mean without getting caught," he had to somehow get the information to Nate.

"We meet in the Boiler Room. No one goes down there after hours, and the noise down there hides Kike screams real good," Alfred answered.

Tony nodded in what he hoped passed as admiringly. "Brilliant. Who knows, maybe you'll beat enough sense into him that he'll get Nate to withdraw from the fight!"

Hans raised his hand. "No, no. We don't want that."

"You don't? But wouldn't that be a victory?" Tony asked innocently, hoping to trick Hans into revealing more of their plans centered around the fight next month. "I mean it would show how yellow bellied the Kikes really are."

Hans nodded. "Yes, you're right, but that demonstration during the fight is going to set a lot of other things in motion. I can't tell you everything, but I promise you, no one's going to see this coming. No one."

Alfred's eyes were wide with excitement. "The fire power alone that we've-"

Hans interrupted him, his voice echoing through the hall. "Alfred!"

Alfred blushed and stammered out an apology. "I didn't mean…"

Hans closed his eyes and recomposed himself, forcing a serene smile back on his face. "It's okay," he said, reassuring the now quaking teen. "We're just not ready for a broad announcement."

When Tony left the meeting, he had only one thing in mind. He had to find Nate. He looked behind him to see if he was being followed for the fifth time–he couldn't be too careful. When he was satisfied that he was alone, he sought out Arte Bella. He'd know how to find Nate.

Tony walked to Guido's, the headquarters for the Cantalupo family. It was ten o'clock at night, but he was sure someone would be there. Walking in, he received a nod from a wiry man near the door. "Hey, Tony," he said. He brushed his hands through his hair in an effort to straighten it, which had no effect on the unruly curls.

"Hey, Michael. You know where Mr. Bella is?"

"You're in luck. He's in the black. Wait here." He bounded off the stool he'd been sitting on and jogged to the back room.

Thirty seconds later, Arte Bella came out, hurrying to meet Tony. "Something happened," Arte stated with a nod. Tony never came by the restaurant uninvited.

Tony nodded. "I need to talk to Nate. Now. I don't know where he lives. I figured you might. Do you?"

"Yeah, of course. Come, we'll go together."

As they drove to the Rubin household, Tony sketched out everything that had transpired in the meeting. The talk of ammunition earned an eyebrow raise from Arte. "Those fuckers," he said under his breath. "If they're looking for a fight, they've got one."

When they arrived at Nate's home, Arte bolted out of the car and ran to the door. Tony lagged behind him only a few seconds. Forgetting what time it was, Arte rapped on the door calling Nate's name loudly, making Tony cringe. This neighborhood looked to be in bed already.

Nate opened the door a crack and peeked out. He combed his hair with his hands when he saw who was there. "Arte, Tony. Come in." He yawned and opened the door.

Tony could tell that they had woken him. The house was quiet and dark. "Sorry to brother you, Nate. It's important."

"Want some tea?"

Arte sat on the cluttered couch, ignoring the stray papers that crinkled underneath. "There's no time for fucking tea," he said. "Sit. Tony's got something to say."

Nate was immediately alert and fully awake. "What? Did something happen at that meeting tonight?"

Tony sat down in the chair across from Arte and nodded. "Yeah. There's a subgroup of Nazi's going around selecting out various Jews for special treatment. They're 'educating' them on the Nazi way," Tony said carefully.

Nate looked confuse. "What you mean, 'educating them'?"

Tony clenched his fists. "They're forcing them to recite things from their catechism. The German National Catechism."

Arte continued to look confused. "What the fuck's that?"

"Shit!" Nate exclaimed. "Oh my God. My father has one of those. It's brown about this big, right?" He indicated a small book with his hands.

Tony shrugged. "Don't know, never seen it. But tonight, they were talking about working over your father. I think they've been making him memorize things from that booklet."

"What's in that thing?" Arte asked.

Nate sighed. "I read what I could from it when I found it in Pop's pocket. Father doesn't know that I saw it. I didn't know how to ask him about it. His copy was in German, but it had English notes in the margins. It looks like a kid's school book with questions and answers, but it's all about how the Jews are trying to take over the world. It's pretty horrible."

Arte's face turned red. "And they're making your Dad read it?"

"Not only read it, but recite it. I think they've been beating him up too," Tony said gently. "I'm sorry, Nate."

Nate sat down and put his head in his hands. That explained a lot of things. Why his father looked cowed at work, why he was coming home with bruises, and why he had that God forsaken book. He wondered why his father didn't ask him for help?

"What are you going to do?" Tony asked.

"He's going to give those son's of bitches what they have coming," Arte answered before Nate could say anything. His voice was deep and menacing, making the hairs on the back of Tony's neck stand on end. "And I'm going to help you."

"Thank you," Nate said meaningfully.

"My pleasure."

CHAPTER SEVENTEEN

Nate looked up at the sky and wondered if it was going to rain. The bleak dark skies had been threatening to pour down on the city all day. He knew that this was one of the days his father would be kept behind for "lessons" by the Nazis. Jules was a poor liar. When he had stammered to his son that he would have to work late into the evening, Nate knew that the propaganda booklet would be gone from its hiding place when he looked for it.

Nate walked into the Provision house just before the end of the day shift and found his way down to the Boiler Room. Arte and his boys said they'd meet him here, but he didn't see any of them. A semicircle of six folding chairs had been set up, which was obviously the Nazi meeting room. Looking around for a place to hide, he found a dark corner. It wasn't hard considering that the area was lit by a single light bulb dangling from a chord in the center of the room.

Twenty minutes later a loud horn sounded, signaling the end of the work day. Nate didn't have to wait long before the door opened, gleeful voices through the cavernous Boiler room. Nate clenched and unclenched his fists in anticipation of their arrival.

"Jules," one of the voices taunted. "I hope you're better prepared today."

Nate peaked around the large furnace to see his father being prodded down the stairs. He held his breath, hoping his father wouldn't lose his balance. Jules' eyes were trained on the ground in front of him. He remained silent.

When they reached the floor, Jules stood before the chairs and waited silently while the men filled the seats.

"What have you learned this week?" a young wiry blond man said as he slouched down in his chair, his long legs crossed in front of him. Nate wondered if this was Alfred, mentally matching him to the description Tony had given him.

"I…tried real hard…," Jules stammered.

"You hear that Joey," the blond said. "The poor Kike's trying. Does that mean anything?"

Joey laughed. "Not to me Alfred. All that I care about is that he don't fuck up his lessons. It's disrespectful."

Alfred grinned. "Yeah. It sure is. Okay, Kike, let's get started. From the top. What is a race?"

Jules stuttered through an answer to the question, defining the word. The answer was accepted to the relief of Jules. Nate found himself holding his breath. He wondered when Arte would be there with his men. He didn't want to botch this by attacking the Nazis too soon. He needed back up.

Alfred continued. "What race must we fight against?"

Jules cringed. "The Jewish race," he answered faintly.

"What's that? I can't hear you!" Alfred said, sitting forward in his chair. "Speak up, loud and proud or be punished!"

Jules cleared his throat. "The Jewish race." His voice rang out through the small room.

"Good!" Alfred said, leaning back again in his chair. "And why is that?"

Again, Jules' voice trembled. As if in a trance, he recited, "Because the Jew wants to make himself ruler of humanity. The Jew wants to destroy the culture. He is a destructive spirit and opposes creativity."

Nate cursed to himself silently behind the furnace. Where the fuck were Cantalupo men? He couldn't take on all six men himself.

"That's quite enough!" The strong assertive voice of Arte Bella rang out through the room. Nate sighed in relief.

Alfred bolted out of his seat as did his comrades. They each turned sheet white as they looked around at the dozen fierce faces of the Cantalupo men who had surrounded them. Nate jumped out too, gasping in surprise.

Arte grinned at Nate. "You look surprised."

"Shit yeah. I wondered where you were!"

"Nate!" Jules cried out. "What are you doing here?"

Nate walked over to him and embraced him fiercely. "Father, why don't you go home? We have some unfinished business here."

Jules looked around and asked, "Who are these men?"

"They are Minutemen," Nate replied calmly. "We are Minutemen, Pop. Someone has to take care of these Nazi scum."

Arte looked at the Nazis and pointed to the seats. "Why don't you boys have a seat? We're going to be here for a while."

The men sat down. They looked more like boys now then men. A couple looked on the verge of tears. They seemed to understand at the moment that none of them would live to let Hans know there was a resistance movement.

"I can't believe you're here," Jules said, dazedly. "All of you."

Arte turned to Nate and said gently, "Take your father home. We'll take care of this. It will be our pleasure."

Nate looked around and debated to himself. Although he'd love to stay and help Arte finish these boys off, but his father needed him. He slowly nodded his head and sighed. "Okay. Thanks for your help."

Arte nodded. They all watched Nate and Jules ascend the stairs to the top. When they got to the street Jules broke down into tears. Nate ushered him into his car and let his father unburden his grief. He offered comfort and listened to the horrors his father had endured over the last few months.

Finally, when the tears subsided, Jules sniffed. "What are they going to do to those men?"

"Do you want to know?" Nate asked.

Jules stiffened. "I'm not a child. Tell me."

Nate sighed. "They must be silenced. Permanently. It's a good thing they're in the boiler room. The furnace will hide all traces of their bodies."

Jules shuddered at the though. "I guess I'd rather not know."

"Let me take you home, Father."

The next day, Tony got word that Mr. Cantalupo wanted to see him first thing. His pulse quickened as he checked his books, wondering if he erred in the last pickup. No, everything checked out. Then why did the boss want to see him?

He walked into Guido's and looked around for Mr. Cantalupo. Michael stood and said, "He's expecting you in the back. Follow me."

"Sure thing," Tony said, wiping his hands on his jeans. Maybe he should have worn something else. Cursing himself he hoped his casual wear didn't offend Mr. Cantalupo.

He had never seen Philip Cantalupo's inner sanctum and was curious what the legend's office looked like. When the door opened, Tony gaped at the beauty before him. The large room was filled with mahogany antiques. The large desk with the intricate carvings was undoubtedly the boss's. Only Cantalupo could carry off that desk.

Without thinking, he turned around to make sure the red and white checkered tablecloths and multicolored candle wax decorated wine jugs was still behind him. Turning back, it felt like he had been magically transported to an executive's lounge in Manhattan.

A familiar voice came from his right. "I like elegance." Tony whipped around to face Philip Cantalupo. He had been standing by the back wall, as if keeping from view on purpose. Tony wondered if he enjoyed seeing people's initial reactions to the room. "The front place is just that, a front. As I've built up my business, I've been able to afford some niceties. But enough about that. You're here because– do you even know why you're here? I'm curious."

"No," Tony said, wiping his hands on his hands on his jeans again, cursing himself for bringing attention to them. "No, sir. Did I do something?"

Cantalupo smiled. "Yes, you did. I heard what you did for Nate Rubin's father."

Tony nearly let his body drop to the ground with relief. "Oh, right."

Cantalupo shook his head. "You worry too much." He indicated an oversized burgundy leather chair. "Have a seat. Can I offer you anything?"

Tony shook his head and took a seat. "No, sir, I'm fine."

"It is kind of early for a drink. Okay, how about I pour us a couple glasses of juice. You want some breakfast?"

"Sure, sounds good." The conversation was nothing like had been expecting. He watched as the most powerful mob boss ordered Michael to run down to the local bakery to pick up an assortment of pastry.

When Michael had left the room, Cantalupo leaned back in his chair. "Did you hear how it all worked out?"

Tony shook his head. He'd been dying to know, but didn't know who to ask without drawing suspicion. "No, sir. What happened?"

"You're good man to keep your mouth shut. Nice. Hard to find someone like you. Arte and his men dispatched those creeps. They just disappeared. Figured you should know about it, considering you have another meeting in two days."

Tony's mouth went dry. "Disappeared?"

"Yeah. You want to know the details?" Cantalupo raised his eyebrow at him.

Tony nodded thoughtfully. "I need to know something about what happened. And some sort of plan of what I should say if anything at the meeting."

Cantalupo filled Tony in on the ambush at the provision house. "The boys cried for their mommies in the end," Cantalupo said. "Arte and his men cut the bodies up and burned them in the furnace."

Tony couldn't help but shudder. "Did you get any information from them?"

Cantalupo shook his head. "Unfortunately, no. They didn't know much."

"Do you think the Nazis will find out?"

"It's important they don't," Cantalupo said leaning forward in his chair. "Right now, their biggest weakness is their overconfidence. They have no idea we're out there. No idea that they have any resistance."

"Won't they suspect something when the kids don't come to the next meeting?"

Cantalupo smiled. "They might, but you'll be there to help them sort it out."

"How?"

"Maybe suggest you saw them heading out of town."

Tony nodded. "Throw them off."

"That's right."

Concern etched Tony's brow. "Don't you think they might start suspecting me?"

Cantalupo shrugged. "I don't think so. As I said, downfall is their inability to conceive there might be anyone willing to stand up to them. They rely on strength only."

Michael came in with the pastries and set them down. With one look from his boss, he left quickly, closing the door behind him.

"They're not going to link you to this," Cantalupo said. "Just do what you've been doing all along."

Tony nodded and sat back in the chair. "Okay." He reached for an odd- looking roll, shaped like an L with powdered sugar on it. Inside was a white creamy filling.

"You like the La Santarosa?" Cantalupo asked.

"Hm?" Tony asked his mouth overly filled with the sweet dessert.

Cantalupo laughed. "It's called La Santarosa. Lobstertail. It's from Naples. Not too many places you can find it. Drew's Pastry has it. The man's not Italian, but he knows how to bake."

Tony grinned sheepishly as he swallowed. "Whatever it is, it's good. I'll have to bring some home to mamma."

"You're good boy. You'll be okay. No go, get back to work."

CHAPTER EIGHTEEN

"These pastries are amazing!" Teresa exclaimed. "Where did you get them again?"

"Drew's, Ma," Tony replied with a grin. "Pretty good, huh?"

"How did you find this Drew?" Teresa asked skeptically.

Tony froze momentarily. He realized he couldn't be completely truthful as Teresa didn't have any idea of his new mob connections or the dangerous game he was playing. "Uh, it's just a bakery," he said a little too defensively for his own ears.

"Since when have you been exploring new bakeries?"

Danny guessed that Cantalupo was Tony's source and jumped in to save his younger brother before he stammered out a complete confession. "Ma, I told Tony about it. It's no big deal. Just discovered it on one of my runs."

"Oh," Teresa said. "Okay. Well, it's nice that we can afford good pastry again."

Tony sighed in relief, looking over at his brother with a grin. It was the little unexpected lies that tripped him up more than anything else.

Maria looked over at Danny with a nervous smile. "What do you know about your opponent, Nate Rubins?"

Both Danny and Tony stared at her. "Why?" they asked in unison.

Maria shrugged, staring down at her plate, unwilling to give either eye contact. "No reason, really. I just wondered what you thought of him?"

The two brothers looked at each other for a moment debating what to say. Finally, Danny said, "He's a stand-up guy." He looked to his father to gauge his reaction. Donato just stared at his plate with a blank sort of look. "You feeling okay, Pop?"

Donato lifted his head and nodded. "Sure, why not?" He looked tired to his son's eyes.

"You sure?" Tony asked. "You don't look so hot."

"What a thing to say!" Teresa chided. She put her hand over Donato's and asked, "Everything okay?"

Donato nodded. "Go on with your conversation," he said waiving his hand toward Maria.

Although she was concerned about her father's health, she was also interested in her brother's opinion about her suitor. "So, you think Nate's okay?"

"Okay for what?" Tony asked. "Okay to receive punches from my brother? Yeah! I'd say so."

Maria still didn't meet his gaze. "Okay to date me."

"What?" Donato asked. "You won't date a Kike while you're under my roof." Although his words were harsh, his tone had none of its usual bluster.

Danny looked at Maria and said, "You could do worse."

Tony hesitated and nodded. "I have to agree with that."

"You have to *what*?" Maria asked, completely surprised.

Donato stared at his son with a bewildered expression. "What did you say?"

Tony sat up straight in his chair and glanced over at his scowling mother. "I'm just saying he's an okay guy. I'm not suggesting she marry him or anything."

Donato leaned back in his chair and closed his eyes. "I don't feel so good," he finally admitted. "I think I'll go upstairs and rest."

Teresa was up on her feet immediately. He never complained about his health and never went to bed before the meal was finished. "I'll help you."

"I don't need any help," he said gruffly, as he allowed her to usher him up the stairs.

"You three stay down here and finish your coffee and pastry," Teresa called back over her shoulder.

Maria stared after them. "Is he going to be okay?" she asked, fear lacing her voice.

"Pop'll be fine. He's stronger than anyone else I know," Danny said reassuringly. "Tell me how you met Nate." He wanted to take his mind off his own worry about his father.

Maria looked back at him with a soft smile. She told him about the brief encounters they shared and how Nate had asked her to go out with him. "It's been so long since I've dated anyone."

Tony nodded. "Too long, my sister. Now don't get me wrong, I don't think any man will be good enough for you. However, I really do want to see you happy. I agree with Ma that a girl can't be happy without a man."

Danny grinned at Maria's expression. "Mixed blessings, huh?"

Maria smiled. "As long as you both are okay with my dating Nate, I guess I'll give it a try."

✥ ✥ ✥

Maria waited for Nate at the same spot she had left him last week. It was an unseasonably warm afternoon for February. Feeling anxious, she leaned against the brick wall, staring down the street. Nate had asked her to come, but would he show? She'd made it difficult; not every man wanted to play games.

"Penny for your thoughts," a gentle voice caressed her ear.

Maria turned around, smiling a relieved smile. "You came."

Nate laughed a deep rich laugh. "You though I wouldn't? I've spent more time on this corner than I have on my own front porch."

"I'm glad you're here," she said.

Nate said looking deep into her eyes. "You're different," he said searchingly.

Maria held his gaze. "How so?" She knew how, but was stalling for time.

"You're not looking away from me for one thing."

"Anything else?"

"You tell me."

Maria shrugged. "Let's go somewhere."

"I know the perfect place." He guided Maria to Branch Brook Park. It was beautiful even in the winter, with various trails leading through forests and meadows. Nate's favorite path went around the large lake.

Nate waited for her to speak. When she didn't, he realized he needed to start the conversation. "I've been thinking about you all week."

She blushed and looked away toward the lake. He was so close. She shivered, suddenly uncomfortable with his proximity.

Nate stopped walking abruptly. "Okay, what's wrong? I don't get it. One minute you're looking unflinchingly into my eyes and then next…"

Maria groaned. "It's not you."

He couldn't keep the growing irritation from entering his voice. "Having second thoughts about dating a Jew?"

"No!" she exclaimed vehemently. "That's not it all."

Nate smiled in relief and nodded. "Okay, then what is it?"

"I…," she didn't know where to begin.

Nate led her over to a bench facing the water. It was a good distance away from the main path, affording them some privacy. He reached out and took her hand in his. She tried to pull back, but he wouldn't let her. Finally, he won the small battle and held her hand against his chest. "Trust me."

"I do," she said without hesitation, surprising herself as much as him with the declaration.

"Can you tell me why you look like you're ready to bolt again?"

Maria took a deep calming breath and then another. She looked out onto the water and then back into Nate's eyes. "I've never talk to anyone about…" He eyes fell to their interlocked fingers against his chest.

Nate waited a moment and then prodded gently. "About?"

"About that night."

Nate nodded, pretending to understand. She fell silent again, and he searched for words to help. Finally, he asked, "What can I do to make things easier for you?"

"The only thing you can do is listen."

"Then, I'll listen."

His warm attention made her feel safe and she began. "Which I was in high school, I was a very different girl. I was popular and had many friends."

"Many boyfriends too I'd imagine," Nate said with a grin, trying to lighten her mood.

Maria shook her head. "Not many, just one. A boy thought I was in love with him. He was so handsome. All the girls wanted to date him. He'd just transferred from some country in South America. I never imagined that he'd noticed me–I mean he was always surrounded by pretty girls. I'd steal glances toward him when I thought he wasn't looking.

"Then one day, out of the blue, he asked me to the prom! I was beside myself with joy. For the next few weeks, he was so kind to me, so considerate. Each morning he'd bring me little things, like a buttercup he picked or a little candy. He was gentle, thoughtful and always a gentleman.

"I knew my parents would never allow me to go with him, so I lied to them," She bowed her head in shame. "I know that was wrong, but father is very against anyone who isn't Italian. Unfamiliar accents don't sit well with him. So, I told my parents that I was going to prom with a group of girls. Well, that was true, but we all had dates."

She hesitated in her story and so Nate squeezed her hand reassuringly. "Then what happened?"

Maria took a deep breath and continued. "After prom, some of the girls and their beaus were going to spend the weekend at the Jersey Shore. Johnny's family had money and owned a vacation home on the beach at Seaside Heights. All my parents knew was that I was going with my longtime high school girlfriends for a weekend vacation. They trusted me without question. To this day, I wish I had deserved that trust."

Maria closed her eyes and was transported back in time, remembering that day as if it were yesterday. "The prom was divine. So beautiful, everyone in their finest. My dress was amazing. Mamma had spent four months sewing. It had little shiny beads all over it. She was so proud of me.

"We all danced and laughed and had so much fun. Again, Johnny was the perfect gentleman, keeping his hands where he should, treating me like a lady. When the dancing was over, he leaned over me and whispered that we should go. Breathless, I looked up into his eyes and nodded. He gave me a sweet kiss and ushered me out of the room.

"He explained that the other couples would be meeting us down at the house. I agreed and rememberd being even a little relieved that we might have a few moments alone together before the others arrived. How naive I was."

Nate groaned. "The others never came." he predicted.

"No," Maria said quietly. "I found out later that Johnny offered them another house, one further down the beach. I don't even think they knew where we were."

Nate felt her hand tremble, and his heart beat faster. "What happened?" he asked with dread.

It was no longer an option for Maria to stop telling her story, to keep this part of her past hidden. She hadn't realized how much she needed to talk to someone, anyone about that night. "When we arrived at the little cottage on the beach, the moon was shining bright and the stars were clear in the sky. The sound of the water lapping on the sand was mesmerizing. I was so excited.

"Johnny gave me a warm kiss and told me to enjoy the moonlight on the back porch while he went inside to get surprise. After a few moments, he came out with a bottle of port from his home country, along with two beautifully cut crystal glasses. I'd never had alcohol before that night and was a little nervous about it. But I think my curiosity won out more than anything and I accepted. Besides Johnny was so excited about sharing this bottle with me; I didn't want to disappoint him."

Nate closed his eyes against her words. He felt nauseous as he predicted what was to follow.

Maria said looking down, pulling her hand back. Tears started streaming down her face. "I don't remember much after the first drink. It was laced with something strong. It was all just a haze,"

"What did that son of a bitch do to you?" Nate asked, wrapping his arm around her.

Hiccupping through her tears, she continued as best she could. "I woke up the next day around noon. Johnny was just staring at me." She shuddered violently. "He was so different from the boy I knew. He gave me a lewd smirk up at down until I noticed that I was naked in his bed. I hurried to cover myself up, but he just laughed. 'A little late for that,' he'd said.

I knew something was dreadfully wrong, but my head felt like it was made of lead and my mouth was dry as cotton. I started shimming off the bed, looking around for my clothes. My beautiful dress lay in a tattered heap on the floor. I wrapped the sheet tightly around me and walked out of the bedroom.

"I was determined to leave that house, even if it meant walking out that door without clothes. I just didn't anticipate what I saw next. My legs didn't seem to want to do anything but root me the ground."

Nate gave her shoulder a small squeeze. He desperately wanted to help her, but he didn't want to hear anymore. It was too disgusting, but he knew she had to get this story out of her. It had sat festering too long. "What did you see?"

"All over the kitchen table were p...p...pictures of me." Maria cried, her hands covering her face in shame. "Doing things you'd never imagine," She couldn't continue for a few minutes; she just sobbed. Finally, she calmed and continued. "I had never kissed a boy before Johnny and suddenly, I was ruined. It wasn't just that I wasn't a virgin anymore, but I'd become a whore."

"You're not a whore," Nate said firmly, pulling her into him, wrapping her up in his embrace. "Do you remember anything else?"

"My memory of that evening was sort of like a broken movie. Little snippets of pictures of me doing unspeakable things pop into view when I try to remember, but it doesn't seem real. At all. It doesn't seem like me doing them, if that make sense."

Nate nodded. "How did you get out there?"

Maria shook her head. "I went a little crazy. I started ripping up the photographs as fast as I could. Johnny just laughed, saying he had plenty of copies. He told me not to worry that he wouldn't expose me to my family and friends. He would just keep them to himself, for his private little collection.

"He threw me some old clothes and told me he'd drive me home. I wanted to get so far away from him, but I was stranded and still in shock, so I agreed. He was no longer interested in me. He'd gotten what he wanted.

"Mamma asked what happen to the dress. I had to lie again. I told her I had spilled punch all over it, and that Betsy Anne had taken it home to wash it for me." Her voice trailed off.

"I'm so sorry," Nate said as he rocked her comfortingly.

"So that's why I can't be with you. I can't be with anyone."

Nate winced against the finality of her statement. "I understand." How could she ever accept the touch of another man after having been so betrayed?

Maria tensed at his words. She never expected him to still want her after hearing about her sordid ordeal, how she had been so vilely used, but some part of her still hoped he'd miraculous still desire her.

Nate felt her tense and released her a bit, not wanting her to feel confined in his embrace. He felt helpless. He wished he could erase that evening from existence forever.

Maria felt him loosen his hold on her and lifted up from his embrace reluctantly. He was disgusted by her, but too polite to leave her alone. "Thank you for listening. I'm sorry."

Nate was appalled. "You're sorry? What do you have to be sorry about?"

She looked up at him with confusion. "You know."

"No, I don't. You did nothing wrong!"

Maria shook her head. "I did plenty wrong. I shouldn't have been there. I shouldn't have lied to my parents. The list goes on."

"It wasn't your fault. It was that scumbag," Nate said sharply. "Hey, you're not talking about Johnny Martens are you?"

"Yes," Maria said.

Nate reeled at the thought of that little Nazi punk touching his beloved, "I'm going to kill that bastard!"

"No, you can't!" Maria cried in alarm.

Nate looked at her with confusion. "You want to protect him?"

Maria felt bile rise up in her throat. "No! Are you kidding? I'd love to see him dead!"

"Then what?"

"Weren't you listening? He has photographs. Of me. Lots of photographs. If those got out…"

Nate groaned. It would ruin her. He nodded. "I forgot about that. Damn!" His mind searched for ideas of exacting revenge without compromising her. Nothing came to mind.

They felt silent. Finally, Maria tentatively looked up at him and said, "Did you mean what you said?"

"Huh?" Nate asked, still trying to sort out how to kill Johnny and recover the pictures.

"Did you mean what you said about it not being my fault?"

Nate give her his full attention. "Of course, I mean that. It absolutely wasn't you fault."

Maria sat there and digested that piece of news. Could it be that he might not find her revolting? It was too much to hope. "I always assumed any man would blame me."

Nate shook his head. "Never." He saw the relief flow through her and smiled reassuringly at her. "And now I understand your reluctance to enter into a relationship."

Maria nodded. "I don't know if I can."

"There's more to a relationship than physical. I love you, Maria. I can wait."

"You love me?" Maria asked, her voice wispy as if afraid she misheard him.

"Yes," Nate chuckled. "I would have thought that was obvious by now."

Maria shook her head. "I mean, now? Still? After everything I told you?"

Nate became very serious. "Yes. I love you wholly and unconditionally. I am sickened by what you had to endure, but that doesn't affect how I feel about you. And mark my words Johnny Martens will get his in the end. But you're right; we have to tread carefully. But never doubt that I love you."

"But how do I not disgust you?" Maria asked.

Nate ran a finger across her cheek. "Because I love you. Trust me when I say you do not disgust me in the least. Quite the opposite. I'd love nothing more than to kiss you, but I promise not to make any moves on you until you're ready."

Maria looked into his sincere eyes and believed him. Moments ago, she wouldn't have dreamed it possible, but he really didn't hold it against her. Slowly, she leaned into him, dropped her gaze to his lips. Her heart began beating quickly, and she contemplated what she was about to do. Did she dare?

Yes, she decided in an instant. When her lips touched his, it felt so natural, much more than she would have thought. She pulled away and looked at him. The restraint she saw in his eyes made her giggle. Her eyes fell to his lips once again, and she sighed as pleasure surged through her. Finally, she understood why Sonya was so obsessed with men.

CHAPTER NINETEEN

Teresa, Maria, and Danny Petrucelli were all at in the visitor's lounge of the St James Hospital waiting for Donato's test to be finished. Teresa was incensed that she was not allowed in the room during the tests, but the doctors were adamant it was hospital policy.

Tony rushed into the waiting room, wide eyed with terror. "What is it? What happened to Pop?"

Teresa stood up and gave her son a hug. "Thank God you got my note! Pappa's going to be alright. He's just getting some tests."

"Tests?" Tony asked, looking around for Danny. When his eyes locked with his brother's he asked again, "Tests?"

Danny stood up and shook his head. "Pop was feeling bad and so Mamma decided to bring him here. I was coming in the front door when they were leaving."

Maria stood up and gave Tony a hug. "He hasn't been feeling too good lately, you know."

"I know, but that's nothing to take him to the hospital for," Tony cried. The waiting room was fairly deserted. Only one other family sat quietly toward the back, obviously waiting to hear back from a doctor. They looked over at Tony with a mixture of sympathy and curiosity.

Maria nodded. "It was worse than the usual. He was complaining about his heart."

"His heart?" Tony asked, his initial fear doubling. "Are you sure? Maybe it's heartburn."

Teresa shook her head. She brushed a tear from her eye and said, "You know Pop. He's not one to complain. He said his chest was aching and felt tight, not like anything he'd felt before."

"Oh God!" Tony cried, collapsing into a nearby chair. "Please…" he pleaded into his hands. "Please don't take Pop away from me."

Teresa's tears fell onto Tony's head as she held her son against her chest, "We don't know anything yet, Tony. He'll be okay. He's made of strong stuff."

Danny ran his hands through his hair. He felt so helpless. He was the eldest and couldn't do a single thing to stop his family's pain. "I'm getting some coffee. Anyone want any?" Maria shook her head. Danny didn't expect a response from Tony or his mother, so he started for the door.

"Mr. Petrucelli?" A middle-aged man with graying hair asked him as he was leaving. He wore a white coat and had a stethoscope around his neck.

"Are you my Pop's doctor?" he asked.

The man nodded and guided Danny back over to the rest of the family. "Dr. Palmieri. I'll be your father's chief cardiologist."

"That sounds a bit like he's not going home tonight," Danny said dropping his body into the closest chair.

"No," Dr. Palmieri agreed. "He needs to stay for observation."

Tony's sobs grew in intensity, and Maria sat back down looking ashen. "Is he going to be okay?" she asked, her voice shaking with fear and dread.

Dr. Palmieri's shook his head. "I can't answer that at this time. I call tell you that your father suffers from cardiogenic pulmonary edema."

"Cardio-what?" Tony asked, lifting his head. His eyes were red from crying, but he was focused intently on the doctor.

"Cardiogenic pulmonary edema," he repeated patiently. "Simple put, your father's lungs are filling with fluid because his heart isn't pumping the liquid out as it should."

'Why?" Maria asked.

"We don't know that yet."

"What do you know?" Tony asked angrily.

"Try to stay calm. We'll do everything we can, and I will report back to you when I know something. For now, I would suggest you all go home. Your father needs his rest, and you'll be of no use to him if you're sleep deprived," Dr. Palmieri replied.

Teresa looked up at the doctor. "Thank you. We all appreciate your help."

"Yes, thank you," Maria repeated, taking her cue from her mother.

Tony looked disgusted, but Dr. Palmieri took no offense. He was used to dealing with grieving family members. It was the burden of every doctor in the hospital. "You are very welcome," he said to the women. "I'll call you later."

Danny stood for a moment at Sarah's door. After her father had heard of his heroism with Anton the other night, he had extended an invitation to Danny for dinner. It was a huge honor, but one that brought a certain level of trepidation. Staring at the door, he wondered if this would be the right time to ask for permission to date Sarah.

He raised his hands to knock and decided he could wait a few more moments and lowered it again. He noticed a rectangular box affixed on the doorpost on the right and wondered at it. There was an unfamiliar symbol on it. Tentatively, he reached out to touch it when the door opened suddenly.

A tall thin man with a long flowing beard of gray greeted him. "Hello. You must be Danny."

Danny redirected his hand to shake the man's hand, feeling guilty at almost touching the box. "Yes, sir. Pleased to make your acquaintance."

"I'm Morris Greenberg, Anton's father," he said grasping Danny's hand firmly. He indicated the box in the doorway and said, "And that, my son, is a Mezuzah. Have you ever seen one?"

Danny shook his head. "No sir. I was curious about it."

"Curiosity is a good thing. It is how we learn about each other and the world around us. You are Catholic, right?"

"Yes," Danny answered. "I'm afraid I know little of the Jewish culture."

"Your desire to know more warms my heart," Morris said approvingly. "The Mezuzah holds a scroll containing God's scripture. It is placed here to continually remind us of God's words as instructed to us in the Bible. We wish to keep him in our minds at all time."

Danny nodded. "That's beautiful. May I ask another question?"

"Of course, my son."

"Why is it at an angle?"

Morris laughed. "You know, I've never been asked that before. Come in, and I'll answer you. You have a keen mind."

Danny entered the house and looked around for Anton or Sarah. Both were standing in the living room. They both looked like they'd been holding their breath, waiting for their father's approval. "Hi," Danny said to them both with a nod.

"Hello," Anton and Sarah replied in unison.

"I like him very much," Morris said with a twinkle in his eye. "You two can relax."

Anton smiled and sat on the couch. Sarah still stood in the middle of the room, her hands behind her back, fingers snaking in and out of each other. Her father may like him, but he still didn't know she wanted to date Danny.

Morris cocked his head at Sarah. "Sit, my child," he commanded gently.

She immediately complied, dropping to the couch next to Anton like a stone. She sat rigidly on the edge of the cushion, while Anton leaned back into the pillows. He pulled her back in an effort to relax her.

"Danny was asking me about the Mezuzah. He asked a very good question. I wonder if either of you know the answer," Morris said with a smile. His voice was soft but held authority. Danny could tell that there was a lot of love in this household.

"What's the question?" Anton asked.

Morris looked at Danny and raised an eyebrow. Danny coughed and repeated his question, feeling a little silly.

Anton grinned. "I've never thought about it. It's just like that. I don't know."

Sarah looked at her father and then her brother, before answering Danny. "It's a compromise," she said quietly.

"A compromise?" Danny asked.

"Yes," Sarah replied, feeling more comfortable. Morris smiled proudly at her as she continued, "See there have been different interpretations of the Talmud. Some rabbis felt the Mezuzah should be vertical and others felt it should be horizontal."

Danny smiled in understanding. "So, they compromised and put it on a slant."

"Very good, my daughter," Morris said. "That is exactly right."

"She always seems to know the answers," Danny said casually as he sat down on a chair across from Sarah. He leaned back against the padded back and smiled fondly at her.

Morris studied him for a moment before he took his seat. His voice took on a frosty quality. "So, you know my daughter as well as my son."

Danny's spine stiffened. "Yes. You didn't know that?"

"No," Morris said with a heavy sigh. "No, I invited you here to thank you for saving my son's life. We are all extremely grateful to you."

"I was just glad to be there at the right time," Danny replied.

Morris continued. "I had wondered what had brought you to our doorstep that night." He held Danny's gaze, his voice showing concern.

Danny realized how it must look to Sarah's father. "Oh, no sir, I can assure you there has been no inappropriate behavior between me your daughter. See we work together at the bakery and-"

Confusion wrinkled Morris' brow. "You work together?" he interrupted. He looked to Sarah. "How is that possible?"

Danny looked helplessly to Sarah. It was becoming obvious that there was nothing he could say that would make the situation better. He opted to remain silent and wait for Sarah to speak.

Sarah felt Danny's gaze on her, but kept her eyes on her lap. "He works at the other bakery, Father. He comes daily to our shop to collect all the financial statements."

"Look at me, my daughter," Morris commanded. Although his voice was firm, it was laced with love and patience.

Sarah immediately obeyed her father, looking him directly in the eye. "Yes, Father?"

"Why was he outside your door?"

"I…," she faltered. Her mouth opened and closed a few times as she searched for the best explanation.

"I think you'll find the truth is always the best solution," Morris offered gently.

"I walked her home," Danny supplied. "Sir, I just walked your daughter home. That's all."

Morris studied his daughter for a few moments before he turned to Danny. "I see. When you say 'that's all' are you telling me that you have no romantic intention toward Sarah?"

Danny was baffled. Why was he making such a big deal about walking Sarah home? In light of the incident with Anton, he would have thought Morris would be relieved for Sarah to have protection.

As if reading his mind, Morris nodded. "You do not understand. I can see that. We come from two very different worlds."

"Not so different," Danny said.

"Different enough that marriage is out of the question."

"Father!" Sarah burst out. She was mortified. Morris looked at her with a frown, and she immediately apologized for raising her voice.

Morris nodded in acknowledgement of her apology. "This is an emotional topic."

Danny wasn't ready to give up without a fight. "I'm not asking you for Sarah's hand in marriage. I am simply interested in dating your daughter."

"Danny," Sarah groaned. She knew he had no idea how volatile this subject was with her people.

"No, no," Morris replied, waving his daughter's attempts to silence Danny away. "I do like his honesty and interest in good open communication. We're more like you."

"But I'm still not good enough to walk your daughter home," Danny replied sullenly.

"Please don't misunderstand," Morris replied. "That's not what I'm saying at all. You are a fine young man, and I meant what I said when I spoke of my gratitude. I am in your debt."

"Then why…?" Danny began. There was no point in repeating his thoughts.

"Well let's look at this logically. You obviously have feelings for my daughter, do you not?"

Danny nodded. "I do," he said sincerely.

"So, let's say I allow you to date Sarah. What then?"

Danny shrugged. "Sir, I can't tell you that. There is no way to know."

"Yes, but bear with me here. What would happen if you fell in love with her?"

Danny felt a surge of defensiveness flow through him. "I'd do the right thing. I have far too much respect for your daughter to treat her any other way."

Morris leaned forward in his chair. "Of that I have no doubt. You are a good boy. So, tell me what would you do?"

Danny looked over at Anton with a stunned look as if expecting him to answer for him. Looking back at Morris, he said, "I'd come to you asking for her hand in marriage."

"Right," Morris agreed. "I do believe you'd do that. And at that time, I'd have to decline your offer."

"What?" Danny exploded. He closed his eyes and worked to calm his emotions. Opening them, he relaxed his shoulders and asked. "But why? You've said you like me. You've said you're grateful to me. You've even gone as far to say you owe me. Then why would you make that sort of blanket decision now? Because I'm not Jewish?"

Anton looked over at him with sympathy. Sarah was steadfastly staring at the floor.

"Precisely," Morris said.

"But why is that so important? I just don't understand."

"Interfaith marriage is possible," he said simply.

"But why?" Danny knew he sounded stubborn, but he didn't care. This was far too important. Although he didn't want to admit it, he had fallen in love with Sarah. It sounded silly, but he couldn't bear the thought of not being with her.

"There are many reasons," Morris explained. "For one thing, a Jewish marriage must be between two Jews. In our eyes, it simply would not be a marriage."

Danny fought for the

right words. He didn't want to sound like he was belittling the Jewish beliefs but that explanation didn't satisfy him.

Morris chuckled. "You don't need to walk on eggshells with me. You don't understand, do you?"

Danny shook his head. "No. Although, Sarah has explained on a few occasions that not everything is always understandable. Some things are based on faith alone."

Morris smiled. "She is right. But if you search you can usually find the answers to explain questions you have. In this case, let's take an example and explore it. If a Jewish man took a non-Jewish woman to wed, do you know that their children would not be Jewish?"

Danny shook his head. "No, I didn't. but in this case a Jewish woman would wed a non-Jewish man, so the children would be Jewish." he felt a glimmer of hope.

"That's true, but how would they be raised?"

"I don't know," he answered honestly.

"Well, I do," Morris replied. "Statistically speaking, they probably would be raised Catholic and would be lost to us. Being Jewish is not easy. There are a lot of traditions, a lot of study. It is unlikely that you would invest that kind of time and energy into a religion you did not believe in."

"I might," Danny replied.

"How would your parents feel about that?"

Danny's mind reeled with thoughts of his father bellowing at him for even considering sending his children to a synagogue, let alone celebrating Hanukkah. "I see your point."

"There's a lot to think about."

Morris stood up. "I'm sorry, I've been a terrible host. Dinner is ready, is it not, daughter?"

Sarah immediately stood up, relieved to have a new topic of conversation. "Yes, just give me a moment in the kitchen to do the final preparations. Please go into the dining room. I shouldn't be long."

As they all enjoyed the meal, they tacitly agreed to talk about other things, including Danny's boxing career and upcoming fight against Nate Rubin. It surprised Danny to learn that Morris was up on the fights in the area.

When the meal was over, it was late and Danny extended his hand to Morris. "Thank you very much for your hospitality."

"You are always welcome in my home, my son," he said warmly.

But not in my daughter's heart, Danny thought. "Thank you," he said instead. He turned to Anton. "I had a favor to ask of you. My father fell ill and is at St James Hospital. I wondered if you could stop in and take a look. The doctors there are treating him, but he doesn't seem to be getting any better."

Anton looked shocked. "Why didn't you mention this earlier?"

"I didn't want to be a burden or seem to be taking advantage of our new found friendship…"

"Are you kidding me?" Anton asked. "I can't believe that I'm just hearing about this now. How long has been there?"

"Two days."

Anton looked at his watch. "Visiting hours are over now, but I'll meet you there first thing in the morning. 9a.m., I believe they allow guest in."

"But you're not a guest."

"Neither am I completely welcome," Anton said sadly.

Danny nodded with understanding. "Prejudice runs deep."

"Never mind though. We'll get your father well."

CHAPTER TWENTY

Danny paced the corridors outside his father's room at St James Hospital. Maria and Teresa remained in the room chatting with his father. He glanced at his watch for the third time in the last two minutes. It still said 9:15am. Where was he?

"Danny!" Anton called out. Danny whipped around, relieved to see his friend. "Sorry I'm late. I just wanted to check a few things before I came in."

"No problem," Danny replied, letting out his pent- up breath. "I'm just grateful you're here at all. What did you find out?"

Anton grimaced. "They weren't exactly forthcoming with information. I did find a nurse I knew from high school though, and she showed me the records. I don't want to say anything before I see him. Can I go in?"

"Certainly," Danny said. He held the door open for Anton and followed him in. "Everyone, I'd like to introduce you to Anton Greenberg."

"Greenberg?" Donato's voice was weak, but the rasp in his voice didn't hide the snide overtones.

"Father," Danny chided gently. "Anton's a doctor. He's here to help you."

Donato glared at his son and opened his mouth to say something. Teresa gave her husband's arm a warning squeeze. "Enough," she whispered. "Just lie back and relax." Donato reluctantly obliged. His closed his eyes wearily and fell asleep almost instantly.

Anton looked him over, his face showing concern. "Is he always this lethargic?"

"Pretty much since he's been admitted," Maria answered.

"Can I see you all outside?' Anton asked after studying the bedside chart.

Teresa cast a glance at her husband who was in deep sleep, before nodding her head. They all tiptoed out to the hall.

"What do you think, Doctor?" Maria asked. She looked him in the eye, wanting to communicate her appreciation and respect.

Anton ran a nervous hand through his hair. He hesitated a moment before answering, "Danny was correct in his assessment. Your father's not doing well. He's not responding to their treatment."

"Why?" Danny asked, aghast.

"Because their giving him morphine along with a few other drugs," Anton said bluntly.

Teresa looked confused, "The doctor told us it was all necessary."

Maria shook her head. "It seemed like a lot of medication to me."

Anton smiled at her assessment. "You're right. It is. At Beth Israel, the hospital I work at, we have a different approach."

"Really?" Teresa asked. Her voice reflected the doubt she felt. It seemed logical that her husband needed medication. And after all they were in a hospital and these doctors treated sick people on a daily basis. They must know what they were doing.

"I'm not saying that medicines couldn't benefit him," Anton said, as if reading her mind. "I'd just cut back–a lot. And I'd implement some other options."

"Like what?" Danny asked.

"Like dietary measures and exercise. Oxygen has been proven to aid in recovery. We need to boost his energy and his body's ability to heal itself. Lying in bed all day, half comatose from morphine isn't going to help him recover any time soon."

"Mamma?" Maria asked. "What do you think?"

Teresa shook her head. "I don't know."

"Let me help you," Anton said softly. "I owe your son that much."

"You do? Why?" Her confusion was apparent.

Anton looked at Danny with a puzzled look, almost accusatory. "You didn't tell her?'

Danny held his look. "I didn't want to worry her," he said pointedly.

Anton closed his eyes, berating himself for overlooking that possibility. "I'm sorry, I'm just to used to -"

Danny held up his hand, "Don't worry. You don't need to explain."

Teresa stood there with her hands on her hips glaring at her son. "Will someone please tell me what you're talking about?"

Danny sighed and explained what happened the night he saved Anton. Maria and Teresa gasped throughout the story. They each had very different reactions. Maria threw herself into Danny's arms and kissed his check a dozen times. "You're a hero! My brother's a hero!"

Teresa glared at her son. "You could have been killed!" she nearly shouted. The nurses at a nearby station looked over at them, and one indicated that she should lower her voice. Teresa nodded embarrassingly. Lowering her voice, she gritted out. "And you didn't think to tell me?"

Danny extracted himself from his sister and turned to his mother. "I wonder why I didn't tell you," he responded lightly, trying to charm her out of her bad mood.

Teresa grasped his chin in her hand and pinched him hard. "You do that again, and I'll beat you senseless."

Danny didn't want to argue with her so he just nodded within her grasp.

Mollified she gave him a hug. "I'm proud of you, my son," she whispered in his ear. He felt wetness on his neck and held her tight.

"Thank you, Mamma."

Anton watched the scene with a smile. He redoubled his commitment to helping their patriarch. Hopefully, Donato wouldn't protest that help too much.

Maria held her breath as she dusted a nearby end table for the fifth time that day. She glanced nervously to the dining room table, which was all set for five.

Danny watched his sister from a nearby chair. He stifled at grin at her frantic puttering. "It'll be fine," he whispered calmly, looking up from his book.

Maria whispered back, "How do you know?"

Danny laughed, causing Maria to look hurt. He immediately looked contrite and stood up to give her a hug. He squeezed her tight when he felt her trembling. "Aw, sweetie, don't worry so much. I'll be there, and Tony'll be home soon."

Maria clung to her brother and resisted the impulse to burst into tears. She had never brought a suitor home to meet her family before this night. Her father had been transferred to Beth Israel Hospital two nights ago and was resting easier now. This was a good opportunity to introduce Nate to her mother without worrying about her father's reaction. She felt immediately guilty that she felt so much relief that her father wouldn't be there. Pulling back away from her brother, she quickly crossed herself and asked God for forgiveness.

Danny looked puzzled by this but assumed she was praying for tonight. Smiling, he patted her on the head saying, "God will be watching over you tonight."

Maria nodded and studied the door to the kitchen, wondering what her mother was thinking. Teresa had been unreadable all day. The night that she had confided in her family that she was considering Nate for a beau was the night her father fell ill. She never had a chance to ask her mother for advice or her opinion. She could, however, guess that Teresa would not be pleased; every Italian mother dreamed of her daughter marrying an Italian Catholic, not a Jewish prizefighter.

She did not jump out of her skin when the doorbell rang. She cast a quick glance up at her brother and walked to the door. She wiped her hands on her dress before opening the door, her heart all a flutter.

"Hiya, sis!" Tony's cheerful voice boomed out. "I forgot my key again."

Without a word, Maria walked back to the end table and began dusting in earnest again.

Tony popped his head in the door, looking puzzled by Maria's lack of greeting. Almost afraid to come in, he glanced over at Danny. "What?" he mouthed, shrugging to emphasize his confusion.

"You're not Nate," Danny explained with a suppressed grin.

"Oh, yeah, that's right. Tonight's the night, isn't it?" Tony asked. He took a few tentative steps into the house.

"Yeah, tonight's the night," Maria said, her voice brittle with irritation. She didn't look up from her task of cleaning the table but continued to rub the same spot with her rag. "And thank you so much for making sure to come home early so that you could help prepare the house for dinner."

"I hope you're not going to any trouble," Nate said poking his head in from the door.

Maria jumped at the sound of his voice. "I…I didn't know you were there," she cried. "How long have you been standing there?"

Nate smiled warmly at her. "I just got here."

Maria glared at Tony, silently berating him for not letting her know Nate was standing there. Tony looked completely flummoxed. "What did I do?"

"Nothing," Maria bit out icily. "Apparently."

"May I come in?" Nate said, shivering in an exaggerated manner. He was still in the door frame. His grin melted Maria's frost.

"I'm sorry. Of course, please come in." she walked to the door, pointedly pushing her brother out of the way as she passed him. She waited for him to enter before closing the door behind him. "Here, let me take your coat."

He handed his woolen coat to her and added his gloves and hat to the pile. "Thank you," he said softly.

Maria's heartbeat quickened at his intimate voice. She stood for a moment just staring into his aqua eyes, relishing his warmth.

Tony coughed discretely into his hand and said, "Come on in, Nate. Have a seat. I think dinner should be ready soon."

Maria cranked her neck around to her brother. "And how would you know that?" she asked. Her voice was more playful than irritated now, and Tony silently thanked Nate for his ability to tame his sister's ire.

Danny took Nate's garments from Maria so that she could accompany Nate into the parlor. He hung them in the hall closet and then joined the group.

"Would you care for a glass of Chianti?" Maria asked Nate.

"No, thanks, I don't drink," Nate replied.

"Neither do I," Maria agreed. After that fateful night with Johnny, she made a vow to never to touch alcohol again. She smiled at Nate, relieved that he would never expect her to drink.

"Well, I do," Tony said, taking the cork off the bottle of red wine. "And you, Danny?"

"Not while I'm training," Danny said shaking his head.

"Right," Tony said. "Okay. Well, there's no point drinking alone." He put the stopper back on the bottle.

Teresa came out with a tray of cheese puffs. She glanced over at Nate as she put the tray down in the center of the coffee table. "Hello, I'm Maria's mother, Teresa," she said stiffly.

Nate immediately stood up and said, "It is a pleasure to make your acquaintance, Mrs. Petrucelli."

Maria also stood. "Mamma, this is Nate Rubin,"

Teresa nodded. "Welcome to our home," she said with a perfunctory smile. "I need to get back to dinner. It should be ready soon." She turned and walked back into the kitchen.

The four in the room watched her leave in silence. When the kitchen door closed, Nate sat back down. He whistled low, "I have my work cut out for me, don't I?"

Maria smiled reassuringly at him. "She's not the least of your concern."

Nate looked a little alarmed. "She isn't?"

Tony shook his head. "No, she's right. Pappa's not going to like you. No offense."

Nate nodded grimly. "None taken."

Danny leaned forward and said indicating the closed kitchen door, "She'll come around, don't worry."

"And Papa Petrucelli?" Nate asked with a grumbled in his voice.

"Let's take it one parent at a time," Maria said. "Now, how about some water?"

Nate nodded. "Sure."

When Teresa called them into dinner, they all filled the seats at the table. They each filled their plates from the hot steaming serving bowls in silence, no one wanting to be the first to initiate conversation.

After Nate took his first bite, he said, "This is a wonderful meal, Mrs. Petrucelli."

Teresa studied him for a moment before replying. "Thank you," she said politely.

They fell silent again; the sound of cutlery on china filling to the vacuum of sound. Nate struggled to find something to say to ease the tension. He could ask about Mr. Petrucelli, but that might remind Teresa about how much her husband would disapprove of him. There wasn't a safe conversation he could come up with so he remained silent.

Danny rolled his eyes at the uncharacteristic quiet that hung over the table like an unwanted table cloth. "How's your training coming along?" he finally asked, deciding that any conversation was better than none.

Nate cast a nervous look at Teresa who kept her gaze on her plate. He shrugged his shoulders and answered. "Good and you?"

Danny nodded. With a playful glint in his eye, he answered "Great. I'm in the best shape I've ever been in. Word on the street's that I'm a shoe in."

Nate couldn't help but grin as he relaxed into the playful banter. "Depends on the street you're on, I guess."

Teresa had trouble repressing her smile. She looked up at the two and saw a friendship beyond the bond of competition. "Sounds like a draw to me."

Danny pretended to be affronted. "Mamma! How could you?" he asked.

Teresa smiled and said, "He's our guest, Danny."

They all burst out laughing. Part of the laughter was genuine mirth but most was a release of all the pent- up tension that had built up. The conversation of the rest of the evening was easy and comfortable. They steered clear of religion and no one mentioned the possibility of Maria and Nate dating so as to keep things light. By the end of the evening, Teresa had forgotten her distrust of Nate and gave him a friendly hug to say goodnight. Maria walked him to the door, but stayed inside the house. Nate silently agreed with her decision. The evening had gone far better than anticipated, and he didn't want to do anything to mar that.

CHAPTER TWENTY-ONE

The East Ward Club was humming with activity. Both rings were occupied with boxers training as spectators looked on. Danny was waiting his turn as he pummeled a worn punching bag. His punches were sluggish, and his rhythm was off. Grimacing, he looked over at his frowning trainer.

"What's the matter, kid?" the old man asked gruffly, tugging at the brim of his cap.

"Nothing," Danny said with a shrug. "I'm tired, that's all."

"That's not all," Willie flashed back. "There's something going on here. What is it?"

Danny moved away from the bag and pulled off his gloves. "I've been training nonstop. I need a break or something."

Willie grabbed the gloves from Danny and threw on the ground. "Take a break. Take a good long break then. I'll just call Manny and let him know that my boy's too tired to fight."

Danny groaned. Don't be like that. I'm just saying I'd like a night off."

Willie sighed. "I'm sorry, kid. Is it your Pop? Is he doing okay?"

Danny nodded. "No, Pop's doing better."

Willie smiled. "That's good. Wise move, moving him to Beth Israel. They've got the best doctors there."

Danny nodded. "We got lucky."

"Okay then, what's going on? I've never seen you so distracted."

"I keep telling you-"

Willie interrupted him with an impatient wave of his hand. "I know–nothing, right?" He paused and studied Danny. "If I didn't know better, I'd say it was a girl."

Danny blushed and quickly looked away. He tried to think of something to say but couldn't. He glanced up into Willie's irritated gaze and winced.

Willie didn't try to hide his disgust. "I've known you for how many years? Never had a girlfriend. I worried about you but thought you'd find the right girl eventually. But now? This is the time you decide to get all tangled up with romance? Weeks before the biggest fight of your life?"

Danny closed his eyes against his trainer's words. "I didn't do it on purpose," he said, sounding like a petulant child.

"But you can undo it on purpose," Willie retorted. "End it. For now, at least. She'll understand. If she really cares for you, she'll understand."

Danny looked at the floor. "It's not like we ever really started."

"Then it should be easy to end."

"Maybe."

Willie pulled his blue Giants cap off his head scratched his skull. "Take some time. Go for a walk. Think it over. If you're here kid, I want you here. Not with your heads in the clouds. Got it?"

Danny nodded. "Got it." He picked up his gym bag and walked out into the cold night.

Danny was still thinking about his trainer's words as he stared out the window of his father's small hospital room at Beth Israel Hospital. He glanced back when he heard the loud snoring coming from his father's bed. Smiling, he sent a grateful prayer to God that Donato was finally looking better. His color was improved, and his sleep looked far more restful than the drug induced one at St. James.

Donato was transferred three days prior. In the beginning, the old man protested loudly but in the end, he couldn't deny his entire family who was united in their recommendation to give Anton a chance. Ultimately, Donato muttered a reluctant agreement and signed the paperwork needed to move to Beth Israel.

The nurses at Beth Israel were selectively deaf to the poorly veiled racial slurs he'd whisper to his family in a voice the entire room could hear. At every turn, Maria apologized for her father's words, which made Donato even angrier. Anton kept a pleasant demeanor despite Donato's uncooperative attitude. His questions were answered by whichever family member was visiting at the moment who would inevitably receive a mutinous glare from their patriarch.

Maria came into the room just as Donato let out another rumbling snore. She giggled behind her hand. "It's good to see him getting back to his old self."

Danny opened his arms, embracing his sister. "I know. It is amazing. He's really responding to Anton's treatment."

"We owe your friend a lot." Maria said, sighing against her brother's chest. "I just wish Pappa would see that."

"Give him time," Danny replied.

Maria pulled away and looked up at him. "How's training?"

Danny shrugged. "Fine."

"Fine?" she asked intently. "Somehow that doesn't sound so fine."

Danny sighed in frustration. "Willie thinks I'm distracted."

"Are you?"

"I don't know."

Maria studied her brother. "What does Willie think's distracting you?"

Danny glanced back over at father's resting form and whispered, "A girl."

"A girl!" Maria exclaimed excitedly. "Really? Since when?"

"Shhh… you'll wake him," Danny said, nervously. He waited until he heard his father's reassuring snore before he continued. "It isn't anything yet, and it might not become anything. Sarah's father doesn't exactly approve."

Maria had intended to lower her voice to a whisper but was so taken aback by her brother's words that she found herself shouting even louder. "Doesn't approve? Are you kidding me?"

"Maria, will you please keep your voice down?" Danny burst out. He groaned as his father stirred, slapping his hand against his forehead in frustration. He held his breath praying that his father wouldn't wake up. After a few moments, it was clear that Donato was still slumbering peacefully.

"Sorry," Maria whispered. "I just can't believe…I mean how could anyone disapprove of you?"

"It's a cultural thing."

"How so?"

Danny paused. "She's Jewish."

Maria's eyes opened wide. "Really?" she whispered. "Why that's…"

Danny frowned. "What? What is it?" he asked defensively.

Maria smiled. "Ironic. That's the word I was searching for. I'm dating a Jewish man, and you're dating a Jewish woman. I think that's amazing."

Danny returned the smile. "Yes. It is. But I'm not really dating her. I'd like to, but-"

Maria nodded as she comprehended the situation. "But her father doesn't understand. I suspect that it isn't that he doesn't approve of you personally. It's just that you're Jewish."

"Yes, that's it exactly," Danny agreed. "It amounts to the same thing though."

"No, not really. He's not finding fault with you."

"Just my religion, my background, my beliefs," Danny replied sulkily.

"Well, can you see his viewpoint?"

Danny sighed with resigned irritation. "Yes."

"Give it time," Maria said giving her brother a gentle squeeze on his arm. "If anyone can change his mind, it's you."

✤ ✤ ✤

Manny scowled as he watched Nate in the ring, trading indifferent punches with Rudy, who was giving it all he had. Although Nate blocked a punch here and there, his weak jabs weren't hitting their mark.

"Okay, okay. That's it," Manny growled in frustration. "Nate, come here."

"Yeah?" Nate asked, confused by his trainer's curtailment of the session. He gave a quick acknowledging wave to his long time sparring partner before stepping out of the ring. "What's up?"

Manny glared at him. "We're a month away from your biggest match, and you're looking like a limp noodle out there."

Nate stared at Manny in disbelief. Manny was always slow to criticize him over the years, opting to train with the carrot approach rather than the stinging whip-like tongue of some trainers. "I don't know what you mean."

"Don't you?" Manny asked shaking his head.

Nate's tone became defensive. "No, I'm working hard."

"Uh huh." Manny wasn't fooled. "Whatever it is that's eating at you, go handle it and come back tomorrow fresh, okay?"

Nate glared at Manny. "You got it," he growled, turning around to walk away. Taking a few steps, he sighed and turned back. "I'm sorry, Manny."

Manny nodded, relief flooding through him. "As long as you take care of it, we'll be fine. You're still the best fighter I've ever seen."

Nate grinned at the compliment. That was more like it.

"You're Lights Out. Don't forget that."

Nate walked out the door into the bitter cold. He pulled up his collar to shield himself and jogged purposefully to the place he knew he could resolve all his woes. Fifteen minutes later he arrived at the stoop of the Petrucelli family. He paused on the landing as he wondered about the wisdom of knocking unannounced. Rubbing his hands together, he paced back and forth.

"You stalking my sister now?" Tony asked from the driveway.

Nate spun around in surprise and grinned. "Seems that way."

"No one home?" Tony asked puzzled.

"Haven't knocked yet."

"Why?"

Nate shrugged. "Don't know."

Tony pretended to understand out of politeness. "Well, come on in. It's freezing out here."

He opened the door and shivered one last time as he entered the cozy home. "Hello!" he called out.

"Hello," Maria called back. She came around the corner and stopped short when she saw Nate. Her hand automatically shot up to smooth out her hair. "Nate, what are you doing here?"

"Nate's here?" Danny asked, coming around to greet them. He grinned at his sister's discombobulation. "This is a surprise."

"Yes, well…," Nate wasn't sure how to explain his appearance.

"It doesn't matter. Come in. Are you hungry?" Danny asked.

"Sure, I could eat," Nate replied. As they walked to the dining room he asked Maria, "How was your day?"

She looked up at him and found herself lost in his eyes. Shaking herself, she replied, "Good. And yours?"

"Okay," he replied uncomfortably. He looked away but felt her gaze still on him.

Danny indicated a seat for Nate. "Sit," he offered. "Mamma's still at the hospital, but she left us a casserole in the oven."

"Smell's delicious," Nate murmured. He sat down, feeling a little awkward as the rest of the family buzzed around the table, putting the dinner out. He smiled broadly as he watched the three siblings work together.

"What?" Tony asked as he placed some rolls on the table.

"Nothing," Nate replied. "It's just… I grew up an only child and you all work so well together. It's just nice to see."

Maria smiled. "There's nothing like family."

They all finally sat down and enjoyed a few bites of food. Tony looked up from his plate and asked Nate, "You've seen the paper recently?"

"Which one?" Nate replied with a grunt. He wasn't a big fan of publicity. Manny was forever trying to get his name in the paper, something that made Nate extremely uncomfortable. He preferred being in backrooms, unnoticed. Still with publicity came larger purses.

"Yeah, we're all over the headlines these days," Danny said with a grin. "Isn't it great?"

"Not particularly," Nate replied.

"But isn't that what you want?" Maria asked.

Nate shrugged. "I supposed I should. It's hard to explain."

Maria nodded trying to understand.

Nate saw her confusion and sighed. "They call me 'Lights Out'. I'm not exactly a pillar of my community, if you know what I mean."

Danny nodded in sympathy. "Must be hard now with the press pitting us against each other, emphasizing your religion. 'The Jew vs the Italian'. Not exactly what I would have asked for either."

"Are you getting hit with it too?" Nate asked.

Danny shrugged. "Just mostly racism. The articles seem to bring out the worst in people. Can't go down the street without someone cheering me on with 'We're counting on you to knock that Jew boy on his…', you know what." Danny glanced over at his sister.

Maria rolled her eyes. "It isn't as if I haven't heard what they say. I'm often right next to you."

"Still, there's no need to repeat it," Danny replied.

Tony looked from Danny to Nate. "You guys can't defend one another, you know. You know that right?"

"Why on Earth not?" cried Maria, looking at Tony as if he'd suddenly gone mad.

Nate smiled at her. "Because your brother and I are supposed to be mortal enemies," he explained patiently.

When Danny saw that Maria still didn't understand, he supplied, "This fight's so big because people expect us to be against each another. The tension's the reason for the early seat sales."

"Oh!" Maria exclaimed as understanding dawned on her. "I guess that makes sense. I guess it might be easier to fight if you're not worried about hurting each other's feelings."

Nate and Danny laughed. "Maybe if you're a girl." Danny said. Tony joined in their laughter.

Maria blushed in irritation. "What was I thinking? Men are about as sensitive as goats."

Nate struggled to stop chuckling when he caught Maria's glare. "Sorry, it's just funny to think about. I mean worrying offending my opponent." Thinking of the brawls in the smokers, he burst out laughing again until tears streamed down his face. Waving his hands, he tried to apologize, but the words came out as hiccups.

Maria looked at Nate as if he had truly turned into a goat. Tony and Danny struggled to sober up, but watching their typically deadpan friend lose the battle to regain his composure sent them over the edge again.

Finally, the three settled down. Maria crossed her arms mutinously across her chest, refusing to look at anyone. She wouldn't say a word for the rest of the evening. Maybe next time they would think twice about laughing at her and behave less like insensitive cretins.

Danny looked over at Nate, judging he was ready for conversation again. "Seriously though, if we really want this to be a big match, with lots of people watching, we need to avoid each other socially. That means you shouldn't be visiting here."

Tony nodded in agreement. "And you probably shouldn't be seeing our sister right now either."

"What?" Maria asked completely forgetting her vow of silence.

"Just until the fight's over. That'll be next month. Not that long to wait," Tony supplied.

"But, I don't…" Maria didn't want to sound too disappointed, but she felt like her world had just collapsed.

"Bubbeleh," Nate said soothingly, placing his hand on hers. "It's just for a little while. Tony's right. Besides you are a bit of a distraction."

"I am?" Maria's wide eyes sparkled with joy

Nate grinned broadly at her reaction. "Yes. You are most certainly that."

✣ ✣ ✣

The next day as Danny was walking Sarah home, he was lost in thought, not sure what to say to Sarah. He looked at the trees and houses, carefully avoiding Sarah's eyes.

"What's wrong?" Sarah asked without preamble.

Danny sighed and shifted his gaze to meet her inquiring one. "I'm sorry."

Sarah nodded. "It's okay. How's your training been?"

"'Good. Tiring," Danny replied. "It's a big match coming up."

Sarah nodded. "But that's not all. That's not the only reason you've been so withdrawn from me, right?"

"Right," Danny answered without hesitation. He groaned. "There's something about you that makes me truthful to a fault. I am usually more capable of tact."

Sarah smiled up at him. "That's what I admire most about you, you know. You're honesty. You don't try to hide behind socially acceptable norms. I can always count on you to tell me how you are really feeling. What you're thinking. That's special, Danny."

Danny grinned like a fool. "You know I'm in love with you. I can hardly think of anything else. Even when you're not right in front of me."

"I'm sure your trainer has suggested you stop seeing me," Sarah said nodding.

Danny's mouth dropped open. "How did you know that?"

"It makes sense. He's looking after your best interests."

"Willie's a good man."

"But that's not the only reason," she said as her gaze dropped to the pavement. "I haven't seen you since you came to meet my father."

Danny nodded and looked away. He tried to think of something to say but couldn't. He coughed as tears threatened to surface. Not being with Sarah wasn't something he wanted to consider. Not now, not yet. It was easier just to put the relationship on hold until after the fight. Then they could think about what to do.

Sarah studied him and nodded. "I've told you how I feel about you, but I don't know how to make my father understand. I always thought, always assumed I would marry a Jewish man. I never considered marrying a Christian."

Danny looked back at her.

"That is until I met you," she added softly.

Danny pulled her into a side ally and kissed her hard on the lips. Sarah melted into him, returning the kiss with a longing passion. Danny broke off and looked into her eyes. "After the fight."

Sarah nodded. She touched his cheek with her hand and pulled out of his embrace. She walked backwards a few steps, looking him over as if memorizing every line in his before she turned around and walked briskly home.

CHAPTER TWENTY-TWO

A week later, Donato was sitting up in his bed, chatting amicably with his children. Maria stared at her father as he laughed at Danny's joke. The jovial sound roused a distant memory of her father from her youth.

"You're looking at me as if I've grown a new head!" Donato declared after a few moments. "What do you stare at, child?"

Maria instantly looked away. "It's …nothing. I'm sorry."

Donato lifted her chin with his hand. "What is it?"

"I just haven't seen you this happy in a while. That's all," Maria whispered. She didn't want to do anything to disrupt the moment.

Donato burst out in laughter. "And that is cause for your worry?"

Maria smiled. "Not worry, just…"

Teresa learned in. "We're just all so happy to see you well. This new treatment's working. We have a lot of people here to thank."

Just then a nurse bustled in. "Time to take your temperature, Mr. Petrucelli."

"Donato," the old man corrected. "I think we should be on a first name basis by now, don't you, Becca?"

The nurse froze for a moment before she recovered from her initial shock. Blushing, she said, "Why yes, Mr., I mean Donato," She took his blood pressure and temperature quickly and left.

"Nice girl," Donato said fondly.

Tony and Danny exchanged looks of shock. Maria's mouth dropped open. The siblings looked to their mother who smiled knowingly. "I think you've managed to surprise your children," she said to her husband.

"Ba!" he exclaimed dismissing their stunned looks with a wave of his hand.

"Does that mean…?" Tony couldn't figure out how to finish the sentence.

When he didn't continue, Danny offered, "I think what he's trying to say is…um…that is…"

Donato's eye twinkled at his children's discomfort. "So, you don't think an old man can change his viewpoint? You think I'm so dense as to ignore what these fine doctors and nurses have done for me?"

"No," Tony and Danny answered quickly in unison.

"Well good, because I realized I maybe wasn't seeing things as clearly as I could. Do you know that Becca there has family in a concentration camp in Germany? And Anton has a cousin who's been missing for a year now. It's hard to ignore all the pain of these good people."

Maria leaned in and gave her father a kiss on the cheek. "I'm proud of you Pappa. I love you."

Donato's eyes misted as he patted her daughter's head. "And I hear that you have found yourself a new beau."

Maria froze, wondering what he would think of her dating Nate. She glanced at her mother who nodded her head reassuringly to her. Looking back at Donato she gulped. "Yes," she said quietly.

"I look forward to meeting him," he said gently. "It might take me a while to get used to my daughter with someone that isn't Catholic. Or Italian for that matter. But if you're happy, I'm happy."

Relief flooded Maria as she threw herself on Donato. "Oh, Pappa! Thank you. Thank you!" Tears rolled down her down her cheeks as she realized that she had her father's approval, something she never expected to get.

The air popped in the hall as if electricity filled the air. The Minutemen murmured amongst themselves as Philip Cantalupo and Abraham Greenburg consulted off to the side of the podium. Finally, Philip addressed the crowd. It took less than a minute for the crowd to settle and await news.

"We're a week away from the big fight," Cantalupo began. "We do not know many details but thanks to Tony Petrucelli, we know enough. The Nazi's are planning a blood bath, that much we know for certain."

A murmur went through the crowd.

A young Jewish man shouted from the back, "Do we know anything about the guns they have? Anything about members?"

"How are we to fight?" a frightened voice called out from the center of the group.

Cantalupo looked Abraham and nodded. Abraham rose and walked to the podium. Again, the crowd became silent.

"Whoever said this would be easy?" Abraham's voice was quiet but held the authority of his many years of experience. "Freedom is something that is earned, not given away. These men want to take our liberties away. They dare come to our country, our home and try to steal our way of life! Are we going to stand up to them?"

The room erupted into cheers. "Yes!"

He waited for them to subside. "Can we defeat these monsters, these devils poorly disguised in brown?"

Again, the room cried back in one voice, "Yes!"

He stood silently in front of the room surveying the crowd. "You are all worthy of the fight. You understand the preciousness of that which you fight for. Never forget it. Next week, we must not back down. We must stand up and cry 'We see you! Go home!'"

The group cheered loudly and started chanting, "Go home, Nazi pigs! Go home, Nazi pigs!"

Abraham stepped down from the podium and motioned for Tony to come join him. He stood with his back to the wall and waited for the young man to join him. Cantalupo joined them as well.

"So, do you have anything else for us?" the old man asked.

Tony shook his head. "Nothing more than I had last week. They've clammed up."

Cantalupo frowned. "You don't think they suspect you, do you?"

Tony shook his head again. "No, I've been careful. Very careful."

Abraham leaned in and said, "There is a thing as too careful. You don't think you caught anyone's attention?"

"No, I'm sure they still trust me," Tony replied. "Last meeting, Nick was so warm to me it made my skin crawl. He'd clap me on the back every few minutes. He's the kind of guy that doesn't touch you if he's pissed. Pretty open about that."

Cantalupo nodded. "We trust you Tony, but we need more. Anything. Any little bit of information you might have forgotten?"

Abraham said. "Go over it again. What's the plan as far as you know?"

"They're going to come to the fight, outside the building and rally in the street. They're going to arrive before the bell rings and wait. When the fight's over, they're going to target the Jews. Throw things at them.It' s what they've been talking about, but I'm not sure that they need guns for that," Tony said with a shrug.

"And you're sure they have guns?" Cantalupo asked.

"Yes," Tony replied. "I'm sure. Nick told me a few weeks ago. He took me aside and whispered that the backup arrived. I asked what he meant by that and he said 'you know–*backup*'. He put his hands out like he had a rifle in his hand, and he was shooting something.

"Hans gave him a dirty look, and Nick dropped his hands immediately, whispering to me, 'Don't tell anyone okay? It's our secret, right? I reassured him that I would take the secret to the grave and thanked him for having faith in me, you know, telling him what he wanted to hear.

He likes to think I look up to him, so I play on that as much as I can. Yes, Mr. Martins. Thank you, Mr. Martins. 'Call me Nick, kid,' he says constantly, but I keep calling him Mr. Martins, because well that's what he wants to hear really." Tony's voice trailed off as he realized he'd been rambling.

Cantalupo grinned at him. "So, you're sure they have guns then."

"Yeah," Tony said returning the smile. "I'm sure. Nick's not that good an actor."

"Okay, well we've got to anticipate the worst."

Abraham nodded. "We have to get there before them; be ready for them. And be sure the community knows what to expect."

"Yeah, not everyone's in the know," Cantalupo said with a sigh. "It's tricky. We don't want to show our cards too soon. Can't afford a leak. But we need to make sure everyone's safe."

"It needs to be done quietly, privately, one on one in people's homes," Tony said.

"Hm?" Abraham asked. "What's that?"

Tony found himself having more and more confidence. He looked the old man squarely in the eye and said, "Now's the time to start a message. Our people, your people, they all need to know. That's going to be our biggest threat."

"What's going to be our biggest threat?" Cantalupo asked.

"Our numbers. Our conviction," Tony replied with confidence. "If everyone in that boxing hall all stand up in unison and say, "Go home Nazis!" there's nothing they can do. We'll outnumber them 10 to 1. Even with guns, that's good odds."

"But what if there's a leak?" Abraham asked, shaking his head.

"We know who's a part of the Friends, right?" Tony asked.

"We think we know," Abraham replied. "Yes, we probably do."

"We need to get the information out through people we know and trust and instruct them to tell only people they know and trust. We might not get everyone but if we get most, it'll do the trick."

Cantalupo clapped Tony on the back. "Good kid. Yes, that's the way we'll beat them. It's as you say, Abraham, all we really have to do is stand up and say ' We see you! Go home!' If they have no audience, they'll have to leave. These snakes in the grass only succeed when people pretend they aren't there. Never mess with a man from Newark. We'll teach them.

"We have a week. Let's tell everyone, tell them what to say, who to go to. In a week, we'll be prepared. During that time, we'll come up with a few surprises. If you know there are snakes in the grass, it's just a matter of lighting a match, right?"

Abraham smiled for the first time that night. "Right!"

✤ ✤ ✤

"Tony," Nick said in a hushed tone. "Come here."

Tony's heart beat faster as he approached him. Fear crept up his spine, making the small hairs on the back of his neck stand on end. "Yeah?" he asked, doing his best to mask his fear and look like the recruit Nick expected him to be.

"It's the day before the big rally," Nick said, glancing around the room making sure the other recruits were not within earshot. "I think it's time we let you in on the plan."

"Really?" Tony didn't need any acting skills to convey his eagerness at the news. "That's great. How can I serve?"

Nick patted him on the shoulder. "Know how to use a gun?"

Tony's mouth went dry. "I...I shot my Dad's shotgun a few times."

"Good. Most of these kids don't know which end fires."

"You gonna to teach them?" Tony shivered at the thought of kids wielding guns for the first time, aiming them at his friends.

"No," Nick said, his eyes perusing the crowd of young initiates. "Nah, we don't need that many armed men. I mean we might not need the guns at all, you know? We just want them there in case. These Jew bastards don't even know we're coming, right?" he laughed derisively.

Tony coughed up a week laugh. "How could they? Stupid Kikes," he added for safe measure.

Nick nodded in agreement. "So, the fight's going to be at the East Ward Gym. We're going to send these boys out with uniforms and picket signs. Teach people the way it is. The community needs to understand they don't need to put up with Jew scum. Right now, they don't know better, but we'll teach them. If we can do it without guns, so much the better. The point is to recruit and educate, not scare our people."

Tony nodded. "Where do you want me?"

"You'll be outside with us. We're stashing the guns on site tonight. That way if we don't need firepower, we don't have to use them. If we do, well they'll be right where we want them to be."

Tony's mind raced. Where were they hiding the ammunition? If he could get that information to the Minutemen tonight, they could end the fight before it began. He didn't want to appear too eager. He still needed to be careful. He opted for his old fall back. Forcing his eyes to shine with fawning adoration he said, "Thank you so much for allowing me to serve the brotherhood tomorrow night. I am so proud that you have asked me to stand by your side and that you trust me with your confidence."

Nick grinned and ruffled Tony's hair. "You're worthy of trust."

Tony opened his mouth to try to form the words to ask for the location of the guns when Hans came up to them. Although Hans seemed to trust him, the old German was a little bigger than Nick, and Tony didn't want to risk anything. "Good evening, sir," he said instead.

"Good evening, son," Hans said in a clipped voice. "Pardon me, but I need to steal Nick for a few moments. Why don't you go over to the others?"

"Yes, sir. Thank you, sir," Tony replied quickly and departed.

"How much did you tell him?" Hans asked.

Nick shrugged. "Just that we were going to arm him tomorrow night."

Han's sharp eyes bore into him. "You didn't tell him anything more? Nothing classified?"

Nick shook his head. Judging by the look in his eye, his leader would not like to learn that he'd told Tony that the guns were on site. He didn't feel like a lecture on the eve of his biggest conquest. "Of course not," he reassured his leader. "What do you take me for?"

Hans continued to stare at him and then satisfied he let out a sigh. "Good. Keep it that way, okay? I'm sure he's fine, but all these new recruits are just that- new. I trust you and few others. The rest, well we'll see."

"There's nothing to worry about. These Jew's are in for a surprise tomorrow. Tomorrow will be our shining moment of glory," Nick said with sincerity.

Hans nodded and grinned. "You're right. Tomorrow is the beginning of a new era. Our names will go down in history."

Tony passed the time listening to the idle chatter of the other members. The room was buzzing with excitement. The more experienced members were regaling the younger ones with stories of their youth. Tony waited until he could politely excuse himself Walking back over to Nick and Hans, he was relieved to see that Hans appeared more relaxed, almost jovial. "Sirs, if it is okay with you, I'd like to go home."

Nick nodded. "Good idea. We should all do the same."

Hans patted Tony on the back in an unusual display of affection. "We'll see you tomorrow," he said, his eyes shining bright. "Tomorrow will be a good day."

Tony walked briskly from the hall. He had grown accustomed to checking for tails, although he had never been followed. Although he was confident in Nick's trust in him, he knew not to let his guard down. It was better to be paranoid and alive.

Guido's had a closed sign up on the front door. The lights were out in the small restaurant and the chairs were up on the tables. It looked deserted. Saying a small prayer, Tony tried the door and sighed in relief when it opened. He glanced behind him to make sure no one was there. It was pretty deserted and quiet.

The floor boards creaked as he made his way back room. When he got half way across the floor, he heard the unmistakable click of a revolver's hammer locking in place. He slowly raised his hands and said. "It's Tony. Tony Petrucelli. I need to see Arte."

"Shit, I almost shot you," the gruff voice stated. "I'll let Arte know you're here." The man opened the door to the back, shedding light into the main room. When he closed it again, the room plunged back into darkness.

"Thanks," Tony muttered into the darkness. He marveled at his calm considering what the man had just said. How much his life had changed over the last few months.

The door opened again and the man motioned him in. Tony hurried forward and saw the back office was filled with men. Closing the door behind him, he searched the room for Arte; he found him sitting next to Cantalupo. They waved him over, and he maneuvered his way across the room.

"What happened?" Arte said without preamble.

"They'll have the guns hidden on site tonight," Tony replied. "Nick told me just now. I couldn't get where. I couldn't ask without drawing attention from Hans, but I figured that was enough. If we're lucky."

Cantalupo nodded. "I know the area. It might not take too much luck to find their stash. Have any idea how many guns they have?"

Tony shook his head. "Not an exact number, but I can tell you they plan to arm me. And they're not giving guns to the new guys. If I had to guess, I'd say they had two to three dozen. Just a guess."

"Sounds about right," Arte said. "Those cocky sons of bitches. They think we're all going to just roll over and die, don't they?"

Tony nodded. "Something like that. They aren't expecting a fight. And they certainly aren't expecting me to turn on them."

"We have that going for us," Cantalupo said with a twinkle in his eye. "Okay, we have to find those guns."

Tony looked around the room. "Looks like you've got the manpower to find them."

"That we have. Wait until tomorrow. You'll be amazed," Arte promised with a wink.

CHAPTER TWENTY-THREE

Danny's heart was pumping hard. His hands felt clammy and he wasn't sure he remembered how to breath. Not only was this the biggest fight of his career but if all went as planned, it was the night the Minutemen sent the Nazis packing. He wished he could find out what was going on outside, but Willie gave strict instructions to anyone within earshot of the dressing room that Danny needed to concentrate on the fight and not the outside turmoil.

"Just...," Danny started, in another attempt to glean some information from his trainer.

"No," Willie responded tersely. "Concentrate, will you? This is your career, your future in the ring."

"Do you know what's at stake out there?" Danny cried. By now the entire neighborhood knew the plan. He'd been happy to finally let Willie in on the goings-on of the group this last week. He'd also been able to let his family in on it. Maria had helped them spread the word to her close friends at the Provision House.

Willie had been relieved to know that Danny's distraction was not simply due to a girl. Still, he wasn't please that his fighter had such a monumental cause to fight at the same time as this pivotal match. If only Danny's energies for both fights could be channeled together. But they weren't. They were divided, on many fronts.

Danny and Nate were now more than friends; they were brothers in the battle against the ultimate suppressors. This didn't make for exciting action in the ring. Willie prayed that he could pump Danny up enough to initiate the fight of his life.

"You think I don't know?" Willie asked aghast, "Are you kidding me?"

Danny grimaced at his stupidity. Of course, Willie knew. He knew firsthand. Willie had family in Europe. Two of whom had been missing since last November. "I'm sorry. It's just…" He didn't know how to end that sentence. Danny slumped back against the bench.

"It's okay. Don't worry about it," Willie said, fighting back the tears. He had to drive the images of his sweet cousin out of his mind right now. Images of a girl with large brown eyes playing with him in the grassy fields of his youth streamed uncontrollably through his mind. He prayed every night that she was safe but deep down, he couldn't deny the probable truth.

"Looked, kid, you're just gonna have to trust your pals out there tonight," Willie said, keeping his voice low. "Your fight's important in here too. You and Nate. You both can win, you know."

"Huh?" Danny asked.

Patiently Willie laid a hand on his shoulder. "If you both are at your best, giving it all you got with your fists and your mind, you can't lose. Even if Nate wins the match, you'll have a career made tonight."

"Yeah, but winning's better," Danny said with a grin.

Willie laughed. "Yeah, winning's better."

Outside, the cold air wasn't what made Tony shiver. He breathed into his woolen gloves to warm his face. Nervously, he looked around him as the Nazi's prepared for battle. It was like he was in some bad dream. He wore the dull brown uniform along with the Friends. It was important that he fit in. The young men shifted nervously in place as they waited for the demonstration to start, their picket signs dangling from their hands. The more experienced members were looking confident and eager. No one seemed to anticipate any resistance.

Tony wasn't precisely sure of his role in tonight's event. He had the element of surprise on his side, being that no member of the Friends of New Germany would ever suspect him. Arte had told him to just follow along until it made sense to split off and join his brothers. But when and how? Tony's nerves were frayed. He wished he had a concrete plan.

He also wished he knew for sure about the guns. He hadn't dared meet up with anyone today. The Friends had convened their group early in the day to rehearse. Mostly, practicing a march planned for the demonstration. It required timing, precision, and coordination, something the younger members had difficulty mastering.

He was sure the Minutemen had found the small arsenal, but doubts stemming from fear crept through, and Tony found himself looking around for any signs of his compatriots.

Nick appeared at Tony's side. "Stay in formation and you'll be fine. There's nothing to worry about."

Tony jumped, stifling a scream. He covered with his best imitation of a smile. "Sure," he said.

"Don't be so nervous!" Nick said reassuringly. "You're with a winning team."

Tony was relieved that Nick attributed his jumpiness and nerves to the rally. He nodded and said sincerely, "I sure am."

"It's straightforward," Nick said. "We're going to start by showing this neighborhood what we're about. And if any dissenters show up to cause trouble, well, we have a solution for that." He looked meaningfully at Tony.

"Speaking of which, when do I get a gun?" Tony asked. The more Tony knew the better he could help his people. He still had no idea where the guns were stashed.

"About that...," Nick said sheepishly. "We had more people turn up than we expected. Word got around and, well, we don't have enough."

Tony looked around again and began mentally counting. How many were there? One hundred? Two? He couldn't tell from his vantage point, being in the middle of a pack of brown. He suppressed his revulsion at having to don on the Nazi garb, but there was no way around it. He prayed his brothers wouldn't mistake him for a Nazi in the heat of the moment. "There's a lot of people here," he said, his voice quiet as bile threatened to rise again.

"Three hundred and fifty," Nick said proudly.

"Really?" A thrill of fear shot down his spine. That was more than he'd thought, more than the Minutemen had expected. Still, they had done everything to inform the community and gain supporters. If they had decent numbers, they'd win. Good guys always won in the end, right?

"Really," Nick replied reassuringly. "So, don't worry. You gonna be okay here?"

"Sure," Tony said with a wave of his hand. "You go on ahead. I'll be fine."

As he watched Nick walk to the front of the pack, he caught the reflection of something up in a second story window across the street. He stared at the window hoping to see it again, but it didn't reappear. He looked around to see if anyone else had caught it, but the others were concentrating on the upcoming rally. He turned to look in another direction not wanting to draw attention to what he was sure was a hiding spot for the Minutemen.

Danny's adrenaline soared as he stepped out into the large room of the Easy Ward Club. Camera flashes blinded him from all sides as he made his way to the ring. The cheers were deafening. Looking out, he saw his mother and sister standing by seats just behind his corner of the ring. Their cheers rose above the cacophony of the crowd and eased Danny's nerves. He wished his father was well enough to be here, but he knew he was glued to his radio in his hospital room. Danny prayed that he'd make his Pop proud tonight.

Danny looked up. Nate's confidence exuded from his stance inside the ring as he waited for him to arrive. As agreed, they were mortal enemies for the evening. Still the twinkle in Nate's eyes gave away their friendship. Danny quickly looked away afraid he would greet his friend with a smile. Composing himself, he looked back up to give Nate his best glare, but Nate had turned his back to talk to Manny. Danny bent down and entered the ring. He nodded to Willie, who gave him some last-minute words of encouragement.

As if synchronized, the Nazis' formed lines began to move out just as the first bell rang. The young goose steppers marched the streets carrying picket signs. Some depicted young Aryans frolicking in the great outdoors with swastikas in the background while other showed the might and force of the Nazis through images of tanks. The staccato sound of their feet hitting the pavement exhibited their dedicated practice. "Sieg Heil!, "Sieg Heil!" the older men started to chant, the younger ones following suit. It was as if they were imagining the skulls of their foes under their feet as they stomped through the streets.

Tony had managed to maneuver himself so he was in the rear right of the pack. That way he could duck out when the opportunity arose. The goose step made him ill, and he wondered how much longer he had to stay in formation. He needed to find somewhere he could hide, somewhere out of sight that wouldn't draw attention.

His heart pounded as they approached an alley. It was perfect. Feigning a twisted ankle he limped to the side, turning into the alleyway. No one seemed to miss him; they were all intent on their march, wanting to impress the leadership with their prowess. Tony leaned against the wall and waited for a sign.

Nate's powerful right hook made Danny's head jerk back. His vision blurred for a moment before correcting. The crowd cheered as Danny pulled away. He should have known better than to get within arm's length of Nate for too long. Shaking his head, he stabilized himself and maneuvered around his opponent. Three consecutive jabs to Nate's ribs earned him the groan every fighter lives to hear.

The bell rang, signaling the end of round three . Exhausted, Danny fell onto the stool and allowed Willie to clean him up.

"Save your energy, kid," Willie whispered. "You still have seven rounds to go."

"I'm fine," Danny mumbled stubbornly.

"Sure, you are," Willie said reassuring as he pressed a silver coin against the latest cut on his left cheek. "You're doing great."

"You think I'm winning?" Danny asked hopefully.

"'You two are neck and neck," Willie said. "But my money's on you."

"Any news?" Danny asked hopefully. He desperately wanted to hear that his brother and friends were okay.

"'Keep your mind on the fight," Willie growled.

Danny looked over to Nate who shot him a quick glance. Nate still looked strong and vigorous, nothing like what Danny felt. He wondered if Nate was just better at hiding his fatigue.

The bell rang again, and Danny stood up, looked back at Willie and said, "Okay." He needed to forget what was happening outside and focus on the fight. He had to trust his brother and the other Minutemen to pummel the Nazis the way he was going to cream Nate. With a grin he launched himself toward Nate.

Tony could see Nick looking around for him as he hid in the shadows. Time crept by too slowly. Tony's skin tingled with fear. The longer he awaited the better the chance he had of being discovered. How would he explain his retreat? The Nazi's had cleared the block once already and were coming around for the second go. He hated waiting, feeling like a coward.

Suddenly, a flurry of rotten vegetables shot down from the sky, looking like a hail storm directed at the Nazis. The tomatoes left satisfying red stains on the pristinely pressed brown shirts and pants of the Friends of New Germany like bloody marks of war. Rotten eggs joined the fray and splattered all around the boys in brown's feet.

The effect was perfect, making Tony grin. The perfect formation scattered as the young, inexperienced men shrieked with terror.

The people of Newark had come out in droves. Looking up on the roofs, he could see neighbors and Minutemen working together to pitch tomatoes and eggs off the edge at the demonstrators below. Windows were flung wide open as people leaned out to curse the Nazis. Chorus of "Go home you, Nazi swine!" echoed through the neighborhood. Dozens of Minutemen were on the ground prepared for battle, rubber hoses and batons in their hands slapping against their palms.

Although Tony was too far away to see anyone's face, he could imagine the outrage of the older Nazis as they realized they had underestimated their foe. It was as Cantalupo had said–their overconfidence would be their downfall.

Tony realized this was his chance to join his compatriots. He shot out of the alley and ran over to the center of the battle.

Danny swayed on his feet as they called round seven. He stumbled over to his stool and slumped. That round hadn't gone well; he'd lost it to Nate. He'd blocked most of Nate's punches but hadn't landed a single one of his own. His arms felt like jelly, and he wondered how the hell he was going to go three more rounds. Danny didn't have the energy to open his eyes to look at his trainer, let alone lift his head.

"You want to give up?" Willie asked, his voice laced with concern and sympathy. "I can tell the ref to-"

Forgetting his fatigue, Danny jerked his head around to glare contemptuously at him. Give up? Was Willie suddenly addled? "Not on your life!" Danny gritted out. "Are you crazy, old man?"

Willie tried to hide his smile, but failed miserably. "Good. Go out there and wrap this up, will you?"

The Nazis were overwhelming overpowered. Once their new recruits had realized their childhood friends were fighting back, they immediately switched sides and began attacking the Nazis. It was like they had all awoken from a bad dream. The Minutemen allowed them to escape without harm.

The streets had turned into a chaotic battlefield. All around the East Ward Club were pockets of Nazis, each surrounded by dozens of Minutemen and townspeople. Arte and his gang had allowed Hans and Nick to recover their guns. They laughed as the two smashed the rifles to bits in frustration when they realized they were irreversibly jammed.

They tried to flee but found all exits barred. When Nick saw Tony standing by the sidelines he shouted, "Tony! Come help us!"

Tony folded his arms and glared at the man. After all this time of having to pretend that he was one of them, he left tremendous relief at finally being able to reveal his true feelings. "Not on your life! You think I'd help you, you Nazi scumbag?"

Nick's expression of utter bewilderment was comical, making the other Minutemen laugh. The raucous laughter shook Nick out of his stunned reverie, and his face turned into a mask of unadulterated rage. He lunged at Tony only to be stopped by a blow to his knees by Arte, who had expected this response.

"They're kind of like dinosaurs, aren't they?" Arte said casually as Nick rolled on the ground in agony, clutching his knee in his hands. "All brawn and no brain."

The crowd laughed. "Now let's make them extinct," Cantalupo said, effectively giving the order to end the cat- and- mouse game once and for all.

Nate's swing whiffed past Danny's ear. Danny could now tell that Nate was as tired as he was. He hoped more so. They had made it to the tenth round and both men had lost all bounce to their step, limiting their footwork to necessary movement. Danny threw a weak punch that was easily deflected. He stepped back, and Nate stumbled forward. They both threw simultaneous punches and fell into an embrace of exhaustion.

Danny prayed for the bell to ring and wondered if Nate was doing the same. Pulling away, Danny shot his left arm out to give Nate a weak jab in the ribs. Nate grunted, giving Danny a boost of energy. He tried to give him another punch when the bell rang. They both sagged in relief and dropped into their respective corners. The match was over.

The thunderous roar of the crowd was deafening. Each side was convinced of victory. Never had a match been so close. Minor fistfights broke out amongst the fans in the aisles as the three judges debated who was to win. Nate and Danny stared at each other from across the throngs of fans that had surrounded them in the ring. Too exhausted, both fighters could barely hold themselves up.

Choruses of "Dancing Man" and "Light's Out" clashed against each other in the hall. Maria leaned against the ropes to hug her brother. She looked over at Nate who winked at her.

Maria blushed and turned her gaze back to her brother. She motioned for Danny to lean in toward her. "There's someone here you might like to see," she shouted.

"Huh?" Danny asked, his head spinning. He wondered what was talking the judges so long. He'd never seen such a delay in declaring a winner.

"There's someone…," Maria shouted again. Then she stepped down and pushed Sarah forward.

Danny's heart leapt in his chest. She looked so soft and vulnerable in this brutish setting, her eyes wide and innocent, looking up at him with adoration. He grinned, grimacing as the action stung his split lip. "'Sarah, you came!"

Sarah nodded. "You were magnificent."

Danny blushed. "Thank you."

The referee's voice boomed over the microphone that the decision had been reached. The room hushed immediately as all eyes turned to face the small wiry man. "The judges," the ref said, enjoying his moment in the spotlight. "'were *not* unanimous in their decision. In a two one split vote, the winner of this fight is…," he paused a moment for effect. "Danny Petrucelli!"

The crowd erupted as the ref lifted Danny's arm high into the air. Nate congratulated him with a bear hug, and Danny felt himself lifted into the air. He looked around for Sarah, but she had disappeared among the throng of people.

CHAPTER TWENTY-FOUR

The streets around the East Ward gym looked war-torn. Bodies lay on the ground, some moving, some not. Rotten eggs and vegetables dotted the sidewalks and walls, their smell permeating the area. The police were nowhere in sights, a tribute to Cantalupo's power. By the time Nate and Danny exited the gym, the riots had settled down, occasional moans vibrating against the brick walls.

Tony raced over to Danny as soon as he spotted him leaving the gym. He embraced his brother fully, eliciting a groan of pain. "Sorry," he said contritely. His face beamed with pride. "I heard the news, Champ. You did it!"

Danny grinned as various Minutemen roared their praise. Looking around at the brown shirts prone on the pavement, he said, "Looks like a victory out here, too."

"Yeah," Tony said with a relieved grin. "Not much of a fight."

Nate's arm rested comfortably on Maria's shoulder. He leaned down and kissed the top of her head. "I'm sorry we couldn't be out here to fight alongside with you."

"We didn't need you out here," Arte's voice boomed from behind him, causing them to turn around. "We need you in there. What you two did for Newark tonight was just as important. You did good."

Nate smiled. "Thanks."

"So, did you get them all?" Danny asked Arte.

"Yeah," he answered. "Every last stinking one of them."

"Any dead?" Nate asked coldly.

Arte's eyes fell to Maria. "We can go over that later. There's a lady present."

Maria shook her head. "I'd like to know," she said, raising her chin a notch.

Arte's right eyebrow rose. "Anyone in particularly?" he asked.

Maria shrugged and looked away. "Never mind."

Gently, Nate turned her face to look back at him. "You can trust Arte," he said.

Danny and Tony looked at each other with equally puzzled expressions. "What are you two talking about? Who?"

"Johnny Martens," Maria whispered.

Tony's mouth gaped open. "Did that mother fucker…?" he couldn't bring himself to finish the question.

Danny tried. "He didn't…?" but couldn't do much better.

Maria looked down to the ground in shame, tears streaming down her face. It was humiliating to know that others knew a hint of that evening. "Please don't ask me to tell you anymore. I can't bear it."

Nate reassured her with a protective embrace while looking over her head at Danny and Tony. "Suffice it to say, if he were to die tonight, it would be a just end to that sorry life."

Arte Bella rarely showed emotion. He'd been Cantalupo's right-hand man for over a decade now and had seen almost everything. Violence was second nature to him. But when he looked at Maria's tear-stained face and heaving body, he boiled over in rage. Women and children were always off limits.

"I hope he's still alive," he bit out as he tore through the streets looking for Johnny's body.

Tony and Danny exchanged looks, "Go," Danny said. He didn't have the stomach for revenge.

Tony nodded and took off after Arte's retreating form. Nate's body tensed as he considered going after them, but he quickly realized that Maria needed him by her side more. She calmed, looking up at Nate and then Danny. "I'm sorry. I feel like such a ninny."

"You're no such thing," Danny reassured her. Part of him wanted to ask her what Johnny had done to her, but the other half didn't want to know. Sensing that Maria felt more comfortable talking to Nate, he added. "I'll see you at home, okay?"

Maria nodded, and Danny kissed her cheek before leaving.

Nate nodded a farewell to Danny, not wanting to let Maria go for second. When Danny was out of earshot, he whispered, "One thing I can assure you is that after tonight, you'll never need to worry about Johnny Martens ever again."

Maria's entire body relaxed against Nate. "I never thought I'd hear those words."

Tony and Arte finally found Johnny's body a few blocks away. His brown uniform had been ripped to shreds, and his body was covered with welts and bruises. He moaned as he saw Tony. "You traitor," he groaned. "I thought you were one of us."

Tony leaned down, staring Johnny directly in his eyes. "You complete imbecile," he gritted out. "You really thought you could get away with what you did to my sister?"

Although Johnny had lost a lot of blood, he still paled a few shades. "I…I…," he stammered. Instinctively, he tried to get up and flee, but he couldn't move his body. Terrified, he defecated himself.

Tony relished his fear and played on it. He jabbed his index finger in a choice wound, enjoying Johnny's abject moan of pain.

Arte knelt down on the other side. "Do you mind if I join in?" he asked Tony, keeping his voice casual.

"Be my guest," Tony answered.

It was hours later that Johnny gasped his last breath. Tony looked down at the inert body and felt sickened. He looked up at Arte, who nodded his head in understanding. "Go home, take a shower, and go to bed. Things will look better in the morning."

Tony stood up. "Sun'll be up in a few hours," he said. "Not sure I can sleep."

"Try," Arte said. "Take the victory. We massacred our enemy tonight. They're not coming back."

Tony turned and walked home. Image of the carnage from the night plagued him as he took each step. He picked up the pace and started running. Moving his body, feeling his blood flow through his veins, helped. When he got home, the house was dark. He crept up the stairs and closed himself in the bathroom. He stood under the hot water until it turned cold.

The next morning Danny came down the stairs to find Tony sitting on the couch staring off into space. "Want some coffee?" he asked.

Tony looked up and nodded. "Sure."

"You get any sleep last night?"

"Nah."

Danny disappeared into the kitchen and came back with two steaming mugs. Tony welcomed the bitter taste of the black coffee.

Danny studied him for a moment and then said, "Oh shit, I forgot. You take it with cream and sugar. Here, I'll fix it." he reached to take back the mug.

Tony shook his head. "Not today. Black works for me."

Danny nodded, leaning back into the couch. "You want to tell me about it?"

"Not really."

"Okay," Danny said, allowing the conversation dip into silence. After a few moments, he tried again. "I take it you found Johnny."

"Yeah," Tony clipped. "Look what part of 'I don't want to talk about it' do you not understand?"

"I just think it might help. That's all."

"Well, it doesn't!" Tony shouted. "Nothing's going to help." He dissolved into tears. Danny put his mug down and embraced his brother. After his sobs died out, he said, "I was so angry. Don't get me wrong I hate that punk with every living fiber of my being for what he did to our sister. I'm glad he's dead."

Danny pulled back and looked at him. "So, what is it then?"

"We tortured him," Tony said, his voice a haunted whisper. "I tortured him. Brutally keeping him alive to inflict more pain. For hours. I just wasn't myself. I turned into some craven beast. It scares the shit out of me."

Danny nodded. "It's over now. And the fact that you feel remorse is all I need to know that you're still my little brother."

Tony looked at Danny and paused. He finally nodded and said, "I guess so."

"You should get some sleep," Danny said pulling the mug of coffee from his brother's hands. "Why don't you go upstairs?"

"But I wanted to go see Pop."

"We'll go later. For now, get some rest. You need it."

Tony nodded his head and plodded up the stairs. He fell into a deep sleep the instant his head hit the pillow.

"Pop? You awake?" Danny whispered to Donato. The only mar to his victory last night was the fact his father couldn't be by his side.

Donato's eyes popped open. "Son!" he shouted as maneuvered to sit up in the bed. "You're here!"

"Take it easy," Danny said.

"I'm fine," Donato reassured him. "They're going to let me go in a few days. Can you believe it?"

"That's great!" Danny said, sitting by his bed.

"My son, the champion!" Donato cried with tears in his eyes. "'I'm so proud of you; I don't know what to do with myself."

"So, you heard the fight then?"

"Are you kidding me? Of course, I did. I was just sorry I couldn't be there with you mom and sister."

"Me too," Danny said giving him a hug.

Maria and Teresa peeked their heads into the room. They had wanted to give Danny a chance to have a moment with Donato. "What a son we raised," Teresa said proudly.

"I'll say," Donato's muffled reply came over Danny's shoulder.

Two days later, the neighborhood was almost back to normal. The Walnut Club was deserted. There was talk of it becoming a community center, but no one seemed interested in going near it for a while.

Battered and bruised, the Nazis had left the city quickly. Cantalupo's men killed Hans Reuther along with Johnny but let the others live to warn the rest that Newark was off limits.

Canatalupo pulled his woolen coat tight across him as he walked into a nice residential area. He wanted to handle this last piece of business on his own. Too often, Arte and the others protected him, not allowing him much action, so he had taken matters into his own hands. He wondered how long it would take for the others to realize he wasn't in his office. Grinning, he imagined the scramble as Arte tried to find him.

Turning the corner, Cantalupo approached the beautifully manicured home of Stephen Larson. He wondered why Stephen didn't have any security. He could certainly afford it. Shrugging, he rang the doorbell and waited.

The door opened, revealing a disheveled Larson still in his robe with a cup of coffee in his hand. He gasped at the old man before asking, "What are you doing here?"

Cantalupo withdrew a revolver from his pocket and pointed it at Stephen's heart. "Guess I don't need to come in."

Stephen dropped the cup of coffee, wincing in pain as the liquid scalded his feet. "Www..what are you doing?" he asked.

Cantalupo looked him directly in the eye. "I know, Stephen."

Stephen shook his head. "You know what?"

Cantalupo cocked the gun. "I know everything," he said simply. "Your men didn't take long to talk. They're not terribly bright. Or, loyal for that matter."

Stephen backed up into his home. Cantalupo followed, matching him step for step, never taking his eyes off his prey. He kicked the front door closed behind him as soon as he crossed the threshold. It was better not to disturb the neighbors.

"Whatever you think you know…," Stephen began.

Cantalupo shook his head. "Don't try it. There's no reason those Nazi scum would lie. Besides, I know you well enough. You were always a snot-nosed punk. Nothing like you father."

Stephen's eyes were fixed on the gun. He licked his lips nervously and croaked. "What now?"

Cantalupo leaned against the wall, looking as casual as a man waiting for the bus. "I'd like to know why. But first, I have a little paperwork to handle." He pulled out a stack of papers and indicated that Stephen should sit down.

Stephen took out his glasses and looked over the papers. He paled. "What's the meaning of-"

"Just start signing," Cantalupo said quietly. "You don't have a choice."

Stephen's trembling hand signed page after page, only looking up to glance at the gun leveled at his head from time to time. When he was done, Cantalupo nodded.

"You can put the gun down." Stephen's eyes flicked up to meet the old man's. Maybe there was a chance to plead his case, reason with the old man. "They're a menace, you know," he said quietly. "A plague on our people. They must be stopped."

Cantalupo's brows knitted in confusion. "Of course, the Nazis are a menace. They were stopped last night. But no thanks to you! You bastard, you're the one that funded them. Gave them the money to unite and arm themselves here in our own backyard. And now, you're trying to tell me-"

"No!" Stephen shouted in frustrated contempt. "The Nazis aren't the threat! They're our salvation. They're our only real hope. They're the only ones doing something to rid ourselves of the disease of the Jews. The Jews are the menace. Don't you know? Allowed to roam free, they're going to be the end of us all."

"You're demented," Cantalupo said, sighing in resignation of the fact. He had somehow hoped to find a different answer, one that might lead him to more sympathizers, more financial backers.

"Demented? Me?" Stephen asked in disbelief. "You're the one that's-"

The gun blast ended his sentenced. Cantalupo shook his head as Stephen's body dropped to the ground by his feet. "Waste of a good bullet," he muttered as he put the gun back in his pocket and walked out the door.

CHAPTER TWENTY-FIVE

The day was a routine working day for the Larson employees. Maurice O'Donnell and Tony Petrucelli walked up to the second floor marching straight into the executive area of the company. As the two walked from one department to another, the stares Tony received would have unnerved most.

Tony knew that all eyes were upon him as he walked to the president's office. They had no appointment and the normal thing to do would be wait and allow Katherine, Stephen's personal secretary, to announce their arrival.

But they didn't wait to be announced. As Tony opened the door to Larson's office Katherine half stood, uttering a spluttering cry. Tony's commanding look quelled her speech and prompted her to sit back down. Tony nodded briefly at her and walked in, O'Donnell trailing behind. The door closed and Katherine looked around at the other secretaries in wonder. No one dared speak a word, not even a hushed expression of surprise.

After a few minutes, the door opened, and Tony signaled Katherine to join them. Looking to the other secretaries in disbelief, she silently asked them for direction. When no one even looked at her, she slowly got up from her desk and entered the office. She wondered why these two men were taking over Stephen's office. Where was her boss?

Tony's authoritative voice directed her. "Katherine come in and sit down. I'm guessing that Stephen hasn't forewarned you of the changes that are taking place in this company."

Katherine shook her head briefly, looking at Tony questioningly. "You're Tony Petrucelli," Katherine said quietly. "And Maria, who works in our accounting department, is your sister." She looked Tony up and down, realizing that the double-breasted suit he wore probably cost more than her last month's paychecks. Two weeks ago, this man worked somewhere in the shipping department and now looked like he, well, owned the place. No one climbs up the ladder to president that quickly.

He allowed himself the luxury of perusing her lovely form, reciprocating her look before answering. "That's right. Do you have a problem with that?"

Katherine shook her head and turned to the only person who could make some sense of this, Mr O'Donnell, the company's corporate council.

Tony looked to O'Donnell for help, "Moe, perhaps you can shed some light on this for Katherine."

Moe was what the Larsons had always called him. Very few others ever used that nickname. O'Donnell had started as corporate council for the Larson's over twenty-five years ago. He began with Larson senior and quickly found himself overseeing all corporate matters, including the Kosher operation.

He picked up a chair and slid it next to her "Katherine, there are some changes coming. Some pretty big changes. Are you going to be able to handle that?"

Katherine found herself nodding.

"Good girl," the man replied. "The man sitting across from us is the new president of Larson's bakery."

"But…," Katherine burst out. "How?"

Moe shook his head. "That's privileged information and not for you to ask," he chided stiffly.

Katherine blushed and looked down at her lap. Tears began to well in her eyes.

Tony's heart melted at the sight. He stood up and shooed Moe from his chair giving him a brief scowl. He pulled out a pristinely pressed cream handkerchief from his pocket and handed it to her. "Don't cry," he implored her gently.

"But what's to happen to me?" she asked not looking at him but accepting the cloth. She dabbed her eyes daintily.

O'Donnell rolled his eyes and said, "Tony is the new president of this company. I'm here to back him up. Whether you stay or not is up to you."

Tony glared up at Moe and said, "What Moe meant to say is that whether you stay or not is up to *me.*"

O'Donnell sat down in a nearby chair. "Of course," he grumbled.

Tony nodded to Moe, acknowledging his concession. "That's right and Katherine, don't worry, you're not going to replaced." Katherine turned grateful moist eyes to him, and he grinned like a schoolboy. "I need your help for this transition to go smoothly. Will you help?"

She nodded. "Of course, I can help you."

"Good," Tony said with a grin. He winked at her, and she blushed. He felt so powerful, invincible. Just last year he had gazed longingly at her whenever he had the chance. Now he was in a position of power over her. Good thing his intentions were honorable.

Katherine looked at Tony envisioning what type of boss he might turn out to be. Stephen had made numerous attempts to seduce her, using her position in the company as blackmail. He'd invited her on weekend getaways and extravagant dinners. Katherine had managed to sidestep his clumsy attempts because Stephen wasn't very bright. She found herself wondering if she would mind if Tony made the same attempts. She had hardly noticed him before, but now she couldn't help but admire how his suit molded to his fit form perfectly. Blushing, she looked away.

Tony hid his grin behind a hand. "Katherine, I'll be an easy boss, I promise. I drink Earl Grey in the morning with cream and one teaspoon of honey. You are to sit in on any and all conference concerning the company with Mr O'Donnell and certain staff in the office. From here on out, we're all a team, and all I expect is for you to be a part of that team."

Katherine nodded her head and gave him a small smile. "I can do that, Mr. Petrucelli."

"Good," he responded. "Oh yes, I almost forgot, Katherine I want everyone in the company to know that Stephen Junior will no longer be a part of Larsons in any capacity. The company name will stay the same, and there will be no layoffs. The company will be very similar with some improvements made here and there. Katherine, I need you to get the word out, if you know what I mean."

Katherine nodded. "Yes, sir. I'll send out a memo informing everyone that you are the new president of Larson's Bakery." She gave him a coy look before saying, "And I'll make sure the entire staff knows it before the memo hits their desks."

Tony laughed and said, "Perfect!" He turned to O'Donnell and said, "Moe, can you give us a few minutes?"

O'Donnell stood and bowed to his new boss before he left the room.

Tony stood up and took up his position behind his desk. "I know it must be odd for you having me as your new boss."

Katherine knew exactly what Tony was alluding to, the invisible wall separating office personnel and factory workers. She nodded.

"It is important to me that my past position doesn't interfere with my ability to run Larson's. Again, I'll need your help."

"Of course," Katherine said as she looked around the office. A puzzled expression crossed her face as she looked at the many pictures of Steven still scattered around the office. He had attended many fundraisers and made sure to get photographs to commemorate the event each time. Appearance and propriety were extremely important to her old boss. It had always been her job to rotate the photos and include the latest most prominently.

Tony watched Katherine look over the gallery of photos that adorned Stephen's wall and froze for a moment. Seeing things from her vantage point that looked very strange. Finally, Tony realized he didn't want to lie to her, but he also couldn't tell her the truth. "I don't think Stephen has any use for these pictures anymore. You can dispose of them.

Katherine looked skeptically at him. "Are you sure?"

Tony nodded. "Where he's gone, he'll have no use for these photos."

Katherine shrugged. That made sense. Wherever he was working now, he probably didn't want reminders of his past. "Will you be keeping the furniture?"

Tony nodded. "Yes, everything, but let's take those photos down. I'm hoping that you and I can create a new set of photographs. Those worthy causes still need benefactors." He winked at her and smiled.

Katherine returned the smile and found herself pleased that Tony was including her in creating the future for the company. Many of her friends, who needed to support their family, lived in fear of losing their jobs to a man. There were too many employers who took advantage of those fears, subjecting the women to every indecent act that any unscrupulous boss could inflict. She looked at Tony and knew she would never need to worry about him.

Tony saw her relax, and so he leaned back into his chair. He began to share with Katherine his vision for the company. His words were soft yet deliberate as he spoke of honor in the workplace.

As Tony spoke, he began organizing the piles of papers on his desk into neat file folders. She noticed one folder was marked "Cantalupo Trucking". Having handled all of the freight contracts before this, she knew that McMahons Trucking had been the only ones Stephen had ever used.

"These few folders represent a new direction that the company is taking," he said meaningfully as he handed the new folder to her. "I need you to handle this personally."

Nodding nervously, she asked, "Do you want me talk to the dock workers directly or shall I do what I did with Mr. Larson and communicate through Mr. Demaio?"

Tony sighed and said, "For now, do things the way you have always done them. Running instructions through Demaio makes sense. I'll leave those decision up to you. Just give me full reports when tasks are complete, okay?"

"Yes sir," Katherine said feeling less confident than she had two minutes ago. "I'll do my best."

"Your best is all I can ask," Tony said. He put his attention back to the papers on the desk, and Katherine realized she had been dismissed. She turned to leave.

"Oh, and Katherine," he said casually, still not looking up from his papers.

"Yes, sir," she replied looking back at him.

"I like your hair like that. It's fetching."

Katherine grinned and turned back to leave. Tony looked up just in time to see her pat her hair as she walked out the door.

CHAPTER TWENTY-SIX
Three years later

Teresa smiled as she put the finishing touches on baked ziti with meatballs. Looking over at the pan sizzling with polenta, she gave it a little shake to make sure it didn't stick. Not stopping in her tasks, she called over her right shoulder, "Donato, are you coming down any time soon?"

Just then, the kitchen door opened, and the newest expectant mother came into the kitchen. "Mamma, we're outside waiting. What's taking so long?"

Teresa in an exasperated gesture, pointed to the second floor. "You know something, Maria? Sometimes, I think we were better off with the old Donato. Mind you, he'd complain about everything, but he was always on time. Now, I can't pry him away from the bathroom mirror. Mark my words, he's up there admiring his waistline and combing his hair." As Teresa uttered the final syllable, Donato came down the stairs.

Bouncing down the steps like a man of twenty, his voice boomed out, "Hey! There's my baby girl! And how's our newest little Donato doing inside there?"

Maria rolled her eyes. "Honestly Pappa, I've told you we don't know if it's a boy yet. And even if he's a boy, Nate and I haven't decided on any name yet. We just want happy healthy baby, that's all."

Donato put his two hands on his only daughter's shoulder and beamed at her with pride and love. "You grew up so quickly," he murmured affectionately.

Maria could see his eyes begin to well with tears and in that instant, all her newfound worldliness melted, and she became again his *bella* Maria. Embracing him, kissing him on both cheeks, she whispered, "Pappa, I'm so happy that you're doing so well."

It had been three years since he took over the helm at Larsons, and Tony wanted to celebrate. What better occasion than to give his baby sister and brother-in-law a spectacular baby shower.

The other reason for the gathering was that it was 1941 and even though America was not involved in the war, everyone knew that it was only a matter of time. Tony, as president of Larsons, had been appointed the official representative of the War Bond movement, helping America's allies by donating provisions to humanitarian organizations aiding the global war effort.

The Petrucelli and Rubin families were on edge waiting for the day that Nate would be called for duty, so a party of any kind would help to take the edge off.

It was Sunday, the Petrucelli and Rubin families had free reign of Larsons. Danny, Sarah and Katherine had arrived early to decorate the cafeteria. Katherine smiled to herself in eager anticipation of the announcement of her impending engagement to Tony. She glanced lovingly over to Tony, remembering his sweet proposal from the night before.

Lost in her own thoughts, Sarah looked longingly at Danny as she pinned a yellow balloon on the wall.

Danny returned the look and squeezed her hand. "Penny for your thoughts?"

Sarah shrugged and sighed. "Nothing new."

Danny understood what she meant. The religion issue between them had never been resolved. Sarah's father likes Danny and never forbade her from seeing him; however, she and Danny both knew that he was vehemently against the match. Danny smiled softly and whispered, "I'm in no rush, sweetheart. I'll be here for you."

Sarah shook her head. "That's not exactly true, now is it?" There was an edge to her voice.

Danny's brow furrowed before he realized she was talking about his leaving for the war. He pulled a paper from his pocket and said, "Actually it is. I just found out today that the review board has rejected me for service."

Everyone in the room gasped.

"Rejected? Why? How?" Sarah exclaimed.

Tony shook his head and cried, "Don't they know that you're one fight away from being the middleweight champion of the world? What on earth could disqualify you?"

Danny opened up the letter and showed it to him. "Believe me it is as much a surprise to me as it is to you. Uncle Sam officially says that my hearing isn't up to par. I guess it happened with all the boxing matches. It says here that I'm exempt from military service. I never knew. When Nate and I enlisted, the last thing I thought was that I'd be rejected." He looked at his brother sadly. "I really did want to join the fight."

"What's with all the long faces?" Tony asked looking around at the suddenly somber gathering. "This isn't all bad. Danny, you're still going to help me raise funds for the war, right?"

Danny nodded, looking at Sarah who was feeling guilty to be so relieved. She molded herself against him and allowed herself a small smile.

"And brother, if you ever want a vice president position here at Larsons, it's all yours," Tony offered proudly. "We could work side by side together."

Danny shook his head. "Thank you for your generous offer, but I could never work for the Cantalupo organization. It just wouldn't be right for me." The last thing he wanted to do was a start a fight today with his brother, so he hoped his rejection was diplomatic enough.

A little stunned, Tony nodded. It never occurred to him that someone might not want to work for the Cantalupos. They offered so much to their people. Shrugging, he looked to Nate. "And Nate, do you think I would let my sister have the kids alone? I spoke to a few people I know, and you'll stay stateside and be near all of us."

Nate shook his head. "Tony, I appreciate all the effort you went through, but I need to go. I need to be where the action is."

When Maria started to cry, Tony lost his composure. First, his brother threw his offer back in his face and now Nate. He jumped up and bit out angrily, "What? Are you crazy? I worked my ass off to pull this thing together, and you say no?! I'm not saying that you don't help out and contribute to the cause, but why do you have to go abroad to do it?"

Nate stood up as did Danny. Nate glanced nervously at Danny, knowing that he would defend his brother if things turned ugly. He was painfully aware that he was an outsider. Still gauging Danny's response, he splayed his hands out and said, "I don't want any problems with the family, but you must all respect my wishes. No offense, but most of you cannot possibly understand how important this is to me personally," he glanced at Sarah who nodded her silent support of his decision. When Danny saw this, he sat back down. Nate turned his attention back to Tony, careful to keep his voice neutral. "Please understand that I love Maria more than life, but what kind of man would I be or American, for that matter, if I took the easy way out? I hope you all can someday understand."

No one spoke. Everyone was utterly stunned by the shift of the mood. Nate shrugged and turned to leave. Donato stepped in front of him, blocking his way.

Nate sighed heavily. In the last few years, he had come to not only respect Donato but enjoy his company. Now, it seemed that the strong bond they had built would be destroyed. Standing tall, he waited for his father-in-law to speak.

Donato looked Nate in the eye and said, "Nate, I cannot express how proud I am of you at this moment."

Relief visibly poured from Nate as his shoulders slumped back to a relaxed position. "Thank you, Donato. You have no idea how much that means to me."

Donato looked at his children, giving each one a stern look. "This man has integrity. You must support his decision and applaud it." he turned back to Nate and said, "Rest assured, we all stand behind you in this. God bless you!"

The two men embraced. Tony and Danny stood up and took turns giving Nate their support. There was not a dry eye in the room.

EPILOGUE
Nordhausen, Concentration Camp, Germany 1945

The cool spring breeze moved swiftly over the barren land as of battle- weary soldiers marched 90 miles from the Rhine. The soldiers were thankful for the ever- increasing wind that was just volatile enough so as to hide the stench of what had just transpired at the camp over the last few years.

The First Army Commander under General George S. Patton was Lieutenant Colonel Arthur Mansfield. He had the dubious duty of leading his troops into Nordhausen to unofficially clean up the mess the Germans had left. The regiment consisting of over 300 men had worked their way into Nordhausen as part of Patton's Germany realignment plan, which called for American troops to clean out any and all enemies throughout Germany.

Mansfield's task was to clean up the few concentration camps still standing and check for survivors.

"Sargent Nathaniel Rubin, reporting as ordered sir!"

Mansfield looked at the man with respect. Mansfield knew how important this day was to his prize sergeant. He had nothing but pride and a genuine liking for this young man who exemplified everything Mansfield had ever learned as a plebe at West Point. Rubin, as part of Patton's army, had fought in both Normandy and on D Day. Mansfield had been Rubin's commander throughout.

"At ease," he said. "I know how badly you want this. I have told all my senior officers that you and your unit would be the first to go into the camp. You deserve that."

Nate knew what lay ahead and tried not to let it get to him.

"Thank you, sir," he replied with choked emotion. "I've been waiting for this for a long time."

The road leading up the gate was all of 75 feet. Local people were walking away from the main gate with food for whatever people that might be left. Nate frowned as he watched two peasants hurriedly walk away from them. As he got closer to them, he yelled, "You two, stop!"

He turned to two of his corporals. "Odwyer, Cassidy, check those baskets those two farmers are carrying."

Nate was about ten feet from the stench- filled front gate when one of his corporals yelled back. "Hey Sarge, come here. You've got to see this for yourself."

Annoyed that these two farmers were delaying him the moment he had been waiting for years to experience, he bit out, "Yes, Corporal? What did you find?" Glancing over at the peasants, he noticed that one was a woman.

The Corporal lifted loaves of bread that were atop the soiled brown cloth and quickly threw them to the ground. Lifting the cloth, Nate gasped. There wrapped in bloodied rags were the remains of extracted teeth with gold fillings still inside. Nate looked at the two men with overwhelming hatred and fury, who were shaking visibly.

The women fell to the ground began sobbing. She grabbed onto one of Nate's boots, begging of mercy. "Please General, please," she wailed. "He made me do it. Yesterday, one of the old Jews called us through the fence, begging us for food. He told us where we could find gold. The German troops left them in haste knowing the allies were coming. We're just poor farmers, and we are desperate for money."

Nate listened in disgust. "Did either you ever consider just helping these poor souls without taking something in return?"

Before the woman could answer, Nate turned and gave a command to his men.

"Get these poor excuses for human beings out of here. Odwyer, go to their homes and make sure they don't have any other souvenirs. I'm going inside. Cassidy, scout the perimeter and make sure that we are free of Germans. Be careful!"

Nate took a deep breath and began to make the fifty foot walk back to the Nordhausen gate. The stench was overwhelming as the winds has suddenly died down. The decrepit wooden gate was filled with notches of all shapes, sizes, and angles. Nate imagined that the notches were probably made by the thousands of desperate fingernails clawing into the wood.

As Nate walked past each building there was tomb-like silence but in his head, he physically felt the screams and pain of what those poor tortured souls had endured. And then he heard a sound that would change his life forever.

"Rabbi! Rabbi, is that you?"

Nate turned, and there standing in the doorway of the last building on his left was a survivor. The tattered cotton shirt he wore barely covered the skeletal remains of a young man.

"Are you a dream? Have you come to save us?"

"Yes, son. We're here to take you home," Nate said, struggling to keep his emotion in check. He was after all a Sergeant in the US Army. "How many are here? How many are still alive?"

The grateful man looked inside the building then back to Nate. "We're six. I don't think there are any women in the camp that are alive. We haven't eaten in days, do you have some food?"

As Nate grabbed the man's hand, he couldn't keep the raw emotion he had bottled up from coming out. They embraced. The survivor held onto him like child holding onto his mother, knowing he would be protected from all the evils of the world. Nate clutched him in a reaffirmation of his belief that God had kept him alive in the war for this very reason.

The entire regimen of soldiers looked as two men from different worlds came together. The historical snapshot would be captured in their minds and hearts forever.

In the next six hours, three hundred troops from the Second Army helped evacuate over 90 concentration camp survivors. Nate and his people ascertained that there were thousands of Jews who were either shot or cremated at the camp. The survivors showed the soldiers the mass graves sites.

It took two weeks before the Army Core of Engineers arrived to assess and document what had happened at Nordhausen. Nate Rubin was awarded medals for valor and commendations citing bravery on both D Day and Normandy. He also received a special honor from the President of The United States for his humanitarian act in liberating the survivors of Norhausen.

www.ingramcontent.com/pod-product-compliance
Lightning Source LLC
LaVergne TN
LVHW021705060526
838200LV00050B/2518